W9-AUE-240

## *Acclaim for*
## Deep Water: A Sailor's Passage

"E. M. Kahn's *Deep Water: A Sailor's Passage* ends with a glossary of nautical terms. The word 'passage' is not included in the glossary, but it could be. One of the meanings of 'passage' in my dictionary is 'a nautical route.' Another is 'transition from one state or condition to another.' There's surely a double meaning in the title of this intriguing novel. The author offers the reader a book of adventure, again with a double meaning—the adventure (often dangerous) of sailing in such places as the waterways around New York City and the islands of the Caribbean, and the adventure (also dangerous) of the life of a gay man in the era of AIDS. The narrator Gene and his 'skinny cowboy' boyfriend Kevin are the main human characters in this book, and the reader joins them as they confront the uncertainties of life and its passages—on the water and on land."

—Allen Young
Freelance writer and Co-editor,
*Out of the Closets: Voices of Gay Liberation*

"*Deep Water: A Sailor's Passage* is a powerfully moving memoir that charts the emotional landscape of a man with stark honesty and surprising candor. E. M. Kahn is as skilled at capturing the complex and shifting passions of life on the sea as those of the life of the heart. Rarely have I read a book that so fearlessly confronts our personal and idiosyncratic responses to the painful losses that many of us endured during the early cataclysmic years of AIDS and the difficult path forward as we find ways to love again. Ultimately this book offers a searching look at men's quest for adventure—adventures of the sea, the heart, and the spirit."

—Eric Rofes, PhD
Author, *Reviving the Tribe:*
*Regenerating Gay Men's Sexuality*
*and Culture in the Ongoing Epidemic*

"E. M. Kahn's *Deep Water* falls squarely into that new generation of 'gay' books that takes same-sex love and longing for granted and moves us into the elemental passions of ordinary human persistence. Sailing through the tides of love, ambition, and loss, including more than a few painful collisions, Kahn invites us to discover with him the current of survival."

—Frank Browning
Author, *The Culture of Desire*
and *A Queer Geography*

"This is one of the most beautiful love stories I have ever read. Eugene Kahn allows us to share two achingly deep and profound passions—the love of wind filling sails, and of one man for another. And remarkably, almost as an afterthought, Kahn helps us make some sense of the inane horror of AIDS. I love this book."

—Laurie Garrett
Pulitzer Prize-winning author,
*The Coming Plague*

"In *Deep Water: A Sailor's Passage,* Gene Kahn offers a fascinating study of small-boat sailing adventures in sight of Manhattan's domineering skyline. Staged around voyages taking place over a fifteen-year period between 1978 and 1993, *Deep Water* is both a valuable collection of adventures on Long Island Sound, the East River, and New York Bay (with an occasional slice of Caribbean warmth for good measure), and a beautifully written love story.

Carefully balanced against Kahn's often poignant tales of two young men experiencing the highs and lows of coastal sailing are stark reminders of the impact of AIDS on our society. *Deep Water* should prove popular among the gay community as well as being a valuable resource for boaters in, or visiting, the waters off New York City."

—Anthony Dalton
Author, *Wayward Soldier:*
*In Search of the Real Tristan Jones*
and Co-author, *The Best of Nautical Quarterly,*
*Vol. 1, The Lure of Sail*

"A sailor's dream—the images and the fantasies. But even if you're not a seaman, you'll be swept up in the wake of this intriguing novel."

—Dan Woog
Author, *Jocks* and *Jocks 2*

"Brisk and refreshing, *Deep Water* brings together the exhilaration of sailing and the mystery of love in a truly distinctive memoir. From navigating through treacherous fog on Cape Cod to negotiating the unruly seas of the West Indies, E. M. Kahn's chronicle carries the reader along on a wave of affability and good humor, and always in the fine company of the author's friends. A tale of love, loss, and renewal, the book also recounts the touching relationship between Kahn and his lover and the devotion and dignity embodied within it. Well-written and absorbing, *Deep Water* is highly recommended for those with a taste for the splendor of the sea and of the human spirit."

—Marc E. Vargo, MS
Author, *Noble Lives: Biographical Portraits of Three Remarkable Gay Men—Glenway Wescott, Aaron Copland, and Dag Hammarskjöld* and *Scandal: Infamous Gay Controversies of the Twentieth Century*

*NOTES FOR PROFESSIONAL LIBRARIANS AND LIBRARY USERS*

This book is published by Southern Tier Editions, Harrington Park Press®, an imprint of The Haworth Press, Inc.

*CONSERVATION AND PRESERVATION NOTES*

All books published by The Haworth Press, Inc. and its imprints are printed on certified pH neutral, acid-free book grade paper. This paper meets the minimum requirements of American National Standard for Information Sciences-Permanence of Paper for Printed Material, ANSI Z39.48-1984.

# Deep Water
## *A Sailor's Passage*

*HARRINGTON PARK PRESS*
*Southern Tier Editions*
Gay Men's Fiction
Jay Quinn, Executive Editor

*Men Who Love Me* by Felice Picano
*A House on the Ocean, A House on the Bay* by Felice Picano
*Goneaway Road* by Dale Edgerton
*Death Trick: A Murder Mystery* by Richard Stevenson
*The Concrete Sky* by Marshall Moore
*Edge* by Jeff Mann
*Through It Came Bright Colors* by Trebor Healey
*Elf Child* by David M. Pierce
*Huddle* by Dan Boyle
*The Man Pilot* by James W. Ridout IV
*Shadows of the Night: Queer Tales of the Uncanny and Unusual* edited by Greg Herren
*Van Allen's Ecstasy* by Jim Tushinski
*Beyond the Wind* by Rob N. Hood
*The Handsomest Man in the World* by David Leddick
*The Song of a Manchild* by Durrell Owens
*The Ice Sculptures: A Novel of Hollywood* by Michael D. Craig
*Between the Palms: A Collection of Gay Travel Erotica* edited by Michael T. Luongo
*Aura* by Gary Glickman
*Love Under Foot: An Erotic Celebration of Feet* edited by Greg Wharton and M. Christian
*Dryland's End* by Felice Picano
*Upon a Midnight Clear: Queer Christmas Tales* edited by Greg Herren
*Barracks Bad Boys: Authentic Accounts of Sex in the Armed Forces* edited by Alex Buchman
*The Tenth Man* by William Podojil
*Whose Eye Is on Which Sparrow?* by Robert Taylor
*Deep Water: A Sailor's Passage* by E. M. Kahn
*The Boys in the Brownstone* by Kevin Scott
*The Best of Both Worlds: Bisexual Erotica* edited by Sage Vivant and M. Christian
*Confessions of a Male Nurse* by Richard S. Ferri

# Deep Water

## *A Sailor's Passage*

E. M. Kahn

the sailing + the
Biggest Part of
my Life

Dave Kahn
January 1st 2009

Southern Tier Editions
Harrington Park Press®
An Imprint of The Haworth Press, Inc.
New York • London • Oxford

Published by

Southern Tier Editions, Harrington Park Press®, an imprint of The Haworth Press, Inc., 10 Alice Street, Binghamton, NY 13904-1580.

© 2005 by The Haworth Press. All rights reserved. No part of this work may be reproduced or utilized in any form or by any means, electronic or mechanical, including photocopying, microfilm, and recording, or by any information storage and retrieval system, without permission in writing from the publisher. Printed in the United States of America.

Henderson, Richard (1972). Illustration of a Typical Sailboat. *Sail and Power: A Manual of Seamanship,* Second Edition. Maryland: Naval Institute Press.

BLUE MOON
Words and Music by RICHARD ROGERS, and LORENZ HART
© 1934 (Renewed 1962) METRO-GOLDWYN-MAYER INC.
All Rights Controlled by EMI-ROBBINS CATALOG INC.
and WARNER BROS. PUBLICATIONS U.S. INC.
All Rights Reserved Used by Permission

WHAT'S LOVE GOT TO DO WITH IT
Words and Music by TERRY BRITTEN, and GRAHAM LYLE
©1984 MYAXE MUSIC LIMITED, and GOOD SINGLE LIMITED
All Rights for MYAXE MUSIC LIMITED Administered by WB MUSIC CORP.
All Rights for GOOD SINGLE LIMITED Administered by IRVING MUSIC, INC.
All Rights Reserved Used by Permission
Warner Bros. Publications U.S. Inc., Miami, Florida 33014

Cover design by Kerry E. Mack.

Cover photos provided by E.M. Kahn.

**Library of Congress Cataloging-in-Publication Data**

Kahn, E. M.
Deep water : a sailor's passage / E. M. Kahn.
p. cm.
ISBN 1-56023-517-9 (soft only : alk. paper)
1. Kahn, E. M. 2. Sailors—United States—Biography. 3. Sailing. 4. Gay men—United States—Biography. I. Title.
GV810.92.K35A3 2004
796.124'092—dc22

2004006523

The more you live, the more you love . . .
The more you love, the more you go away. . . .

A FLOCK OF SEAGULLS

For Kevin Abend-Olsen

A Promise Fulfilled

*CONTENTS*

# ACKNOWLEDGMENTS

I wish to express my gratitude to the following people who made this book possible:

To Jennifer Lyons of The Writer's House Agency, who provided the initial impetus to begin this project; to Frank Browning, author and literary commando, who endured my nonsense and still gave me hope; to David Groff, editor and poet, who made me realize that I was already a writer. I embrace you all.

# Parts of a Typical Sailboat

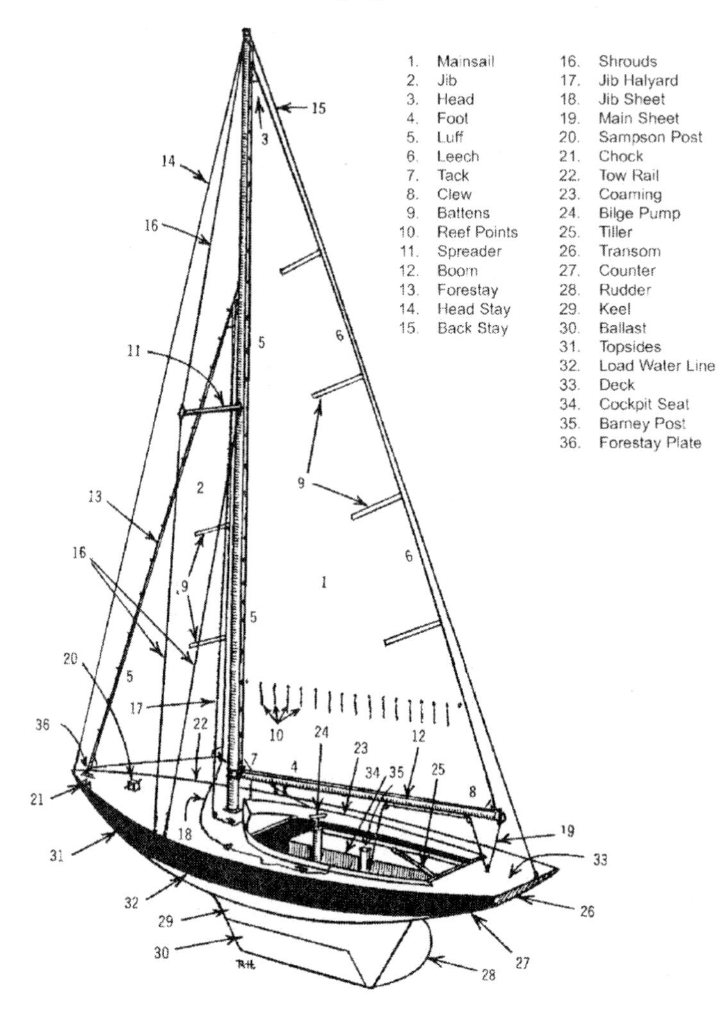

# PROLOGUE

*Departure, August 1995*

Next to me I could hear the water rushing past the boat's hull. The water, I thought dreamily, always the water. It rushed past foamy and alive on the other side of the thin fiberglass. It was my companion as I lay pressed against the hull up forward in the bow.

Kevin was at the helm, of course. I felt him make a sharp correction as a wave, surging up behind us, caused the boat's stern to yaw for an instant. He jammed the wheel over a couple of spokes. He knew what he was doing and I could rest while the boat rushed ahead to its destination.

I closed my eyes, and listened to the sea racing along just above my head. Six knots, I thought, maybe six and a half. Pretty good speed, and maybe we could keep it up all the way through Block Island Sound. Better check the chart, I thought, check the Loran, check our speed and position, update the time to reach the next turning point. The voice of worry nagged at me, threatening disaster the moment I was not vigilant. But instead I closed my eyes again. Kevin did not really need me up on deck.

A moment later the boat heaved sideways and slammed down with the thud of its nearly 10,000 pounds hitting the bottom of a wave. She shuddered for an instant, lifted her skirts with the next following sea, and continued sailing, powerful and unfazed. I smiled, thinking of him back there, alone at the wheel, dealing with all of this without me.

I could picture him with his leg confidently propped across the cockpit for balance. Maybe he steered with just one hand, and held onto the backstay behind him with the other. His blond hair was a mess, all tangled and stiff from wind and salt spray. He loved the sun, loved to think that he was getting a deep tan on his skinny chest and shoulders. He was driven by vanity, and I had even seen him squeeze a fresh lemon right onto his scalp to speed up the lightening action of the sun. He loved the way the sun left his hair all streaky. His dark sunglasses, crusty and spotted with spray, were cinched with a braided lanyard that hung down the back of his neck. In all, he looked like he belonged on a sailboat.

We were only two days into the trip, two days out of City Island, yet it felt like we had been on this boat, this trip, for years and years, and that nothing important had ever come before. Even the destination, another three days further east, did not really matter. We were on our own, inside this boat, this fragile shell, and it seemed we had always been here, together, always sailing. Even from the start it seemed we had been moving through water, together.

I rolled over in my bunk and looked aft through the companionway. I could see one bare foot through the spokes of the big wheel. He was sitting up on the windward coaming. His arms, longer than mine, could easily reach the wheel even while he sat out on the edge. From there he could better watch the luff of the headsail, the wind-sensitive leading edge. How good it felt to settle into the cushion beneath me, to rest my weight against the hull, all the while aware that this boat, with me and all the food and equipment crammed into it, was under Kevin's control. Though he was almost thirty feet away, I felt surrounded by him, his hands, his big red knuckles on the wheel. Around me his smell was mingled with the subtle residue of teak oil and diesel fuel that pervaded the cabin. Even in the berth I was faintly aware of the peppermint soap he washed with. He probably had used this pillow just before me. I closed my eyes again and happily let Kevin sail the boat.

When I looked up again, I thought it odd that the forehatch above me was propped open. When had he come forward and done that? I did not recall opening the hatch. The motion, too, had changed. In fact, there was no motion. Nor were we heeling over any more. And it was hot inside the cabin. I got as far as opening my mouth to call out his name, but said nothing. The boat was at anchor and I was alone.

There was no need to call out his name. The boat was still, lying off City Island, and I was alone on a summer afternoon. I had come out to put a new battery on board. In the thick heat I had stretched out in the familiar v-berth. There was no breeze coming through the hatch. With his name still stuck in my throat I held my breath and let my mind catch up with the past three years since he had died. He was gone, I told myself. He did not exist. It was just memory and longing that had produced this illusory vision. He had been here, before, that I knew, as my mind stumbled with the question, what exactly *is* a person?

I lay in the berth, held on the edge of lassitude and longing. I thought of the heavy marine battery I had just installed, with all its many thin plates of lead immersed in a bath of corrosive sulfuric acid. These two inert substances, put together, could miraculously generate electricity. Something new and measurable was created seemingly from nothing. It had force and direction, and in a way, it was virtually alive. If that could be done so easily, I reasoned, with such common ingredients, why then was it not possible to bring back someone whose reality was already so alive inside my own skin?

Not for the first time had I tried to re-create him. In some simplistic part of my brain I was convinced that I needed only to think hard enough, remember clearly enough, focus, and he would materialize through the very process of my thoughts. This was not matter out of vacant air, I assured myself, for had not some part of him been merged with me? Were there not just enough stray molecules of his voice still surrounding me that I, as the catalyst for this routine act of transubstantiation, could reassemble him again, whole, alive, and laughing?

No, this was merely the persistence of memory, I reminded myself. The memories were real, existing somewhere in my head, perhaps as a chemical bond, maybe as an electrical charge once initiated by his presence. Either way there was something inside me that *looked* like Kevin. But of course, that was not him. He was gone.

Probably I had installed the older battery while Kevin was still alive. Now, after five years, its plates were coated with deposits of lead sulfate, the electrolyte had broken down, and hardly more than a three- or four-volt trickle came from within its heart, like a virtual death rattle.

There was still a lot of work to do on the boat and no way to conjure up Kevin from my mind, no matter how vivid the memories were. Even his ashes had long ago dissolved into the Gulf Stream.

I tumbled out of the berth and immediately remembered all the boxes still in the cockpit, still on the settees, still left on the dock, all filled with supplies for the coming weekend trip. I had come up to the boat to pack away all these things. We would depart at dawn the next morning with three other people on board, people Kevin had never known, people who sailed with me now. If I hoped to leave at sunrise, I had lots of work remaining down below, and no time to continue struggling with the incorporeal nature of ghosts.

Kevin was gone. Now there was Frank, along with Braden and Dennis. All of them would arrive later that night. In the morning we would sail down the East River all the way through the Narrows. We would traverse the great estuary of New York City from one end to the other. I had made this trip many times before, with Kevin, and the novelty had worn off. Still, I knew that the others, my crew, would be impressed by the sight of the city at sunrise from the river. For me the satisfaction would be vicarious as I introduced them to this harbor that I had been pottering around in for over two decades. It would be a world that they had seen only from a distance or in postcards.

Slack water began at Hell Gate at 6:23 a.m. For twenty minutes the water would be still until the pull from the moon, somewhere above the earth, once again caused the waters of the planet to surge toward the opposite hemisphere. Then the current would begin ebbing, southward. At dawn we would slip from our mooring and trust the cool and murky water to bring us downriver, first to the Battery and then to the mouth of Upper New York Bay. We would pass through the Narrows and at last meet the ocean.

The tide, the current, the river, the open bay, and the ocean were all synchronized by the unstoppable phases of the moon. All this was oddly reassuring to me; that all this activity went on totally unaffected by me and my private struggle. Even better, that it was all known in advance and printed in the yellow tide almanac. Like the Bible—or the Torah—it told me how to behave each day, each hour; how fast or slow my voyage would be.

I expected calm weather, a typical summer morning. Yet I had an ominous feeling about this passage tomorrow. As if something important was going to happen, beyond just gliding beneath the Verrazano-Narrows Bridge. I was always nervous the day before a trip, but this time my sense of edginess was not for the safety of the vessel or her crew. That I could take care of. I would face something else tomorrow, something difficult, and the almanac would not have the answer.

How many times had I noticed a blur on the horizon and knew, before I even focused the binoculars, that it was a tugboat pushing a barge? But this time, while I had that same uncomfortable feeling that I was closing with something big, I was unwilling to look at it before I had to.

# 1

## KASHA

*West 38th Street, July 1978*

One day in July he stormed into the shop. "The scumbags took only the new stuff," Kevin blurted out as he arrived for work. He slammed the door and tossed his denim jacket onto a chair. It missed, but he left it there. "All the tools Sue bought for me over the weekend . . . goddamnit!"

The Skill saw, power drill, even the fancy Estwing hammer with its cushioned handle, all were gone before he had used them even once. His stepmother, Sue Abend, had taken him shopping to buy tools to fix up his place. She was trying to support his new life in the city. I told him he could borrow anything that he needed from the shop.

"Right. Yeah. And what happens when *they* get swiped? Forget it," he added as he picked up his jacket and shook the dust off. "It's not worth all this shit. You've gotta have a gun to live in this city. Right?"

He was discouraged but not terribly surprised. He knew that his neighborhood was rife with thieves and drug dealers along with the hookers and pimps. I tried not to think of Kevin as a hopeless loser whose life was just one misfortune after another. Everyone in New York got robbed—or at least taken for a ride—one way or another.

I stayed out of his way until later in the day. Over lunch I told him how my carpentry shop had already been robbed and vandalized twice, how my previous car was stolen from my mechanic on Bethune Street, and how four of my expensive Italian racing bikes were roaming around New York City with someone else's ass perched on the saddle. Even my old tenement apartment, I went on, had been robbed.

"And stupid Auggie," I told him, "she just sat there watching as the creep stuffed my TV set into a pillowcase."

"She probably even licked his hand," Kevin suggested with a conspiratorial smile.

"You know how she is," I admitted. "All you have to do is say 'Paw, paw' and she'll shake hands and give you a kiss. But I never got her as a watchdog, anyway. She's the female interest in my life."

He decided that he needed a dog for protection, a serious watchdog and companion. He already had his two kittens living with him, little snowball-sized things, one gray and one orange, both still nameless. An earlier incident during the spring, when he was held up at gunpoint, also left him nervous about walking around his neighborhood without some kind of visible protection. He was starting to feel a little beleaguered by life in the city.

He told everyone that he was looking for a dog, and that was how he found Kasha. This big black setter was living with Bruce, an old friend of mine from Bard College. He shared a tiny apartment on Cornelia Street with his boyfriend Neil. The dog had, in fact, originally been Neil's dog before he came to New York. She was still quite young and energetic, with puppylike eyes and a silky coat of long black fur.

Bruce and Neil lived next door to Zampieri's bakery in the West Village. They lived with the yeasty smell of fresh bread wafting up from the ovens every night. Their apartment was so small that when Bruce folded out the bed at night Kasha had no room to even turn around. Instead, she had to back up into a short corridor, then find a new spot on the floor for the rest of the night.

I felt sorry for her whenever I stopped by to visit Bruce, long after he broke up with Neil. I sympathized with her plight whenever she nudged her warm snout into my lap. Often she would give me her paw, gravely placing it on my leg as if pleading to be taken away from those cramped quarters.

When he heard that Kevin needed a guard dog, Bruce let her go willingly. Perhaps he felt guilty about confining her so much, or maybe she reminded him too much of his breakup with Neil. So now, Kasha moved uptown to West Thirty-Eighth Street with Kevin.

In a way, Kasha and Kevin were both like orphans on my doorstep, and in that counterculture era of scraggly hippies and loose extended families, I was happy to play earth mother and provide a home for both of them.

When he eventually moved into my apartment on Canal Street, the place suddenly became crowded and the six occupants divided up the living space vertically. The dogs stayed on the floor, most of the time. Kevin and I moved through the middle latitude of chairs, tables and countertops. And the two kittens, now called Jackson and Sven, sought escape from the dogs by leaping from shelves and ledges. Only for Kasha was there a difficult adjustment. Living alone with Kevin, Kasha had grown accustomed to sharing the bed with him. Eventually, with a lot of kicking, we convinced her that she belonged back on the floor with Auggie. Still, some mornings I awoke and reached for Kevin, who always slept close to the wall, and instead of my slender boyfriend I found a mound of fur wedged between us, snoring contentedly.

Although we were all like a family, the bond between Kevin and his dog remained inseparable. And as in all shaggy dog stories, she would eventually die—in his arms—ten years later. I had lived with dogs all my life and had borne witness to their inevitable deaths. In Kevin's case his attachment to his dog extended beyond her parting.

Two years after she died, Kevin himself was near death as he lay in a hospital bed, feverish, disoriented, and weakened by a fungal infection. He knew already where he was going.

"Is Kasha there?" He said this to me one night in a thin voice, childlike yet full of hope. I could easily imagine her sitting outside his room, slouched against the doorjamb with one ear just slightly cocked. It was the first time I had ever been with someone who was already experiencing a vision of his own death. I took what comfort was possible in knowing that he believed he would not be alone.

# 2

## STARBOARD TACK

*Manhasset Bay, June 1978*

"Gene! Look out!" Kevin shouted to me. "Under the jib. There's a boat coming right at us." He was scrunched on the floor of the boat, and staring at a competitor's bow coming toward us at top speed. I looked out to leeward, tried not to panic, and paused to figure out which of us had the right of way.

I am amazed, when I look back now, that Kevin came along that day. Sailboat racing was not like a pleasant day sail; it was fast and competitive, with every move part of a strategy to pass or cover any nearby boat. Comfort and safety became secondary to performance and sailing hard all the time.

"Ahh . . . shouldn't we *do* something?" Kevin asked clearly more nervous. I was used to these close maneuvers at the start, with a fleet of five or more identical little boats crossing and recrossing each other. In the minutes before the final gun went off, the water became whipped up into a *Jaws*-like frenzy of overlapping wakes. It felt like a battle zone and you had to react fast and decisively.

This was my second season racing in a fleet of Rhodes 19 sailboats. We jockeyed around the starting line waiting for the customary sequence of horns to begin: "Preparatory," "Warning," and finally, "Start." Each blast, or "gun" as we called it, was timed exactly five minutes apart.

Kevin could not understand all the frantic maneuvering just before the start. It all must have seemed needlessly aggressive and dangerous, all these boats challenging one another to occupy the same spot in the water. He had scant knowledge of the rules and precedents that were meant to govern every possible situation between boats and buoys. Serious racers, like scholars of the Bible, devoted a lifetime to studying these rules, along with the extensive interpretations and commentaries that were printed in the all-important manual with the blue cover.

"We're on port," I said at last. "He's on starboard. Let's get out of here. Ready about?" Kevin and I, acting more out of fear than naval discipline, sprung to opposite sides of the boat and took positions at the jib and mainsheets. I knew how quickly this little boat could come about. I was pleased to see that when things got scary Kevin was able to rely upon the traditional routine of tacking a sailboat. What might take a British man-'o-war in a Patrick O'Brian novel fifteen minutes and a crew of seventy men to accomplish, we could do in less than six seconds. Still, the basic principle of tacking through the eye of the wind and hauling in the sheets was the same, and it still had to be done with teamwork and precision.

"Helm's alee," I shouted, and pushed the tiller hard over. The sails came slapping across the boat and then made a sharp *woomp!* as they filled with wind. The other boat immediately disappeared behind us. While Kevin nervously watched for more boat traffic, I tried to read a wet and crumpled sheet of paper that listed all the possible courses our race committee could choose from. Each course was given a single letter designation, and twenty minutes before the start a painted sign with the letter for the day's course was hoisted on the mast of the committee boat. Often this was joined by a number one or two, indicating that we would have to sail once or twice around the entire triangular course. Of course during the heat of battle every yard of the Sound looked new and challenging. Then, the final horn went off and we were surrounded by the whole fleet of boats, all quickly sailing past us.

"Gene?"

"What?" I answered Kevin, but did not take my eyes from the red wool streamers on the luff of our jib.

"How come everyone is ahead of us already?"

"We got off to a shitty start. Okay?" I tried not to get pissed at what was a very legitimate and obvious question. We had been too close to the starting line when the final gun went off. The more experienced skippers knew just when to sail *away* from the starting line, then turn around and head back for the imaginary line at top speed just as the final gun sounded. It was a textbook maneuver, I knew, but I did get shaken by all the fast crossings and right-of-way challenges that happened in the last two or three minutes before the gun. The lead boats were already accelerating away while we were stuck in their bad air. I was now also concerned that Kevin would lose confidence in me.

"We still have a chance," I started to explain, but right then the wind shifted and we tacked to take advantage of a lift on the opposite tack. I continued, "If we get a good spinnaker set right at the turning mark, then we can blanket some of the others who are more clumsy and slow with their hoists."

"Does that mean we have to sail right up to their sterns?" he asked, already knowing the answer.

"Well, pretty close," I replied. "Right up their butts, if you get my drift."

I was trying to be flip, but Kevin looked back at me with a disapproving frown. Maybe I had overdone the straight competitive thing. He remained sulky for a few minutes. Maybe the sexual reference annoyed him, and I realized that such dynamics were still far from clear in our own friendship.

"Here," I went on. "You take the helm while I rig up the spinnaker and all the lines up at the foredeck." Shortly afterward, I took the tiller again, and even though we were dead last at the windward mark, we had no other boats in our way. We hoisted the big crinkly spinnaker until with a soft *woosh!* it bellied out with wind and the lines grew taut. It looked like a colorful hot air balloon winged out in front of our mast on a short spruce pole.

"Now watch," I said to Kevin. "Keep letting off your sheet," I encouraged him. He eased the line out to let the sail continue to fill more. We sped up and began to close the distance to the other boats. Coming from behind, with the wind astern, our sail partially blanketed that of the boats ahead of us. Their spinnakers would sag like droopy elephant skin, and repeating the same maneuver we steadily gained on three of our competitors. Kevin shot an astonished smile back at me, and I whispered encouragingly, "Keep playing the sheet. Snap it back in when it starts to collapse."

We had lost the leaders, but were back in the middle of the fleet. Again Kevin turned back and smiled at me with his irregular teeth. This part of racing he was starting to like.

At the next mark, we made a terrible mess and tangle of getting the big sail down and cleared off the foredeck. It cost us distance and we were again at the tail of the fleet. Almost.

One other boat was still close to us, and while we could not touch the leaders, our strategy was to at least beat our nearest competitor over the finish line. Anything was better than dead last. Kevin hiked out on the deck as we sailed upwind toward the starting buoy again. He knew that the more weight we had on the rail the flatter the boat would sail. We needed to cover this other boat—stay close to him at every move, try to get him stuck in our wind shadow, delay and frustrate his movements any way possible that would ultimately ensure our crossing the finish before him.

"You've got him pinned down, Gene," Kevin shouted to me from his wet and precarious seat hanging over the edge of our boat. Beating upwind into the chop, little waves would roll along the side of our boat, giving Kevin a wet ass. But now he was in the spirit of racing hard. "He's getting ready to tack away!" Kevin, his face red and windburned, kept looking over his shoulder to watch the other boat. *Good,* I thought, realizing that my competitor, rattled by our aggressive tactics, was forced to escape from our wind shadow. I heard a rustle of sails and knew that he was going to duck under my stern and sail away on the opposite tack. It would likely cost him speed and several boat lengths between us.

Looking back, I caught the lined and angry expression on the other skipper's face. We stayed on our course this time. Soon enough, we saw him come about once again and our two boats began converging. As we rapidly closed the distance with each other, I kept hoping that my boat would cross in front of his. For the first time I felt the whole boat, small as it was, moving through the water like a racehorse with the two of us riding together on her sleek back. Our bodies rolled and ducked in unison with the rush of the waves under the boat's keel. I was sure we were going faster than the other boat and would cross in front of it.

As the distance between our two boats lessened I heard nothing from Kevin. He gripped the boat's deck and watched as the other boat grew inexorably bigger. He glanced at me, the skipper, for assurance that we were in the right. Already, we could see the red and black Chicago Cubs hat that one of the other boat's crew was wearing. "We have the right of way; we're on starboard tack," I stubbornly hissed to Kevin. "Port tack must yield to starboard. Starboard must hold his course," I recited, as if quoting the Constitution.

"Yeah, but does he know that?" Kevin replied. There was no time to answer him.

When we were only two boat lengths apart I bellowed out the standard hail of "Staaaarboard!"— a flat-out declaration that I was going to hold my course, just as the rules require. I heard Kevin gasp to himself, "He's not doing anything!"

By now we both could see the foamy crest around the bow wave of the other boat. There was still time, I kept telling myself, he could still slam his tiller over and tack away. This was not going to be like the drag racing scene in a James Dean movie. There were rules, after all, and we had the right of way, I repeated to myself.

Sailboat miles per hour are not very impressive when compared to highway speeds. Five knots sounds pretty slow, until the bow of another boat is coming at you. I think the other skipper could not fathom how I had managed to gain on him, and why I was being so stubborn now. I could see a baffled look on his face; his whole expression was frozen and paralyzed.

Then, the unimaginable happened. In one continuous and relentless ballet, the other boat plowed straight into us. His bow punched a hole into the starboard side of my own boat, right amidships. First there was a huge thud, then the splintering of fiberglass, followed by the spranglike howl of the mast and rigging. The sound was just awful as the tall metal spar vibrated like a sine wave. The entire boat reverberated with a sickening lurch, and we were both thrown to the floor of the cockpit by the impact. Racers, in their blasé manner, call this T-boning another boat.

Kevin turned white and threw out his arms as he went sprawling. Even his eyes seemed to have lost all color—all I saw were two black pupils as his face flashed by me. There was a dull thump as his forehead hit the mahogany floorboards. My instincts took over and I uncleated the mainsheet and yelled out, "Drop the main!" There was no time for first aid yet; he was closer to the two halyard cleats at the base of the mast. The boom swung wildly across the boat. I thought I heard Kevin call out, "What's happening?"

I poked my head over the gunwale to see if we were sinking. A loud mechanical clunk from somewhere inside the boat told me that Kevin had at last popped off the main halyard. The sail tumbled down the mast and landed in thick folds over the boom. That in turn dropped with a hollow thud onto the cockpit sole. Further adding to the chaos was the jib that slid like a shower curtain down the forestay and lay in a fluttering heap on the foredeck. Sheets, halyards, and traveler control lines were all tangled around our ankles, but at least now, with the sails down, the boat was no longer being driven into further danger.

"How bad is it? Are we sinking?" Kevin asked. He was still sitting under the boom, waiting for something else to come crashing down around him. His words came out high pitched, and I realized how really frightened he was. I had been too preoccupied with damage control to be afraid yet.

"It's okay. It's above the waterline!" I shouted back to Kevin. I hoped to reassure him that the situation, while clearly a mess, was not critical. A three-inch hole, like a jagged fistula, was punched into the boat's side. It was ugly, but not nearly as bad as all the noise made it seem.

"I think we can patch it ourselves," I said, and I asked him to dig out a roll of duct tape up forward.

Kevin's hand shook as he fumbled with the tape. I realized that I felt more embarrassment than fear when he blurted out, "What the fuck is with that asshole?" By now the two boats had begun to separate and drift apart. The other skipper, a pleasant guy in his sixties, was hanging over his own cockpit, convinced that he had split us in half. I heard him calling to us in a nasally voice, "Are you all right? Are you all right? Do you need help?" He sounded like Elmer Fudd on helium. Clearly he was more shaken than I was, and already I was starting to feel sorry for him.

"He's older, you know," I muttered to Kevin, trying to concentrate on fixing the boat and not get angry. "Maybe he's not used to such aggressive tactics."

"Then he shouldn't be out here racing, the dumb fucker," Kevin said, and his face was twisted with anger. A small red spot was on his forehead, but clearly he did not yet feel his bump.

"Help me patch this. You do the inside," I said, and kept pressing more strips of tape against the hole from the outside. He pulled the tape off the roll and tried to tear it with his thumbs, but his hands were still shaking.

He was probably right, but Kevin did not share the sense of brotherhood that I felt toward the other sailors in this fleet—an understanding that no matter how competitive we became out on the water, we still all needed one another to make the races happen. I appreciated the welcome I had received from the senior racers in the fleet, and I was certainly living up to their encouragement to sail hard and try to beat at least one boat every race.

We pushed the other boat away and hoisted our own sails once again. I noticed that the other skipper had dropped his sails and was going back in with his motor. *Good,* I thought, *at least he won't finish either.*

With the hole taped over we could make the two-and-a-half-mile sail home as long as we did not heel over too hard on port tack. Kevin was sullen and said very little as we sailed back to City Island. I tried to assure him that racing was not supposed to be like Coney Island bumper cars; contact between boats was prohibited by the rules. Still, every time I remembered that awful sound, I felt it had been my fault for putting the boat, and her crew, into such a tight situation.

We were both eager to get off the boat and leave City Island that day. Yet as we drove away, something felt wrong and incomplete.

Kevin smoked in quick deep puffs, and his body still seemed to be all tensed up. Had my pigheaded aggressiveness now soured him on sailing, if not racing, I wondered? The memory of the collision hung over us in the confines of my car even as we joined the flow of southbound traffic on I-95. We looked at each other with nervous smiles, trying to turn the memory of the shock we had endured into something more lighthearted.

"Feels funny, going home so early," I said, mostly to fill the awkward quiet inside the car.

"At least we're not in the hospital," Kevin added, still in a grim frame of mind.

Crossing upper Manhattan on the westbound Cross Bronx Expressway, I had a sudden impulse and exited onto the streets of Washington Heights. I could not let the day end with the memory of the collision haunting us. We were very close to one of the great edifices of the city that I had never bothered to visit. Like most New Yorkers, smug and parochial, I tended to stay in my own part of town—the narrow lanes of Lower Manhattan and the Village. I felt most comfortable in those old streets lined with nineteenth-century row houses, tall ginkgo trees, and dim memories of Bohemian days long gone.

"What's up? This isn't home." Kevin said, perking up. He seemed curious as he looked out of the car window at the unfamiliar apartment buildings along Amsterdam Avenue.

"Trust me," I answered sarcastically, as I nudged the car into a parking spot on 112th Street. We got out and locked the doors. Whatever was in store, it was not going to be boat related, and that alone seemed to cheer Kevin up. We rounded the corner and turned south.

From several blocks away we caught sight of the elaborate spires as they peeked from between the boxy apartment buildings. Finally we stood before the full immensity of the Cathedral of St. John the Divine. Who could absorb in one glance the dizzying layers of arches, rose windows, carved saints, pinnacles, and so much intricate stone detailing? There had to be some limit to all this, I thought, feeling lightheaded by the density of embellishments covering every square foot of the cathedral's front. With a sudden insight, I understood the whole Bauhaus movement, the International style of architecture, the cool discipline of the Seagram Building. Is this what all those talky and cerebral architects were running away from?

"Planning to confess your sins?" Kevin asked, as we stood in front of the great wedding cake of limestone steps.

"I suppose I should, but I think it's Episcopal," I answered. "I just thought it would be a nice change of scenery."

"It's pretty scenic, all right," Kevin joked, then he loped up the steps two at a time.

We strode past the intricately carved bronze entrance doors. Another visitor was reading aloud something about the doors being cast in France by the same foundry that had made the Statue of Liberty. I followed Kevin into the stillness of the cathedral's narthex. The light changed, now filtered through the stone tracery of the windows above us, and the dust particles were illuminated as if from the beam of a projector. There seemed to be a purpose to this light, these ionized clouds of ordinary city dust.

Kevin looked at me and once again I saw that shine of wonder and adventure in his face. Neither of us had ever been here before; thus, we were both to be pilgrims that day, seeking respite and refuge.

We moved into the main body of the cathedral and were dumbstruck by the volume of interior space around us. Standing together in the nave, we inevitably both looked upward to the towering gothic arches.

"Did you know," Kevin asked me slowly, "when I was in school I did a long paper on medieval culture? Sue and Jules took me to the Cloisters, twice. I secretly wanted to grow up and become a knight. You know, wear silver armor, have a great sword and halberd. This is such a trip. It's like the real thing."

I smiled, glad that the gloomy spell cast by the boating mishap seemed to be broken, but also touched that he confided in me this very innocent childhood memory. Color had returned to his face. I indulged my own fantasy about Kevin, but instead of a knight in armor on horseback, I imagined a skinny kid in his flannel pajamas playing with toy soldiers.

We spoke in whispers as we slowly walked past all the side chapels, each devoted to a special saint or some particular human occupation. Tourists were milling and gawking everywhere, yet their voices, like ours, were lost in the dusky complexity of the vaulted ceiling. I felt an awareness of so many people who had come to this place, had shuffled across those marble floors, prayed on those dark benches. An undeniable confluence of energy permeated the place—human energy. As we walked down the great aisles, the disaster of that morning's race seemed to slip into another perspective. It was, after all, just a race, a game, a sport, a diversion.

We separated for a while to study different chapels. When I saw him again he was standing in the center of the cathedral, right in the great crossing. He was staring toward the choir. Light from above filtered around his face and shoulders. I left him alone and continued to wander and examine architectural details.

What was most wonderful about the cathedral was that it was still being built, carved, stone by stone, by young apprentices. Their work area and simple tools, crude wood mallets and dozens of differently shaped steel chisels were laid out on a heavy workbench in one of the courtyards. Thus this architectural anachronism served as a gathering point for a community driven by the most improbable of twentieth-century motivations: to build a cathedral.

I did not want to like the place. I wanted to feel alienated by all the iconography of Christ's passion, and the whole Christian experience. But that was only the wallpaper of the place. Instead I felt that the underlying aspiration of the cathedral was a need to be inclusive and ecumenical. From saints to firemen to pond life, the place spoke out the message: *You are each of you, above all, a part of the whole.*

Kevin walked toward me as I waited back at the portals to the narthex, where we had first entered. He walked slowly down the center aisle of the nave. *How small he looked,* I thought, *how very unceremonial in his denim jacket and rumpled Levi's.* Yet, the light from the stained glass and the clerestory windows seemed to cast his head of blond hair with a caressing glow. His face was lost to me in shadow, and I noticed, a bit perversely, that he didn't even walk like a knight. I heard his footsteps echo on the floor stones. *His weight,* I thought, *his body, his movement, his energy.* They made that sound. Suddenly, I felt this wild desire to call out his name, just as I had bellowed out the hail of "starboard" during the race. I wanted to hear my own voice echo against all these stone columns and arches. I ached to break through the dense solemnity of the cathedral. I wanted to howl like a dog, to jump up and hear my own weight come thumping down against the cold stone floor. I could see the two of us, as if in an overhead camera shot, here in this sacred place, alive among all that cold granite. I pictured us running to meet each other, laughing, exuberant, and irreverent. He was close to me by now, walking with his hands in his pockets, looking upward. I felt so glad we had come here together. The whole race and collision that morning seemed like no more than a small detour on our way here.

"There you are," Kevin said, sounding a little annoyed that I had lingered so long on my own. "I started to think that you had left already."

"Don't be silly," I answered. "I was watching you all the time."

"I didn't see you for a while, that's all."

"Ready to go?" I asked. His blue eyes seemed to glisten from the light bouncing off all the polished granite pilasters. The bump on his forehead now looked like a small red kiss.

"It's really wonderful here," he answered. Then he added, "Yeah, let's go. I'm hungry."

We fell in step, side by side, and still I felt agitated. I had to *do* something, make some kind of gesture, something defiant, willful, and physical. I reached one arm around him and pulled him against me as we walked through the crowded narthex. I turned to face him and said only, "Hey." I felt him lean closer to me, against my shoulder as we kept walking. I felt his whole body, with those long legs, roll into my stride, like a boat gliding comfortably down the trough of a long ocean wave. I tugged him just a bit harder against me. He let his head tilt to one side and drop against mine. We both heard a very soft *bonk* as our skulls collided. When we stepped back out into the daylight, I heard just the smallest sigh from Kevin, before we separated.

# 3

## TO THE ISLE OF DEATH

*Hart Island, October 1978*

"Want to get out of here and go up to the boat?" I asked Kevin one afternoon in late October. I told him we could watch the sunset from the water. It was a warm and sunny afternoon, too nice a day to spend in the fluorescent-lit carpentry shop. As usual, Kasha was with him. She slept patiently in a corner of the shop with a fringe of sawdust clinging to her thick coat.

"What about Kasha? Can she come along too?" he asked me. He pulled a bandanna from his jeans and began to wipe the dust from his wire frame glasses. It seemed like such a fussy gesture for someone so boyish, I thought. Of course, I told him. It would be like a family outing.

Kevin had been working for me as a helper in my woodworking shop for about five months, and during that time he had gone out sailing with me a couple of times. I still considered him just my helper. We left the shop in lower Manhattan and stopped at my own apartment along Canal Street to pick up Auggie. We continued north on the West Side Highway.

"Do you think it's going to be windy?" Kevin asked me as Kasha panted over his right shoulder. In the back of my station wagon Auggie was on the left, behind me. Both had big canine smiles as they gulped in air from the back windows.

"Should be good," I answered him. "There's usually a westerly in the afternoon." In his voice I detected an edge of nervousness. His experience sailing with me included a few pleasant afternoons and that one Sunday back in June when he was my crew in that ill-fated race. For Kevin, it was a terrifying experience, and he would not race with me for another three years.

Weaving around the traffic on the Cross Bronx Expressway, we reached City Island way up in the Bronx by late afternoon. Untypically for Long Island Sound, the perennial late-day westerly breeze had not come up. I borrowed a rowboat and suggested that we explore Hart Island instead. This crooked little island of about 100 acres is just across a half-mile channel to the east of City Island. I clamped my little outboard motor to the stern of the rowboat and we pushed off from the dock at Grant's Boat Club. Kevin sat in the middle of the boat, by the oars, and Kasha sat up in the bow. She wagged her tail and held her nose into the breeze like an old salt. Auggie curled up nervously on the floor of the boat and pressed her body against me for security. The whole trip took about ten minutes. As we landed on a gravelly beach Kasha bounded ashore, eager to romp and explore. Auggie was past her puppyhood and needed more encouragement to clamber over the boat's gunwales.

Unknown to the land-bound, New York's waterways are scattered with small, mostly abandoned islands, from lower New York Bay all up the East River and along the coastline off Westchester. Most had been used for hospitals or military bases or prisons. Hart Island, like all these other specks of rock and overgrown rubble, felt appropriately desolate and creepy that afternoon.

"So who lives here?" Kevin asked, as we trekked inland from the beach.

"No one, as far as I've ever seen," I told him, and added, "I think the last ones here were the junkies from Phoenix House. But they left a couple of years ago. It's just us now," I added with a tentative laugh.

Through most of its history the island had been used for various kinds of prisons and isolation hospitals, dating from the Civil War. During the 1960s it had been used for a Nike missile launcher site and finally in the 1970s a drug rehab center took up residence there. This island had fascinated me ever since I first learned to sail at City Island in 1975. As far as I knew it was deserted; at least, no one challenged us as we strode inland away from our landing site on the beach.

Kevin ducked through some thickets and found what looked like the remains of the island's settlement. The emptiness of the place seemed to echo with all the previous inhabitants: the soldiers, the prisoners, the lame, sick, and even the hopeful young heroin addicts trying to invent a new life on this lonely island.

We wandered among a cluster of old hospital buildings. A street ran down what had once been the main axis, but was covered with leaves and debris. Trees on both sides had grown thick with ivy on their trunks and their dense foliage made all the abandoned buildings appear even more dark and gloomy. Everything had been burned and vandalized long ago. The buildings were just ransacked shells, with weeds growing between their granite foundation stones. At the head of the central street was a small chapel, vaguely Gothic. All the windows were bashed in. Yet inside, the dark wooden pews were still arranged in rows facing a missing altar.

It all seemed so sad and wasteful, and to me just one more proof that my city could not figure out how to make use of its extensive waterfront. We might as well have been examining Mayan ruins, speculating on what calamity caused everyone to flee this lovely setting.

The south end of the island was mostly flat, while the northern part, toward Orchard Beach, rose up to a small grassy hill. I had heard about a cemetery on Hart Island and had always assumed it was over where the land rose up gently. At the top of this hill stood a white slab, like a monument, visible several miles away.

As we came around to the eastern shore of the island, Kevin stopped. He stood for a few seconds, looking perplexed, with his hands jammed on top of his hips. "With this kind of view, really, no one wants to live here?" A frown of bafflement creased his high forehead. Indeed, where City Island had merely a view of the littered beach of Hart Island's western shore, here was the far more breathtaking vista of the entire Sound. Silently, we both stared out toward the numerous headlands of Long Island's north shore, all so clearly visible. On our left the towns of Westchester and Fairfield Counties stretched out to the far horizon. "I'll never understand this stupid city," Kevin said, more to himself, and I followed him as he continued walking north.

Reaching a level area on the eastern side of the island, we came upon some kind of construction or excavation site. We found several huge openings, hardly four feet deep, dug out of the sandy earth—great rectangular shallow pits. My first impression was that the city had begun to scoop out a cluster of vast swimming pools, much like the ambitious municipal pools that Robert Moses had built during his decades as New York City's imperious park commissioner. Perhaps the idea had been abandoned before more money was wasted pouring any concrete. Who would come out here in such numbers to go swimming when Orchard Beach was only ten minutes away?

Stepping to the edge, I saw that these pits were not empty. Scattered in stacks of no particular order were hundreds, maybe thousands, of wooden boxes. These crates of various sizes were all made the same way, as if they had come from the same carpentry shop. Canvas tarps covered most of these crates, almost as if to hide them from sunlight and the curious. The brown tarpaulins were old, weathered, and torn in places. Someone from the mainland probably made infrequent visits here and did not linger long enough to tidy up.

"What is all this?" Kevin asked, as he stood next to me by the edge. "What do they all say?" He pointed at the dark lettering visible on all the boxes. Kasha had already jumped into a pit and was furiously sniffing everything.

Curious, I followed her and read from the nearest box, a very small crate that would easily fit in my hands. I ignored the numerous flies buzzing around. The lettering was stenciled, black, and uniform.

" 'JOHN DOE,' " I read aloud to Kevin. " 'LEFT FOREFINGER.' " This was followed by a date, SEPTEMBER 4, 1954, and some kind of long serial number.

"Oh shit," Kevin blurted out. "This whole place is a graveyard. How creepy. This is neat. Kasha! Get her out of there before she digs something up."

I yelled to Kasha to jump out. I backed a few yards away from the wall of crates and felt behind me for the edge of the pit. I did not want to read any more of them. I sprung back out and looked again at the countless stacks of boxes under the sagging tarps. The full impact of this place began to hit me. This was not like reading the weathered headstones in a quaint New England churchyard. I began to feel that we did not belong here, no matter how novel our discovery was, or how idyllic the setting.

"Fingers," I said grimly to Kevin. "Boxes of human fingers."

"And legs, too, probably," he added, sounding almost enthusiastic.

"And babies, and fetuses," I continued sorrowfully.

"Yeah. And maybe they're not all really dead yet, inside some of those boxes." he added with a grin that showed his chipped front tooth.

"No," I shouted back, "don't say that."

I then recalled that I had heard of this place, years before. This was the designated potter's field for New York City, no ordinary cemetery. The indigent were buried here, their detached and unclaimed body parts or stillborn fetuses. This was the final dumping ground for the genuinely unwanted of the city, this lonely little island with its panoramic view of the Sound. City Islanders occasionally referred to Hart with a reticent nod of their heads in this direction. "Over there," they meant to say, wordlessly sidestepping any connection with this friendless place. And those boxes, of course, came up from the city by truck and then crossed the water by boat. How often did that little funeral procession pass in front of those many neon-lit seafood restaurants on City Island Avenue? The more I thought about it, the creepier I felt. Why had I never realized the purpose of the squat little ferry docked quietly at the foot of Fordham Street with DEPT OF MARINE AND AVIATION painted on its side?

"Kasha! Let's go!" Kevin repeated as we retraced our steps around the tip of the island. Parts of wrecked boats were starting to emerge as the receding tide uncovered all the boulders surrounding the island's perimeter. Over the years Hart Island had also become a convenient dumping ground for unwanted old power boats. The beach facing City Island was littered with their bleached and disintegrating hulks, all permanently heaved up above the high tide line. I scanned the beach looking for our rowboat.

"Hey, where's the fire?" Kevin called from a distance behind me. "Wait for Auggie, or are you afraid of the bogeyman all of a sudden?"

I was almost out of breath when I stopped to ask him, "Do you know what day this is?" I pressed my hand on his chest.

"Auggie's birthday?" he answered, squinting a little at the lowering sun behind me to the west.

"Good try, but no, much worse," I told him. "This is October thirty-first, as in *All Hallows Eve.* And look where we are. Get it? This is Halloween, and we're in a graveyard. I want to get off."

Kevin thought about this for a few seconds, and an odd smile came across his rosy cheeks. "There's nothing to be afraid of," he replied in a slow, flat voice. Then he tilted his head back so that his eyes rolled up into his skull and all I could see were the whites. "It's a lovely island," he continued, "why don't you stay here tonight . . . with me." He gave a sly laugh and reached out with one big hand to find me.

"Stop it," I told him. "You're making me nervous. Let's find the dinghy and get the hell out of here." The dogs were nearby and when I searched a little farther down the beach I spotted our aluminum rowboat. It was now high and dry with its bow painter still looped around a boulder, just as we had left it.

From behind me, Kevin grabbed my arm, hard, with a grip of death and announced in that same Dracula voice, "Why are you leaving so soon? Why not stay here with me, *tonight?*" Again he laughed and rolled his head back to show me two sickeningly white eyeballs.

"Come on, stop it," I pleaded. "You're frightening Auggie." At that moment the dog was rolling on her back on a patch of wet sand. I pulled myself away from the Kevin-monster's grip and trotted the last twenty yards for the rowboat. *Oh stalwart little craft,* I thought, *how happy I am to find you here again.*

Kasha jumped in, gung ho as ever for another boat ride. But Auggie was in one of her obstinate moods and seemed reluctant to trust this tipsy little vessel that smelled of metal and gasoline. I hefted her back into the stern. We dragged the boat to the water's edge. Kevin took up his place in the center seat ready at the oars while I tossed my sneakers and socks into the boat. I shoved the boat out until the water was up to my knees, turned the bow toward City Island,

and climbed over the transom, as Kevin started immediately to pull away from the beach. *We had escaped,* I thought, as I began to prime the outboard motor. Auggie decided to lick between my bare toes.

It was nearly 4:30 p.m., and it would be sundown very soon. A light breeze had sprung up and the bow of the boat made busy little ripples as we inched toward City Island.

I got the motor started and Kevin shipped the oars inboard. I gave the motor more gas and the boat surged ahead. Kasha took up her position as lookout in the bow with her nose bisecting the breeze. Auggie sat close to me in the stern, panting nervously. Kevin remained in the middle, facing aft toward the island. Hart Island was well behind us when he raised his left hand and pointed a stubby forefinger at me. This finger seemed to have a will of its own as it slowly kept getting closer to my face. I gave the Seagull full throttle and hoped that just the sound, that stubborn hammering of its single cylinder, would frighten off any demons. Kevin, though ten years younger than I, had discovered how easy it was to frighten me, or at least to reawaken the frightened little kid inside me. I kept calm, certain that we had enough fuel to make it back to our dock, where I would be safe from the demons of Hart Island. Nevertheless, that forefinger kept coming closer, inexorably, as if saying, "You. You. I'm coming for you."

It was nighttime when I dropped Kevin and Kasha back at his apartment on West Thirty-Eighth Street, not far from the Port Authority Bus Terminal. As usual his street was busy with hookers and transvestites in search of off-duty bus drivers. When he stepped from my car a few of the girls flanking his dumpy tenement waved and hooted with encouragement. "Hello, honey. Is that your big doggie?" Showing off a shaved and muscular thigh, one of them leered, "Want to have some fun?" Kasha jumped to the sidewalk and Kevin slammed the car door.

"Think you can resist the temptation?" I asked Kevin.

He wrinkled his nose, saying, "They never give up, but they're harmless. It's the junkies who make all the trouble around here."

He returned my parting wave as I drove off. I found myself uneasy about leaving him there. I told myself that he was no hick from out of town and he could take care of himself. Driving downtown I could hear police sirens and fireworks exploding, all part of the city's anarchistic celebration for Halloween, and I remembered why I had come to hate this dumb holiday. I was eager to get off the streets and back to my own apartment.

Climbing my stairs, I tried not to worry about Kevin up there on that awful block. It was not the streetwalkers that I was concerned about, but all their attending pimps and hustlers, the drug heads and seductive muggers who worked the dark streets west of Ninth Avenue.

Kasha was supposed to be Kevin's watchdog. Though Kasha was a big dog, she was not much of a killer type. Nor was Kevin. Before he got Kasha he had been held up while crossing the empty parking lot next door. Someone stepped from a shadow and held a gun to his ribs. He handed over a pocketful of crumpled bills, ones most likely, and managed to keep his wallet. When he told me about this, I was glad for his safe escape, but I was left with mixed feelings about getting too friendly with someone whose life had almost been ended in such a random and meaningless manner. Would it happen again?

Coming home that night I kept thinking about Kevin, alone uptown on Thirty-Eighth Street, and me, alone downtown on Canal Street. Lowering the blinds, I remembered watching Kevin some days before as he walked east on Canal toward Sixth Avenue. He was on his way home to walk his dog. It was late and he had stayed around with me until nearly 10:30 p.m. First we had played some Frisbee after work. Then he had joined me upstairs, where we spooned our way to the bottom of a container of Haagen-Dazs ice cream. Like a cat that insists on sitting on the paperwork in front of you, Kevin seemed not to want to leave.

He was just my helper, my employee, I kept reminding myself as I stared out at the empty street. Yet I knew, already, wordlessly, reluctantly, that I missed him.

I thought of the couple of times I had visited Kevin in his apartment. I was amused by the air of urbanity he carried about himself.

He was knowledgeable about fine food, cooking, travel, tobacco, wines. Even though I knew exactly how much money he was earning, he had put on this lavish effort to impress me. He laid out a plate of Scandinavian hors d'oeuvres with thin slices of Danish salami set on little squares of Swedish rye bread, each with a dollop of grainy French mustard. Over a bed of lettuce he piled smoked baby clams, from a tin, and then with a practiced flourish, he gave the whole plate a squeeze of fresh lemon. He was living like a pauper in his walk-up, yet he was entertaining me with the grand pretenses of someone managing heroically under "reduced circumstances."

He slept with his mattress on the floor and kept most of his clothes in a wooden footlocker. He said it had belonged to his father. That was his Danish connection, I learned. Kurt Olsen had been a merchant seaman from Copenhagen away at sea during most of Kevin's boyhood, though Kevin tried to make it sound like a romantic life. Later, Kurt worked on the tugboats in New York Harbor to be closer to his family.

These were the New York Central Railroad tugs that used to be a common sight in the Upper Bay when I was a kid. They shuttled boxcars between New Jersey and all the rail terminals that once lined the Manhattan and Brooklyn waterfront. I had seen then often and by fifteen I knew all the railroad insignias: the Erie Lackawanna, the Pennsylvania, the Baltimore & Ohio, the Chesapeake & Ohio, the Boston & Maine, the Jersey Central, the Lehigh Valley and the New York Central Lines. Of course, that was all history, just like Kurt. He had died when Kevin was barely a teenager. The tugs and railroad barges and all the busy piers belonged to a former generation already.

Kevin talked to me about his trips to Denmark, visiting relatives. I noticed that on an envelope stuffed with photographs he had spelled it "Danmark," like a native, even though, like me, he had been born in Brooklyn. Only later, long after his birth parents had died, did his adoptive family move to Lakewood, New Jersey. I was touched by his need to obscure all that and portray himself as the descendant from a race of Vikings.

As they tumbled out of his hands, Kevin showed me scenes of Copenhagen; crinkled old black and whites of the Little Mermaid gently kneeling on her rock in the harbor, the royal castle at Rosenborg, Tivoli Gardens ablaze with lights. Another yellow packet from Kodak held photos of a robust Kurt with his arms around his shipmates, all of them looking a bit glassy-eyed. Then a snapshot of Kevin's newlywed mother and father posed on board the deck of the liner *Stockholm.* The skyline of lower Manhattan rises up in the background. It was the skyline of the early 1950s, before he was even born.

There were more pictures from later years: Ektachromes of Kevin and his dad rowing on the lake in Prospect Park, Brooklyn. Kevin alone at the oars, maybe twelve, skinny as a candle yet his already big knuckles are confidently gripping the heavy oars. Just a tentative smile plays across his pale face. *He looks embryonic and ill-proportioned, and so vulnerable,* I thought, as I handed him back the picture.

That afternoon as we sat together on his bed, he served me ice-cold Aquavit. Then he dug out a meerschaum pipe from the folds of a soft cloth wrapper. Before coming to New York he had worked as a pipe maker in Virginia Beach. He liked working with his hands, and they were thick and strong. He filled the bowl and lit up. In a moment the room took on the pungent smell of his Borkum Rif mixture. As it slowly burned, the crusty odor smelled like the tarred hemp on old—very old—sailing ships. I listened to him go on about pipe making. All the time I kept asking myself, *Why is he doing all this for me? Why is he pulling out all the stops like this?*

My dreamy recollections of that first visit to Kevin's place were interrupted by the explosions of M-80 firecrackers set off by the teenagers over in Little Italy, many blocks across Canal Street. The young devils would drop fireworks into an empty trash can, and the explosions shuddered like cannon fire off the tired old tenements of Mott and Mulberry Streets.

I fed Auggie and stretched out on my bed, still thinking about Kevin. "Little Kevin," I called him, because once at the shop there had been another helper, a hulking nineteen-year-old whom I called "Big Kevin." Kevin in fact stood nearly a head taller than myself, yet "Little Kevin" seemed appropriate. At least he never complained.

Nothing happened between us during that first visit, though I clearly felt the tension of his desire for me lingering in those empty rooms. I came up again to his drafty apartment a few weeks later when he asked me for advice on renovating the place. He did not know where to even begin; every room was a project unto itself. The place had some potential; four rooms with most of the original moldings still intact, and modest parquet floors under the cheap linoleum.

Again we sat together on his bed. The bed was covered with a dark red blanket that he said was from L. L. Bean. He was proud of the four black stripes sewn into the edge indicating the blanket's weight and quality.

Finally, he turned to face me and gently pushed my shoulders down until I lay flat on the bed with him on top of me. We were still dressed, yet I remember being impressed by how dense he felt. There seemed to be more to him that his wiry body should contain. He began to kiss me, but I resisted. I just did not feel ready for his insistent tongue inside my mouth. He moved lower and opened my jeans. First with his fingers, and then with his mouth, he seduced me, and I did not resist. Afterward I was surprised by what we had done, and a little embarrassed. It would be a long time before I understood his desire for me. I did not think that I was in love with him, and the sex had seemed pretty mechanical. Still, I knew that we had moved closer to each other, and however reluctantly or clumsily, the dynamic between us was changing.

The day after Halloween was just another workday when Kevin arrived by himself at the shop.

"No Kasha today?" I asked him.

"She's still too wound up from last night's coup d'etat."

"The what?" I asked him, turning completely around in my swivel chair.

"You know, the attack, all the explosions. I kept thinking that there were tanks surrounding the building. Kasha kept whimpering every time another M-80 blew up somewhere. It was like in those movies, you know, where the military bombs the royal palace. Then in the morning there's a new dictator and everyone is sitting around in the cafés saying, 'Eh, no problem. It was time for a change, anyway.'"

He returned to the work that he had left the day before. In the afternoon I noticed that Kevin had stopped to fill in his time card for the previous day, October thirty-first, when we had left early. He scribbled in his time and then, in the box for the day's project, he added, SAILING, TO THE ISLE OF DEATH.

I held the card in my hand for a long time, smiling. I decided that he had been such good company I would pay him for the entire day. At the same time I realized that I wanted to live with him.

Despite all the contradictions I began to imagine a life of living and working with the same person. It even seemed inevitable when I thought about all the other times in my life that I had ignored conventions.

Much later that day, as we sat around my apartment, Kevin stood up and pulled on his jacket. He was about to leave; once again he had to head back uptown to walk Kasha.

"You know," I began offhandedly, "if you lived down here you wouldn't have to go back uptown every night just to walk Kasha. No more long trips up to Thirty-Eighth Street." By this time I had been making out his paychecks directly to his landlord. He did not even have a checking account, and I doubted if he could really afford his rent and other expenses. And as for as his renovation work, he was already spending most of his time with me.

"You mean, live here, together . . . like boyfriends?" he asked me, sounding surprised. He knelt in front of me.

"Yeah, I guess so," I answered, and we looked at each other. I smiled and reached for him through his denim jacket. My hands moved up to his neck and I brought his head closer to me. I ran my fingers through his thick hair and I could smell the warmth of his scalp.

"How soon?" he asked me with his face just inches from me.

For a long moment our eyes met, his blue, mine hazel. Then I answered him. "Whenever you want. I'll help you move tomorrow after work if you like. You don't have that much stuff up there anyway."

"What about the kitties?" he asked me in a childlike, almost petulant voice.

"Bring 'em down too. They should have more people handling them. They're growing up too isolated from human contact, alone all day up there." As he looked at me he parted his lips just enough for the tip of his tongue to stick out. I knew what was coming next.

"Uh-oh," I said passively. Slowly and deliberately he removed my eyeglasses and set them aside. "Uh-oh," I repeated, as he gripped my arms and slipped his tongue between my lips. By now, the warmth and weight of his young body felt familiar and welcome.

# 4

## WORKING TO WINDWARD

*Oyster Bay, June 1979*

Okay, we were young and in love and we yearned to go someplace together, to sail away beyond the familiar boundaries of Hart Island and Eastchester Bay. Racing was not for Kevin. He wanted adventure and discovery, not tension and competition. Together we felt safe and comfortable in our little boat. I was still impressed with my boat, the Rhodes 19. She was my first keel boat and felt roomy and stable; I could walk up to the bow or sit on one side and the boat would not roll over. A stout little vessel, weighing about 1,100 pounds, of which almost a third was the ballast in her keel. I was proud of that keel, which represented the difference between a tipsy dinghy with a centerboard and genuine boat that was self-righting.

Though mostly open cockpit, the boat had a little enclosure, called a cuddy, up forward where sail bags and clothing could be kept dry. In rain or rough weather someone could crouch inside for protection.

I was no longer satisfied just to race for a few hours once each week, and then drive home. Moreover, I felt bad about leaving Kevin alone every Sunday morning when I disappeared to go racing. I was afraid he would drift away to see friends down on the Jersey shore, or even worse, go sailing with my old friend Robert, who kept his own boat on Fire Island. Holding onto Kevin became more important than my standing in the fleet. Kevin's idea of sailing was *going* somewhere, exploring new harbors, inveigling ourselves into the WASPY yacht clubs along the Sound. I already knew the names of the most exclusive yacht clubs: Larchmont, Port Washington, Manhasset Bay, Seawanhaka, Noroton, Stamford, Newport. Kevin, too, wanted to sit on those cool verandas sipping drinks, hobnob on the sprawling lawns with other yacht owners, admire the trophies and ship models.

I was determined to do an overnight trip, an entire day sailing to some faraway harbor and then sleeping on board my own boat. *That* was what yachting was supposed to be.

I was dazzled by the charts of Long Island Sound, by the sheer expanse of this great protected bay that stretched nearly 100 miles to the east. My God, I thought, poring over the charts, I could easily spend half my life sailing these waters, exploring all the harbors and anchorages and yacht clubs out there. Grant's Boat Club, even City Island, began to look like only a jumping-off point.

Oyster Bay beckoned to me as a destination. It was about fifteen miles away, a perfect distance for a long afternoon sail. We would make the attempt the following June, when the weather was warm again.

Of course the boat had no berths, no head, no stove, no water tanks. It was strictly a day sailer. We would scoot under the little cuddy enclosure and rig up the canvas boom tent at night for protection. We could unroll an old mattress on the floor of the cockpit for our bed. Like any adventurers, we would have to find toilets and showers once we made our landfall. The history of sailing is rich with similarly audacious and foolhardy voyages.

June arrived, and on the third Saturday we packed sandwiches for lunch and cast off from City Island. Our course was east by northeast. Unfortunately it was flat calm, so we needed the outboard motor for the entire trip. We were not sailing, but we were going someplace, leaving our home waters at last. Within an hour we passed Execution Lighthouse and soon, for the first time in my years of sailing, the familiar towers of the Throgs Neck Bridge dipped low on the horizon. Far ahead, on the other side of Hempstead Harbor, we could just see our next landmark, Matinicock Point, where a finger of rocks projected out from the land.

Kevin worked the tiller in the stern while I made myself comfortable resting against the mast up on the foredeck. If he lifted his head a little he could read the compass mounted on the cabin top, just aft of the mast. This was the first time we were going someplace so far that we actually needed to follow a compass course, and Kevin looked very intent as he held the boat steady on 080° magnetic.

I loved the idea that we could be at opposite ends of our boat. It sounds so pretentious now, talking about the stern, foredeck, cockpit, and cabin of such a little boat. In truth, today I might call it just a dinghy and would scoff at the idea of using it for an overnight trip. Yet back then the boat seemed big to me, and that 400-pound iron keel gave the boat more than stability, it gave it *dignity*. This was no beach toy that a couple of teenagers could pick up.

As we pushed along through the glassy water I was lulled into a malaise from the constant yammering of the outboard motor. Astern of us a V-shaped wake fanned out until it blended with the other ripples.

"Something's wrong with the motor!" Kevin shouted to me. The motor's sound changed abruptly. The rpms raced up and the motor screamed, whined in panic, then slowed down ominously. Stumbling back to the stern I could see that the outboard had slipped off its bracket and was going into the water.

I lunged for it and landed on my stomach flat across the stern. With a frantic grunt of "Gotcha!" I caught the unruly devil. The motor was gasping for life, sputtering water that had gotten into the carburetor.

Kevin watched, amazed to see me move so fast, and instinctively grabbed the legs of my jeans to be sure that I did not go overboard with my beloved British Seagull.

"What now?" Kevin asked after I retightened the motor on the stern bracket. "Will it run again? We're not going to have to paddle all the way there?" This was his first boating mishap since that collision the previous season, and I recognized that worried look on his face.

"Certainly," I told him with confidence. He looked doubtful. "Here, watch," I said, and wound the pull cord around the flywheel. I showed him the little priming plunger and pumped until fuel overflowed and dripped down into the water, leaving little rainbow spots of gasoline. "Okay? Now you just pull. Here, you do it," I said, moving aside to encourage him.

"This better work," he replied, clearly doubtful that the half-drowned engine had any life left in it. He yanked on the cord, the flywheel went around in an offhand way, and the motor sputtered.

"Hold it down with one hand on the top," I showed him, "then pull really hard to get a good spin." I wanted him to see that this was no crisis. Not for a Seagull. He turned around, held the motor as I suggested and, biting his upper lip with concentration, heaved back on the starter cord. The motor spun a few times, producing a few distinct pops of ignition followed by some wet farts out of the exhaust. "Now what?" Kevin asked, frustrated, with the starter cord hanging limply in his hand.

"Keep trying," I said confidently. "It'll start."

Again he yanked on the starter cord and the engine came to life with a loud roar. Blue smoke poured out as all the unburned fuel was blown from the cylinder. I yelled for him to throttle back some.

"It's all yours," I said and slid down next to him in the cockpit. "Steady as she goes," I intoned and gently nudged him in the ribs. He wedged his legs across the cockpit and took up the long mahogany tiller once again. "Amazing," was all I could hear him say over the noise of the motor. The rhythm of the outboard motor returned as we continued toward Oyster Bay.

Two hours later we rounded Rocky Point to starboard. Cautiously, approaching our first landfall, we followed the red buoys that marked the channel as the land continued to fold back toward the right. Oyster Bay lies inside an elbow-like peninsula of land that provides nearly total protection from the Sound. One last mile from our destination, amid a forest of lights on shore, I spotted the cluster of oil tanks indicated on the harbor chart. The town dock had to be a short distance to the right.

Darkness came fast as we navigated through a buoyed channel bisecting a vast mooring field. Around us in the still black water were hundreds of sailboats, all looking very sleek and glamorous. They lay on their mooring lines, haughty and expensive, like pampered race-horses. Searching for the Texaco sign marking the dock, we saw only a bizarre cluster of green and white lights, all whirling through the air in some kind of extravagant display.

Slowing the motor, we continued closer in until at last we could see the lights of a carnival set up in the park just beyond the waterfront. What had so baffled us was a pair of space capsules, spinning around a seventy-foot rotating arm. The whole affair was festooned with flash-ing green and white lights.

Our boat nudged alongside the dock with a quiet scrape, and Kevin jumped ashore with the bow line. A sandy-haired kid running the fuel dock stood there a while just looking at us with his hands in the pockets of his shorts. I came up and said we needed a slip for the night. He gave a bored shrug and told us to just stay where we were. He was ready to close anyway, he added, and said not to worry about any overnight charge.

Kevin looked at me and smiled. I was not sure if he was pleased about our good fortune or hoping the dock boy might hang around a while longer. Kevin usually carried a couple of joints for just such en-counters. But the kid locked up his little shed and said good night to us in a rubber-bandy kind of voice. As I watched his fuzzy legs bound-ing up the ramp I realized I had forgotten to ask him about a key to the head.

Satisfied with our successful arrival nevertheless, Kevin and I climbed the ramp and surveyed the harbor from atop the seawall.

We did not bother to visit the tawdry carnival. We walked into the town and read the plaque on Main Street marking Teddy Roosevelt's summer White House. I soon realized that the glamour of Oyster Bay, the great mansions with their sprawling lawns, was all behind tall iron gates, well outside of the town.

We ate dinner and then ambled back through the deserted streets to the waterfront. Our boat was still there and, in its doughty way, seemed to be saying, "I'm little, but I'm as much of a real sailboat as you big expensive guys." And for that night, at least, she was our home.

Crawling around under the canvas boom tent, we made up our bed on the cockpit floor. In the semidarkness we wiggled out of our clothes and finally lay next to each other, both our heads under the small dome of the cuddy enclosure below the mast. We waited quietly for sleep. We were both tired, but it felt too weird and unfamiliar. I felt vulnerable and exposed without even a door to our bedroom, like a couple of hobos huddled under a flimsy lean-to.

"Kevin?"

"What?"

"Are you asleep?"

"Not yet."

"Are you *about* to be asleep?"

"I doubt it. It's these goddamned cleats you put all over the cockpit floor. They're poking into my back. Why don't you sleep on this side?"

"But I always sleep on *this* side," I answered him. "Besides, the Harken Magic Box is right under me, between my shoulders. Kevin?"

"What?"

"Maybe we should go to a motel? What do you think?"

"Don't be a jerk. Just relax and go to sleep." We both shifted around to find a spot without too many obstructions. Maybe this really was a dumb idea, I thought. It was nearly 1:00 a.m. I let myself concentrate on the sway of the boat lying against the dock. I felt the hull gently press against the rubber fenders and heard the docklines creaking as the current tried to pull us back into the Sound. We were safe, I told myself, and we were together.

In the morning I awoke with a tightness in my stomach. It was a lovely day, with sunshine and clouds and wind. Yet I also felt trapped. We had no choice; having come this far, now we had to sail back again. In truth I had never sailed so far in my own boat, and that day clearly was going to be a sailing day. The outbound trip had been boring but easy.

After breakfast in town I noticed that all the treetops were swaying and it was not even 10:00 a.m. Wind that early meant it would be a steadily building breeze all day, maybe more wind than I was used to or wanted.

We prepared to leave the dock just as things started to get busy. Huge sailboats and towering power cruisers, like fiberglass mastodons, were already lining up to land at the dock, hungry for a day's supply of diesel fuel and ice. The smartassed dock boy was back again, still wearing his faded khakis, and this time, in the daylight, I noticed the woven turk's head knot looped around his slender ankle. It obviously had been braided in place, with deft skill. By himself? By a girlfriend? Like a nun's ring, it struck me as a subtle declaration that he was bound to the sea, and added another layer of cockiness to the lanky kid.

In the channel leading back to open water, boats were already tacking back and forth in the developing breeze. This felt more like a normal June morning with cooler weather and gusty winds from the northwest. We motored away from the dock with our little outboard echoing against the hulls of all the boats around us. We hoisted mainsail and jib and killed the noisy motor. With the wind off our stern we bore off to retrace the channel that led to the open sound. Our speed picked up, the boat heeled a little, and it felt good to be sailing at last.

The boat heeled some more, dug in deeper, and began rushing through the water. A long wake streamed back from our rudder and made a playful bubbling sound. As we swung around Rocky Point we were aware that the Sound was much choppier. We were well out of Oyster Bay and committed to the homeward passage. This was going to be a day of serious sailing, I thought, as I looked up at all the puffy clouds drifting quickly across the sky.

"Are we having fun yet?" I asked Kevin who was sitting up on the windward deck next to me. Wearing a clean T-shirt under his soft flannel shirt casually open at the neck, he looked like he came from the same scrappy genetic stock as our dock boy, only I could talk to him, or kiss him, whenever I wanted. I felt very lucky, and he smiled back at me. Bell Buoy 17 fell astern and we could hear its discordant clanging.

"Can you take the helm for a while? We're trying to do 270 degrees. Watch for the next green bell buoy to port."

"Sure," Kevin answered, sounding confident. He frowned as he stretched his neck to read the compass. As the wind increased the boat streaked along, tossing up spray from an occasional wave. The Sound felt so much bigger that day, a vast body of water, rough and unpredictable, no longer so friendly. There were whitecaps, and spray was starting to kick up and fly back over the cockpit. Kevin's glasses were splattered with dots of salt.

Both of us had to work to keep the boat moving and pointing upwind. The gusts and shifts required quick jabs of the tiller and sometimes one of us had to let out the mainsail in a strong puff. Kevin could handle most of this himself, for a while. He knew the boat and would sometimes ease off a little on the traveler to help keep the boat flat. We were sailing upwind and this required concentration. He seemed to be getting into the rhythm of it. I crawled into the protection of the cuddy up forward and looked at the chart, probably for the fifth time that morning. Bell Buoy 19, marking Oak Neck Point, would be next.

As the morning wore on the waves grew steeper, maybe two to three feet. No squall really, just gusty, and wet going for a boat with hardly more than twenty-two inches of freeboard. We shared a bottle of juice but did not feel like trying to eat any of the sandwiches left over from Saturday.

By noon the wind was steadily picking up. The waves were sloppy and the boat's bow sometimes smacked with a heavy splash that nearly stopped us cold. At other times a rogue sea would shove the bow to one side and I could see that Kevin was having trouble anticipating these sudden shifts. The Rhodes was a well-behaved boat, and did not pound or take solid water over her buoyant bow.

The wind was easily over sixteen knots and puffy. When a fresh gust blew up the boat would suddenly lurch over to leeward and Kevin would almost lose his grip on the tiller. He would spring inboard for an instant and then become disoriented about which way to steer after the gust passed. The boat was starting to heave around, and I could see that Kevin was getting tired and losing control. I kept wondering if I should bring down one of our sails.

"Maybe you better take this now, Gener," he said, eager to be relieved. Steering the boat was quickly becoming an ordeal. I slipped behind him and took the helm. For me this was the first time that the

Sound seemed so big and menacing. I looked out and there were whitecaps everywhere. Other boats, all of them much bigger, had their sails reefed down, and those going in the same direction were heeled way over and, like us, working to windward.

My hands, seemingly on their own, played the helm and eased the mainsheet in and out. In the big gusts the whole mainsail would start to shake wildly, and the aluminum mast would shudder. I began to realize that we were in trouble. The boat was clearly overpowered as the wind began to gust up even stronger, easily over twenty knots. All across the Sound big whitecaps with beards of spray were kicked up everywhere. Kevin grew noticeably unhappy. He looked tense and hunched up, and he no longer played the jib sheet in and out with each puff. "I'm tired of getting wet up here," he announced to me as he moved off the deck and sat on one of the seats. He tried with difficulty to wriggle his head into the neck of a woolen sweater. I had not planned for this kind or difficulty, not consciously. But I had to get this boat home, with both of us in it.

"Get under the deck if you want to avoid the spray," I urged him. "I'm okay up here." While I needed his extra weight up on the high side, I did not want him to think that we had come to a desperate situation. I hoped that I could still balance the boat myself and dodge the stronger gusts. I felt a concern for him that he stay warm and dry. His vision of himself as a stalwart seafaring Viking, complete with his bristly blond beard, was not quite accurate today.

He slid up forward, further into the boat and away from the wind and noise and spray. He curled up against the bulkhead, braced himself into a corner, and faced aft, watching me sail. For the first time since I knew him he looked small and childlike. Not only did he look afraid, but he did not seem to care that it showed, and that troubled me.

"Gener," he called up to me in a voice I had never heard before, "I'm scared."

*Me too,* I thought, but instead I answered, "It's not that bad, Little Kevin; it's just the gusts that are strong." I had to talk to him between the noise of wind and water pounding all over the boat.

He had good reason to be afraid, for in truth, the boat was way overpowered, and most of the time I was easing out the mainsail to spill more and more wind just to prevent the boat from being knocked over on her side. At the same time, I feared that if I dropped one of our sails we would not have enough power to push on through the headseas. The little eggbeater motor would be useless in these conditions. We were on our way home, sailing our asses off, and it was not exactly fun anymore, but there was nothing else to do.

"Don't worry, Kiki," I said, using an affectionate nickname. "I can see Sands Point already." He knew that landmark, knew that it was not much more than an hour's sail from there to the end of Hart Island. At least we were making progress.

Wedged against the forward bulkhead, he pulled out a pack of cigarettes from his jacket and lit one up. The smoke from his Rothman's drifted past me, a sharp smell I had grown familiar with during the past two years. He looked up at me and gave me a tentative smile, just a nervous curl of his lips.

This was *working* to windward in the truest sense, and crabbing steadily upwind, we made it past the familiar landmarks of Prospect Point, Execution Light, and then at last Sands Point. Hart Island was just two miles farther, and already I could see its slender smokestack.

"We're getting there, Little Kevin," I told him. "I can already see Hart Island. Isn't that your favorite place?"

He pitched his cigarette overboard and sat with his knees curled up close to his chest. His eyes were closed, as if trying to rest. He mumbled something that I could not hear, but it sounded happy, or at least relieved.

What had taken seven hours motoring Saturday we managed to cover in less than five that blustery spring day. In the sunlight the decks sparkled with salt, and the sails were glistening wet from spray. It wasn't comfortable, yet there was a rhythm now to the rise and fall, lurch and rush of the boat's motion.

Shortly after we passed the end of Hart Island I bore off toward the north and eased out the main. I aimed the bow toward the crane marking Grant's Boat Club. Soon we slipped behind the protective lee of City Island and everything calmed down dramatically. The wind was fully on the port quarter and we rolled along on a comfortable broad reach.

"We're almost there, Kiki," I said. He looked over the stern and saw the smoother water in our wake. The boat's motion was flatter, and our speed steadier. He pulled himself out from the protection of the forward cabin, sat on his knees and looked around, saying, "We're home already!" How quickly he seemed to have recovered, I thought; he seemed positively jaunty.

He scanned the horizon and saw Hart Island astern of us. He turned back to me with a new look on his face. He gave me a mischievous smile that emphasized the chip on his right canine. Despite his small babylike lips, he seemed to know how to make himself resemble a teenaged werewolf. He raised his left hand and one at a time mechanically folded back each of his fingers until only his forefinger remained outstretched and pointed, portentously, toward me. The finger, with a will of its own, slowly inched closer. It rose and fell as if climbing its own unseen currents.

"Yes," Kevin said with that awful smile. Then he tilted back his head, slowly opened his lids and focused those blind zombie eyes on me again. "Yes," he repeated. "We're almost home."

# 5

## THE MYSTERY OF THE OTHER

*Canal Street, March 1980*

I slipped into bed next to him. Even six inches away he always felt incredibly warm, as if he were burning up energy much too fast. He faced the wall, while I slept on the outside. The two cats occupied the warm valleys between our legs. They were no longer kittens, but now adults each with his own personality and habits that had evolved in response to our routines.

Kevin was almost asleep when he shifted a bit and pulled up the covers. I picked up Jackson, the fatter of the two cats, and placed him on my other side, giving me room to slither up to Kevin's smooth back. The warmth was amazing, like some kind of engine. He raised his head to clear his throat, then settled back down. He wiggled his butt against me and I crossed my arm over his shoulder and let my face rest just near the back of his neck. I could smell his blond hair. He drifted back to sleep with the entire length of his body nested against mine. I could feel Kevin's chest rise and dip under the quilt as his breathing slowed.

I wondered if, at some point on this dark voyage to somnolence, our breathing would fall into synch. Which one of us would be the leader? Or was it a natural process of give and take until a perfect match took place, like two different frequencies on an oscilloscope that eventually merge; the peaks and valleys of the two sine waves becoming one loop, unstoppable. It was all too much to figure out.

Around us all was quiet. Only an occasional car or truck could be heard rumbling outside on the cobblestones of Canal Street. Traffic into the Holland Tunnel to New Jersey had finally ceased. All six of us, two dogs, two cats, and two men, functioned now as a unit, a household. Except Jackson.

Jackson, never a heavy sleeper, was lying next to me when he saw something stir under the covers and presumed it was a mouse. What he saw was my leg moving, with my foot rising up at the end of the bed. In his mind whatever part of me went under the covers disappeared from me and became prey for his hunting games. He leapt up and pounced on my big toe with all his claws at the ready.

"Oow, goddamnit, Jackson! We're not playing mousey now." I yelled at him and sat up, pulling all the bedding apart. I reached to grab the idiot cat. Someone had programmed him to attack anything that moved under the blankets. That had been me. It was another of our bedtime games. I tossed him off the bed and he fell to the floor with a heavy thud.

Kevin sat up suddenly, "Go to sleep, Gener. Do you want me to lock you in the bathroom?"

"It wasn't my fault. Mr. Big attacked me."

"You get him started. Now look, you've disturbed Sven." From between Kevin's legs a gray and white lump of paws and ears gave out a confused "eeeooow."

"I'll be good. I'll be good," I promised Kevin and rolled back over to return to my sleeping position. Jackson leapt onto the shelf that served as our headboard and padded over to lay down above Kevin. I wriggled back into my former position and once again reached my arm around Kevin to pull him closer.

Kevin had never locked me in our bathroom, of course. It was a joke. One time we were horsing around; he was shaving and I was taking a shower. I splashed him, he squirted shaving cream all over me, and then I aimed the shower head at him. He jumped back into the kitchen, and that's when he slammed the door and held it shut while I scratched and pleaded to be let out.

It seemed like innocent horseplay to me at the time. It became a kind of joke between us, being locked in a closet or the bathroom. But for Kevin it had memories and associations that I had to ferret out of him during our first Christmas together. This was the Christmas of

1979, and while we were very happy with our lives I found him frequently bitchy and depressed. He would get touchy and fly off in anger at silly annoyances, things I would have expected him to joke about.

After one particularly furious outburst I got him to tell me about the time his father, Kurt, had locked his mother in a closet as part of a long argument the two had been having. I did not push for many details, but it was clear that they were both boozed up at the time, and it was Christmas. Kurt had been away at sea for weeks. As I listened to this story I could picture all this through Kevin's eyes as a kid, watching his father roughly grab Marqueritte by her pale slender arm and shove her into a hall closet and then snap the key in the lock. That was no game, no horseplay between boys. No. That signaled the end of that Christmas for Kevin and his younger brother Richard. Nor was it an isolated event.

It was not easy for Kevin to talk about any of this history; he was not introspective about his life and tried to make a show of leaving the past behind him. But the buried memories of abuse and disappointment crept through the back door of his feelings all the time. They drove his emotions in ways that slowly became apparent to me. He liked to present himself as handsome, confident, and complete. Which he was. Yet it was his casual bravado in telling me the story of his mother locked in the closet, with a shallow laugh, that alerted me to something more lurking there.

On the shelf over our heads, Jackson stretched himself out and started to purr. He extended his limbs some more, and the purring got even louder. As the cat relaxed he opened his mouth and added a throaty gasping. I tried to ignore it, or pretend it was just a truck parked outside our window with its diesel motor throbbing. That happened pretty often in our neighborhood, whenever the drivers of the private sanitation trucks took a break at midnight and sat in their cabs sipping a bottle of cheap whiskey wrapped in a paper bag.

Jackson reached a state of feline ecstasy, flipped his tail around, and it landed on Kevin's forehead. "That does it!" He shouted and leaped up, and with a big hand he swiped Jackson clear off the ledge. The cat flew over my head and landed again with a thud on the floor. Kevin's face was red, his eyes small and his forehead creased in a frown. Just a couple of seconds ago I had my lips near the back of his neck, all but tasting him. Now he was in a rage, and it baffled me to see so much anger erupt out of him so suddenly from what looked like such peace. Could I ever understand what raged within him? Could I ever handle all that?

"Hey, take it easy; you'll hurt him," I said, trying to soothe Kevin. "You look like a crazy man. You even frightened Sven." The little gray cat was now perched on the far end of the bed, sitting up and wondering how he had gotten there. Kevin was especially fond of him; they fit together so well, those two skinny ones.

"Oh, Svenska, come back here," Kevin said, cooing to the gray cat. His sudden anger seemed to be spent. He bent forward and took up the cat in his hands. Sven began his own soft purring. "Now go to sleep, and no more games this time," Kevin said as he pressed his head once again back into his pillow, his words already muffled.

In another minute all returned to normal. Jackson crawled to the foot of the bed for now, still watching for any sudden movement. I let myself nest again close to Kevin's familiar warmth. We stayed that way for a few minutes until the quiet seemed to hold. But I no longer felt as safe as before, nor could I imagine the rhythm of our breathing merging together. We were different, and maybe I would never understand how his emotions and his anger worked. But I felt committed to him, felt we needed each other and gained a strength from each other that we did not have before.

I drew in another long breath, more of a perplexed sigh. Our tiny house was still filled with the lingering smell of the meal he had cooked earlier that night. It was rich and complex and had tasted wonderful: chicken roasted in curry spices—all freshly ground and intoxicating with their mysterious pungency. In a clay pot he had braised the fowl amid a melange of apples, apricots, and prunes, and the dinner was served on a bed of savory basmati rice. That was an average meal for him. Cooking was his creative outlet, and through it he had created the feeling of a home for me in these two small rooms.

Cooking had been his previous trade. He spent enough time in culinary school to get a job easily, but since he never graduated, he had to accept being hired more as a helper than a chef. He talked with nostalgia of his days working in a café on Bank Street, but he had no desire to return to that world. What he most enjoyed was being a part of an operation, a team, an enterprise that had some direction and a sense of style. Now he had a daytime job, with me, and at night he took over the kitchen while I became his helper and busboy.

It was not for the sex that we moved in with each other, at least not for me. In fact, I was never quite sure what it was that Kevin wanted from me, for I certainly was not a blond clone of himself. Next to him I was shorter, even a little dumpy looking. My hair was still long, and often unkempt. I thought he had everything in the looks department that I lacked, and I assumed he could pick any man he wanted. As a result, I felt incredibly lucky to have him move in with me, along with his entourage of cats, dog, recipes, and Danish souvenirs.

It was not many months before his arrival that I had been wandering the streets of the West Village, lurking in bars, baths, piers, empty trucks, and dark streets. Always looking for some kind of connection: Sex, intense and fast, was the ostensible goal. Like everyone else in that post-Stonewall age of sexual euphoria, I grew to expect that finding a guy to fuck with was as easy as a short walk across West Street.

Two years before I met Kevin, I had been living on West Street itself, where my rickety tenement stood directly across from the abandoned piers. For a time at least, this became a nightly bazaar of uninhibited cruising. The sense of adventure, danger, and conquest each night was close to addictive.

But as good as it was, there was something missing. Friendship, romance, involvement, and the breathless journey taken with a new person toward creating something of permanence. So all those great tricks and one-nighters were never repeated, leaving me baffled and still living alone.

Then Kevin moved in with me. It all just happened so easily—I never expected it. Suddenly I had a whole household: a boyfriend, his dog Kasha, my golden lab Auggie, and the two kittens. Together we started to change the apartment. We built shelves into the walls, made the bed bigger, put up a ladder to the roof.

We fought, and in truth, hardly a week ever went by when there was not some kind of tantrum from Kevin. Like little meteor showers raining down around me, I could only try to stay calm, most of the time, and step aside as the hot cinders hit the floor. Usually, it was because of something I had done, or not done.

Like the time I mixed up the hard boiled and raw eggs inside the fridge. Later that night I heard him yell, "What the fuck?" from the kitchen, and then a metal bowl clattered angrily into the sink. Nervously, I came into the kitchen to see what the problem was. "What did you do with all the eggs?" In the sink was a mess of gooey raw egg along with smashed up hard boiled egg. He had been trying to make some kind of torte and had chanced on the hard egg I had put in the wrong place. I thought it was kind of funny. That's when he flew into a snit at how stupid I was, how he didn't need his life screwed around with like this, and I looked at him like he was nuts.

"Just stay the fuck out of here," he yelled at me, his arms flying all over. I shrank away as he forced me with taunting gestures backward out of the kitchen. *He's crazy,* I thought. *He's threatening me inside my own apartment.* I wasn't even sure if he was going to throw an egg at me. I backed up against a chair at the dining table.

I didn't think I was really in any danger, but I knew our relationship was. He was trapped in some kind of loop that I could never understand, living out some psychodrama he must have witnessed as a boy between his parents. How long would the terrors of his messed-up childhood continue to poison our life together?

He stood over me, fuming, red in the face, glaring. I fell backward into a chair with an awkward lurch. The chair ground across the floor and he was stopped for an instant by surprise. "You're a little shit," I shouted at him. "I've had it with your bratty tantrums." I felt cornered and fed up. I grabbed for his belt and yanked him down. He lost his balance and I held him face down across my lap. "Now you're going to get it," I said, only half as angry as I tried to sound, and I started to spank him.

Surprisingly, he didn't move away as I whacked the seat of his pants. Of course, given his size he certainly had to cooperate in order to continue this charade of punishment. I tried to hit him pretty hard. He squirmed around but made no serious effort to escape me.

I must have smacked his ass six or eight times, probably hurting my own hand more than his ass through those tough Levi's. Finally, he rolled out of my grip and fell onto the floor, landing on his hips, and now he was laughing.

"What are you laughing at?" I yelled. "You think that was funny? You want more? Stop laughing at me," I stammered. "You're supposed to apologize. Besides, you're too big for me to spank."

Finally he rose off the linoleum floor and stood in front of me. His eyes were glistening from laughter.

"My poor little Gener," he said, as he draped his arms over my shoulders and let his head rest against my forehead. His forehead was moist with sweat from all the tumbling around.

"Are you laughing *with* me, or *at* me?" Instead of answering he knelt down in front of me and took my head between his hands and began to kiss me, fiercely. I lost my breath and could feel both his arms holding me around my back, gripping me hard. I closed my eyes as I felt his glasses press against my face. Yet he continued to plunge his tongue into my mouth, wiggling and exploring, eating and penetrating me. I was astonished by his sudden passion, and confused by his feelings for me. What was happening here was not about sex, really, it was about gratitude. Maybe I had found a way to get through to him. Like the unexpected slap from the Zen master, I had somehow opened his eyes to what we meant to each other.

Something did change after that. Something had broken free between us. I had taken a chance with him that could have ended differently, very foolishly perhaps. It changed the course of our time together, I am convinced. Maybe he understood, right through his pants, that this was now, with me, here, that he had to deal with. He could not manipulate me so easily, just because he was so attractive. He really did have a life now that was not just a reprise of his past.

I heard his breathing, slow and regular. The smell of the roasted chicken blended with all the other smells in the small apartment: the dogs' fur, the crisp smell of plywood shelves I brought in the other night, the stack of folded laundry sitting on a side chair, the litter box in the bathtub. I forgot about all those arguments we had in the past, and would have again. I thought only about the mystery of his body, his separate existence, warm with life, pressed against me. He had fallen asleep with both cats once again curled up between his legs. Somewhere on the floor nearby the dogs were both sleeping.

I thought back two years earlier to the first night I had slept in this apartment, the first night I turned off the lights and felt the emptiness of the unfamiliar room around me. I had moved from the West Street walk-up to this place on Canal Street. I had been afraid. Not of ghosts or robbers, but of the cold darkness I felt so palpably around me.

*Is this what it feels like to die?* I had wondered that night. Not a good way to get to sleep. How very different this apartment now seemed. Full of carpets and plants, animals and artwork and sexy photographs. Yet I could not shake the memory of that haunting aloneness.

Inches from my face was the back of Kevin's neck. In the dark I could just see the pattern of hair that tapered down on both sides of the slight hollow called the nape, where the spinal cord enters the skull. I raised my head, and as lightly as a guardian angel, I kissed him there. I did not want to wake him again.

# 6

## THE CRANE FROM HELL

*City Island, July 1981*

"Hey, Kahn. I pulled your boat out." I was hardly out of my car when Frank called to me from across the boatyard. "It was a mistake. I wanted Fitzpatrick's. All those lousy little boats look the same to me. Hey, it's okay. Don't look so worried. I'll put you back in the water in a few minutes. Just stick around."

Frank did not seem tipsy, just harried and unable to keep track of things that a younger person would have less problems with. He was not really that old and befuddled, but he seemed afraid that he was getting there already. Maybe the stories about the brain tumor were true.

There it sat, my little Rhodes 19, perched on a wooden cradle right in early July, as if the season were over already. It seemed so unfair. I felt like such a victim, or at least the owner of one. Kevin had no patience for this irascible old goat, and I was glad he had decided not to come up to the boat with me this trip. At least one of us would get some work done today back at the shop.

It was useless to get angry with Frank Jordeans. *Here was the last of a vanishing breed,* I thought, *a boatyard character.* Frank and his wife Fay ran this dumpy old marina much like a tenement apartment building. Rents were cheap, services were minimal, and amenities were long gone.

Decades ago, the place had been a respectable boat club that specialized in a peculiar sailing canoe, a daring hybrid boat with a tall sticklike mast, a great spread of sail mounted to a slender wooden shell of a hull.

Inside an old clapboard shed at Grant's Boat Club, there were narrow storage racks where these fragile boats used to be kept safe from the weather. Nearby were rows of wooden lockers intended to hold sails and other gear. Everything now was rusted, peeling, and decrepit.

Frank and Fay lived in a dilapidated Victorian house that commanded a view of the entire marina. The property was basically one long jetty, built upon stone rubble, and extending out into the water about 300 feet. They faced east toward Long Island Sound, and this view was really the best part of the place.

A few of the old sailing canoes were still around, and their owners, ages sixty and beyond, did not go out on these contraptions very often. Instead they sat around on splintery wooden benches and complained about getting old and times changing. This was my earliest boatyard experience—Grant's Boat Club, up at City Island, a fingerlike extension of the southeast Bronx.

I had grown fond of the place, nevertheless. It gave me a sense of connection to a long nautical tradition going back 300 years. I knew that the keels of great yachts had first slipped into these waters generations ago, even if the piers and railways were all in ruins. For me Frank Jordeans was a living connection to the glory days of sailing and boatbuilding on City Island.

Frank cranked up his ancient crane and brought the machine up to my boat. Working the controls he lowered a pair of fabric slings under the boat's hull. The Rhodes weighed about 1,100 pounds, which seemed like a lot to me then. For the crane, of course, it was barely enough weight to overcome the rust and friction in all the pulleys. He picked up my little boat, and with the most awful grinding of transmission gears Frank went into reverse and slowly drove back to the water's edge. *Would he stop in time?* I wondered. Gossipy neighbors told stories of how Frank had once driven the crane right off the seawall. Just stories.

But he stopped, the bald tires pressing against a pile of granite boulders. With the engine still rumbling in neutral, Frank climbed out of the truck cab once again and stepped around to the controls for the hoisting derrick. It really did look like a Tonka Toy from Hell. It was all black, dented, and menacing-looking. It was hard to say whether the machine had taken on Frank's grouchiness or vice versa.

"I'll have you out sailing in a second, Kahn," he growled at me as he released the clutch on the winch and slowly, oh so slowly, let my Rhodes 19 down and finally back into the water's embrace. I ran down the ramp to the dock to catch the boat from drifting away, and helped to pull the slings free once the boat was floating on her own again. Now I could go sailing, and Grant's crane would always serve as an easy landmark, the tallest thing on the northeast corner of City Island.

Frank was always difficult to get along with, and his wife Fay did most of his public relations work. Hardly anyone ever casually chatted with him, except some of the old-timers sitting on the benches. He was heavyset, with beefy shoulders and stubby legs. Occasionally he might smile, probably when some secret ailment was not tormenting him, and I suspected that he liked me. Of course, we all knew that there had to be a sporting side to him. He made you feel you were at camp—sailing camp—with a counselor who had been there much too long.

One breezy spring day when God knows what adolescent spirit awakened inside him, Frank went out for a sail on one of those fragile sailing canoes. There he was, with his fat ass perched way out on the helmsman's sliding board, his old knees bent under him Pocahontas style. All of us watched, impressed at how confidently he could come about, then duck under the mainsail, switch over to the opposite side of the plank, and push himself outboard again. All the while he kept steering with this improbable six-foot-long tiller extension. These boats were fast but very difficult to right should they flip over in the water. Of course, there was no keel, but only the helmsman's weight to balance the boat against the force of the wind.

Fay watched her husband, nervously twisting a kerchief in her hands, mumbling to herself, "Okay, Frank, let's start heading back in now."

What made him particularly unique as a boatyard owner was his attitude about money. He was always trying to find ways to save me money. "Don't waste your money at Burck's, Kahn," he would tell me. "We'll find you a mooring; just look around." He'd grope among all kinds of rusted junk to find a 150- or 200-pound mushroom anchor that he could let me use for a season or two. Next he'd rummage among piles of discarded chain, looking for what I could make use of.

"Look at that," he was fond of saying. "There's plenty of meat there." He held the chain wrapped around his fist menacingly, his own knuckles considerably bigger than the links of the chain. He was right, and I would save nearly seventy-five dollars in new chain. It did mean I had to use his giant bolt cutters and cut away all the worn-down links, and then reattach the separate lengths with shackles, also to be found lying around the yard.

It was hard, dirty work and a rough initiation into boating, and not the boating one thinks of for cushy yachtsmen farther east in Larchmont or Greenwich. I grew to accept that a boat owner *should* do all these nasty jobs himself.

It was not so much that I had saved some money. Rather, I was being initiated, learning boatyard tricks, and, mostly, gaining confidence as a sailor who could handle problems. I developed an attitude that there should never be any boat problem that I, as the skipper, could not solve, or at least effect some serviceable repair on. Similarly there should be no place, from under the keel to the top of mast, that I could not get to when necessary. I learned to fold my grown-up adult body into the inaccessible corners of all my boats. Wiggling around like a squirrel brought back childhood memories of rummaging inside my mother's kitchen cabinets in Brooklyn.

I kept the little Rhodes one more year, and then bought a larger boat, a Tanzer 22 with four real berths, a toilet, stove, icebox, a table, the works. After that sleepless overnight in Oyster Bay, Kevin and I knew we were ready for something more substantial.

My first winter after getting the boat I spent nearly every night leafing through marine hardware catalogs. Already, I needed to improve my boat, incorporate some nifty piece of stainless hardware. I read everything I could find about cruising, anchoring, piloting, repairs, paints and varnishes, and, of course, adventure stories by other sailors.

One sentimental account was by an Englishman about launching his first boat. The fellow had saved for an entire year to buy the little wooden sloop. What I most remembered was the picture of an anxious young man running around the bottom of his boat painting those spots where the boat had been resting all winter. He carried a pot of blue paint in one hand and an old brush in the other. It was part of the routine—and tradition—of launching one's boat each spring.

"Hey Kahn, you ready to go in now? Otherwise I got five other boats to launch and you'll have to wait another week." That was Frank welcoming me back to Grant's for the 1983 season. I came up to the yard one afternoon hoping to use the warm weather to do some varnishing. I was not at all prepared, psychologically at least, to be launched yet. It was just me and now I had to paint those bare spots on the bottom of the hull before she went in. Luckily, Kevin and I had already painted most of the bottom the previous weekend.

I assured Frank I was ready to go into the water, even though I did not even have a mooring out there to put the boat on. I'm not sure he could even hear me over the groans and roars of his crane. I trotted back to my locker to find a can of paint, blue paint.

When I returned, the crane was hovering over my lovely new boat like some iron pterodactyl. Frank's teenaged son had already positioned the slings under the shapely hull. With a puff of black smoke from the stack—the crane really did have a smokestack, not just a muffler pipe—Frank heaved on one of the levers to engage the hoisting winch. The boat shook a little as the slings took up the weight. The mast shuddered with a rattle of wires. The slings creaked, stretched, and then the boat was in the air, high above the cradle, looking as vulnerable as a kitten clinging to a willow branch.

Frank shouted orders to his son, something incomprehensible to me over the noise. The boy walked around the boat and tied a ratty piece of rope to the bow cleat, and then pulled the boat around so her bow end faced back toward the crane. I was still trying to pry off the lid of the paint can.

With another puff of smoke the crane began to inch forward. Frank was now sitting in the truck cab steering the whole rig backward, as usual. His big red face frowned as he tried to steer with half his bulky upper body twisted around and hanging out of the window. The crane moved in short jerky fits at first, and my boat shook nervously at the end of the cable.

"Kahn, you got anything you still need paint on, better do it now," Frank warned me as he slowly climbed out of the cab. My ears were still adjusting to the quiet with the crane suddenly not running. It was hard not to be defensive around this man, but in truth he was a sailor and he understood things in a way only another boat owner could. He had just grown old and impatient with trying to eke a living out of a shabby boatyard, where the land was increasingly more valuable than the business on it.

But he understood how his customers, often novice boaters, cared and fussed over their little yachts. For many people in this backwater marina, these were their first boats, their pride and joy. No matter if it was twenty years old, streaked with rust, crumbling with dry rot and with sails blown out and patched.

With the lid pried off my paint can and brush in hand there I was, crouching beneath my own vessel as she swayed lightly in the slings. Only her bow tied horsey-style to the end of the crane kept her from rotating. The underwater profile of the Tanzer was remarkably fish-like, with a swept back keel so like a dorsal fin. How silly my boat looked, though, hanging in midair. How she longed to feel the water support her again.

Frantically I began brushing the thick blue bottom paint onto the spots where the hull and keel had rested all winter. Frank had gone back to his house, maybe for lunch, maybe for some Johnnie Walker. Maybe he would even forget to come back out of the house.

In the midst of all my stooping and scurrying, I realized what I must look like: a nervous man dashing around the bottom of his boat with a pot of blue paint. Just as I had read about during the winter. That story was from England in the 1950s, but the when and where really did not matter.

Today that nervous man with the pot of paint was me. The past four years of hanging around boatyards and listening to old-timers had been like another college education. I was too busy that afternoon to reflect on the sense of belonging to a brotherhood. After a lifetime feeling like a loner, an outsider, I found that I had already become part of a community of sailors—maybe of all time and all places. I no longer felt I needed to make excuses for my complete lack of interest in pro football or the World Series. I knew what mattered to me.

I could hear Frank's lopsided footsteps coming down the gravel yard from his house. From under the shadow of the boat above me, I looked up. He was still chewing something. His face wrinkled as he tried to push a mouthful of Fay's lunch from one cheek to the other. He looked impatient; it was time to launch Kahn's lousy boat and get back to work, goddamnit.

A brain tumor finally got Frank in the end. Fay tried to run the yard for a few years with a more friendly clublike atmosphere, but the heyday of Grant's Boat Club had passed. Then an ambitious real estate developer offered Fay three-quarters of a million dollars for the property. With her pimply son and her synoptic Barbie doll collection she moved into the gabled house just around corner.

Then in 1987 the stock market crashed and the entire property, still with my beloved crane and a handful of derelict boats resting on their cradles, remained empty and forlorn for four more years.

I had already moved across the island to a respectable yacht club. I changed boats twice, each one bigger and more luxurious. Along the way came my election to the club's board of directors, on which I served as the House Chairman and then Moorings and Docks Chairman for two years each. I had a blue blazer with a braided gold emblem of the club's insignia on the breast pocket. I had keys to everything and at board meetings voted in new members and voted out nonpaying deadbeats. For a while at least, I was among the inner circle.

But I never stopped going back across City Island Avenue to Grant's, to the littered yard where Grant's had once been. I made these sentimental pilgrimages on my own, since Kevin always thought the place was just a dump. He had no nostalgia for a romantic past. Fay's old house, a rambling Victorian with various dormers and gables, had been reduced to a pile of plaster lath and studs. The developer, in his frustration with the depressed real estate market, had the house unceremoniously bulldozed simply to elude vandalism and liability problems. All it took was a couple of hours.

It was easy to climb up the rocky jetty to avoid the locked front gate. I would walk down to the far end and look out to the east, toward Hart Island and beyond that the long expanse of Long Island Sound. Sometimes calm, sometimes whipped up and crashing heavily against the boulders below me. So many things had happened here.

I wished the developer would revive his project already. I wanted everything here gone, obliterated, and built over once and for all. I could not stand to see this place that I had loved so much, that had changed my life, looking this way. It made me feel old, ancient, cranky, sentimental, and superfluous. Standing there in the shadow of the old crane, amid all the junk, it made me feel like Frank.

# 7

## IVAN KOLODKO

*Rat Island, Spring 1984*

"Who the hell is Ivan Kolodko?" I asked Kevin as we stood together in the shop. "What the kind of name is that for a boat?"

"Well, then, fuck you. You asked me to come up with a name for the dink and that's my choice." Kevin turned to walk away. I did not mean to step so hard on his choice of names for our latest boat.

"Come on, Kiki," I said, changing my approach. "The name just caught me off guard, you know. It's not like WINDY or WHY KNOT."

"Then don't make fun of what you don't know shit about," he replied. Clearly this Ivan Kolodko person meant a lot to Kevin. I sensed him getting a little less defensive.

"Okay, then, that's going to be the new name on the transom. Ivan Kolodko? You spell it with a couple of k's, I assume? It does have a very dramatic ring, kind of mysterious and foreign."

"What about the hailing port, isn't it supposed to say where the boat comes from?" Kevin asked.

"City Island, of course," I answered, for once trying not to be so smartassed and get Kevin pissed at me. After all, I had given him the opportunity to name his first boat, an honor that I thought appropriate for him now. I wanted this to be a a joint venture, this ten-foot sailing dinghy that we had bought a few weeks earlier.

The little boat was now sitting across two sawhorses in my woodworking shop on Warren Street, two blocks from City Hall. It needed serious work, and this would be a perfect winter project, something to keep me involved in boating during the dreary indoor months from November to the coming spring.

But more than a job for the two of us to share, it was a chance for Kevin to have a boat of his own. I wanted to step aside and let him be the skipper—to hoist sails and tack or gybe as he thought appropriate. I knew he would never really learn to sail well until he had a boat of his own. No matter how small the boat, the concepts were the same. In fact, it was actually better to learn on a small and responsive boat. Bigger boats with all their stability and inertia plowed along no matter what you did to the sails.

We found a ten-foot dinghy, forlorn and deteriorating, in a Port Washington, Long Island, front yard. Despite the boat's neglected condition the owner still wanted 250 dollars. It was too much, but we both knew that under all those weeds the boat had character. I brought it home like a sick turtle, tied upside down to the roof of my lumbering Oldsmobile station wagon.

Looking at the wreck of a boat, Kevin thought it still looked more like a garden ornament than a real sailing dinghy. The wooden seats were split, the transom was detached and a few defiant flowers were climbing out of the centerboard case. He did not see the little boat's future as I did, nor could he imagine what it would eventually mean to him.

We had been living with each other almost four years. We worked together, slept together, went shopping for groceries at Pathmark together, and on the weekends we sailed.

After I got the Tanzer 22 we realized that we needed some kind of dinghy, something to row ourselves ashore in if we anchored in places like Sag Harbor or Block Island. For fourteen dollars at a sporting goods store we bought a tiny inflatable called a Norwood Charger, our first yacht tender. It was so small we had to sit like two insects facing each other with our legs interlocked. Basically it was a beach toy, and what started out as a cheap joke became more of an embarrassment whenever we nosed our way up to the dinghy docks of marinas and yacht clubs.

We needed a real dinghy, a serviceable tender, a versatile rowboat to reach shore whenever there was no dock or launch service. That way, wherever we went, we could anchor for free and get ashore without any outside help.

As work on the boat progressed I asked Kevin to come up with a name. I had already owned and named four boats. I wanted him to feel that this was his boat. I suggested he find some person in his own life whom he thought deserved to be remembered with his name on the stern of a ten-foot sailboat. He thought about it for a day and came back with the name *Ivan Kolodko,* and so it became.

It sounded purposeful and heavy with consonants, clearly foreign yet easy to pronounce. That was important. Mysterious, alien, pregnant with questions about its history, and deliciously presumptuous for such a pint-sized boat. The name was definitely not cute. Best of all, the name managed to bestow on this inanimate object a personality, a bit of character and a curious tribute.

The name worked. In later years we rarely called the boat "the dink," but always *Ivan Kolodko,* or simply *Little Ivan,* and pronounced it "Eevahn." In any case, no one ever forgot that name.

We knew that we wanted a boat that could be towed easily, could row well and could be sailed. We needed to find a design for a sailing rig that would drive the little boat, be easy to set up and yet could be completely stowed inside the ten-foot hull.

We had to find something that was both practical and appropriate for the look of the boat. We ignored the clever and the modern in favor of a rig that for centuries had been a familiar site on coastal waters from Holland to New York. It was called a sprit sail rig, the same kind of sail seen in the fuzzy background of old Dutch paintings.

Rebuilding the little boat was really a project for me. I put in solid mahogany seats along with a new transom. For the mast I shortened a spruce boom that had been discarded from another boat, and for the thin spar called a "sprit," I simply used a long broomstick. At the very top of the mast Kevin put his Danish pennant, a long red flag with a thin white cross.

I built a new rudder from solid mahogany and the centerboard from a plate of quarter-inch-thick aluminum. In both cases I relied upon textbooks on classic small boat designs for patterns to follow. All these details I did alone, hoping that it would sail well and hoping that Kevin would not be disappointed. It was a chance to put to use all my years of looking and feeling and studying about boats.

By the spring I finished the outside with a coat of dark green paint and for the inside used a buff-colored enamel with the evocative name of "Miami Tan." Around her gunwale, I attached a thick canvas rub-rail, and even fastened it the traditional way with short copper nails.

At last it looked like a boat again. Inside the shop we stepped the mast and hoisted the sail. Kevin sat inside the boat, still propped across the sawhorses. His skinny shoulders and mop of blond hair stuck up above the gunwale as he sat on the floor of the boat. Holding the slender tiller and tugging the mainsheet, he looked ready to sail. That's when I asked him about the boat's namesake, Ivan Kolodko. It was in the car, driving home, that I learned as much about Kevin's growing up as I did about Ivan Kolodko.

"Is very tragic story," Kevin said to me, mimicking his version of a Russian accent. "Better to read Dostoyevsky." In his hand he held a cigarette, but now it was conspicuously lying along his fingers in the European manner. He frowned and took another slow drag from his Rothman. He inhaled deeply and then filled the car with clouds of heady tobacco smoke. For an instant the inside of my car, the lumbering old Oldsmobile wagon, felt like a second-class railway carriage, trundling across the vastness of Mother Russia. The light changed to green and I continued up Hudson Street.

"I was very important person. 'Principal Engineer.'" Kevin, as Ivan Kolodko, continued. "Cadres of workers depended upon my decisions. Great hydroelectric project in the Urals. Millions of rubles. Cement was poured continuously. Many workers fell into the unfinished . . . hmm, how do you say, coffer-damn. They were drunk, of course, and fell from scaffold. But . . . we could not stop."

Another slow exhale on the Rothman, and the story resumed. "Party leaders were in great hurry to finish, to meet five-year quota. We had to impress the Politburo. There were great rewards for those who completed the project, and terrible things if we did not. 'Comrade,' they asked me, 'why do you not become party member?' So I said to them, 'Let me serve the people according to my abilities.' Everything was political. You understand?"

Kevin had met the old man when he was living in Lakewood, New Jersey. Kevin was in his teens and was already living with his adopted parents, Sue and Jules Abend. Sue was involved in helping the sick and the elderly, many of whom were from the expanding Russian émigré community of Lakewood. She was trying to find an apartment for Ivan and get him his Medicare card. The old man was well over eighty, Kevin told me, but had a lot of charm.

"It was a matter of superior intellect," Kevin said to me, slipping back into Ivan's Russian accent. "You Americans are like children; there is no discipline in your country. There is no authority or leadership. Your patience it is so limited."

Old Ivan hung around Kevin's house even while the wiry young teen repaired the roof. He was trying to put on new shingles from the top of a long extension ladder and he did not mind having some company.

His parents had come to New Jersey from Fort Greene in Brooklyn, in search of another old house to renovate and then resell, taking advantage of depressed real estate prices during the 1970s. With them he had already learned to repair old lath and plaster, put up drywall, and install new moldings and door trim.

"He sure knew how to supervise," Kevin continued. "He couldn't help himself; he was very bossy. He would sight up to the roof, using his cane, and tell me the rows of shingles were not straight. At first I thought he was a pain in the ass. But he was always right. So after a while I asked him to sight things up for me *before* I nailed them down. That was the first time I saw him smile.

"He told wonderful stories of things he did while in Russia, mostly working in the Ukraine. He had traveled everywhere, all across the continent." That alone fascinated Kevin, who longed to travel in Europe. The old man did not talk much about his family. They apparently had all suffered badly under Stalin. But he was funny, and certainly more interesting to Kevin than the low-life teenagers living in the neighborhood, whose only interest was in getting girls and drinking beer.

What Kevin sought was a sense of refinement, taste, and quality, of knowledge of the world beyond New Jersey, even beyond America.

Maybe Ivan, with his formal manners and supercilious ways, brought to Kevin a way out of the hopelessly bourgeois world of suburban New Jersey.

They certainly were an unlikely pair, a shuffling old pensioner, in his heavy overcoat and battered fedora, giving advice to a skinny and eager adolescent. For Ivan it was a lot better than hanging around the local senior center playing bingo. For Kevin the old man was a welcome source of esoterica.

"So the old man was your role model?" I asked Kevin.

"He was a very sweet person. I think he really cared about me. He had no family. It wasn't sexual or anything, but I felt sorry for him. He was very proud. You had to be very careful not to offend him, and he would never take any gifts. He was the first one I thought of when you asked me to come up with a name for the boat. I like the sound of it, like a Russian battleship."

"Like *Potemkin?*" I asked.

"Yeah," he added, "like something big."

While it was not part of Kevin's story, I realized that he and the old man did have something in common; each in his own way was an orphan. Ivan had no family in this country, and Kevin's birth parents had died.

We launched the boat without much ceremony one day that May, off the beach next to Grant's Boat Club. She floated high, sitting lightly on the water like a bright green slipper.

Unlike the stupid fourteen-dollar inflatable the previous year, the boat was a joy to row. Her design came from a long tradition of little boats. Like two kids, we hopped into the boat and kicked off from the shallows. Kevin hauled in the mainsheet, and off we went. She was really sailing. The rudder steered the boat with just a gentle touch, and the long centerboard plate I had cut by guesswork actually served to keep the hull from making too much leeway. There were a couple of small leaks from the keel, but that was not unusual.

In a light chop, we sailed straight out toward Rat Island lying in the channel off City Island. The bow made this plop-plop-plop kind of noise, as her blunt nose pushed through the water with a doughty self-confidence. We circled that ugly pile of rocks and rusted junk and came back to the beach. I jumped out and pushed the boat away. Off Kevin went again, scrunched into the stern, holding the main sheet between his teeth. He gripped the tiller with just his thumb and forefinger. His big legs filled up half the boat. By the time he came back twenty minutes later, he was actually steering the boat without using the tiller. He found how to shift his own weight, a little forward or aft, to windward or leeward to subtly guide the bow of the boat. It was a total seat-of-the pants experience: No books, no wind diagrams, and no technical blah-blah from me.

Kevin grew to love that boat, and some afternoons he would leave our shop early just to go out sailing on his own. On weekends he would row himself out while I used the club launch to ferry our groceries to our mother ship, the Tanzer 22. The dinghy was always a part of every weekend, even if we did not go anywhere.

*Ivan Kolodko* altered the dynamic of our relationship, for soon I no longer was the keeper of the secrets. I wanted to share sailing with Kevin—the exhilarating times, the monotonous times, the scary times, and the routines of life on the water. I wanted to know he could handle a boat in any condition.

In all the sailing we did together over the years, I always knew I could rely upon him, trust him, know that the safety of the boat always came first, no matter what bitchy domestic stuff might be going on between us. By our second trip to Block Island in 1984, I realized how much I had grown to need him.

# 8

# HARBORS OF REFUGE

*Orient Point, August 1984*

It was a three-day passage from City Island. The weather at the start had been the typical August forecast, hazy, hot, and humid. By the second day the weather conditions began to get progressively rougher as we continued sailing east toward the end of Long Island's north fork. The sea conditions were building up so that the dinghy we were towing behind us was getting filled with water from spray and waves. Weighed down and with water sloshing around inside, it would no longer tow straight, but would skew from side to side and then fetch up on the painter with a sudden jerk. We feared that eventually the line would part.

"How is *Ivan* doing back there?" Kevin would ask me each time I stood on the stern of our boat and looked back at the rowboat. It was about thirty or forty feet behind us, on a long painter. We were both nervous.

"There's definitely water sloshing around inside," I told Kevin. "I can't tell if it's from the spray or coming up through the centerboard case." It was his turn at the helm again. We were taking turns; each of us had the tiller for about an hour. It was hard work, and stressful, but we understood that each of us needed a short rest away from the cockpit. Down below in the cabin it was possible to feel warm and dry and safe for a while, and not think about the weather up on deck.

We were rolling along with a strong following sea and the wind off the port quarter. Our speed had been steadily increasing all day. The sea pushing from astern often kicked the boat off course unexpectedly, or else lifted us up to surf along the back of a wave.

It was my turn to rest down below for a while. Through the open hatch I could watch Kevin and the waves building behind us. When I was anxious I would channel surf on the marine VHF radio for any traffic. Just the voices of other boaters, some nervous, some bitching about the conditions, made me feel less alone out there.

"Can you take it for a while?" Kevin called down to me. He was already getting up from the tiller. "The stern really yaws a lot," he added. "I'm trying to steer ninety-five, but I can't say I'm able to hold it very steady." We switched positions at the tiller. We kept our bulky foul weather suits on, even though the rain had trickled off. The sky, however, was still overcast, and more rain seemed to be in the air. He looked pale and weary, and I felt sorry for him, afraid I was forcing him into something too difficult. His face looked lined and not so boyish that day.

"Do you want to make something hot, like coffee, below?" I asked him.

"I'm not so sure I can do anything down there. You know how the smell of wet foul-weather gear makes me sick. But maybe I'll make myself a drink first. That helps. How about you?"

I told him no, but I was worried. I didn't want to see him get sick, and I knew very well how the cabin took on that funky smell after a long rainy day with the moldy and wet yellow jackets stuffed into a corner of the cabin.

While the weather seemed to be holding we continued to worry about our dinghy, little *Ivan*. If it filled with water that would be a disaster. The previous year we towed it into Port Jefferson harbor while it was half filled. Unstable as it was, a wake caused it to roll heavily, then dip one gunwale completely into the water. On the next roll it sank behind us.

Now, a year later, the thought of this happening again, in these rough conditions, was an awful prospect. We did not say it to each other, but we both knew that such a situation could easily require us to cut the tender loose.

"I just saw a red and green flash!" I yelled to Kevin, who had gone below and pulled off his clumsy foul-weather jacket. He was trying to heat up some water to make coffee. I thought it was a little risky, but at the same time did not want to discourage him. I certainly wanted something hot to drink, something that would feel warm and reassuring inside me. But even more, it was a good sign, I thought, that he was willing to putter around in the cabin, in *his* galley. He wasn't seasick, I thought thankfully, and he was trying to keep busy.

"Hang on, let me look at the chart," he answered me, talking through the main hatch with just the topmost board removed so we could see and talk to each other. I watched him fill our little drip pot with coffee grounds. The stove was gamboled so we could cook, or at least heat up water, even while underway.

"There, I saw it again," I yelled down to him. "A quick red then a green flash. That has to be Port Jefferson light. Take a look for me."

"It's Old Field Point," he called up to me from the dinette table. "Have we passed Crane Neck Point yet?"

"That must be what we are approaching now. How much farther to Port Jeff?" I asked Kevin. He picked up a set of dividers and measured off the distance.

"It's at least two miles to the light, and then another mile or more into Port Jeff harbor. Wait," he added, "there's my water boiling."

We were both thinking the same thing. Did we want to put into Port Jefferson to leave *Ivan Kolodko*? Of course that question easily inspired the next: Did we want to put into there and give up for the day altogether? We did not want a repeat of the fiasco with the dinghy swamping again. The inlet into Port Jefferson would be especially rough today, and that was just what rolled it over the last time. Nor did we really want to stop. The weather seemed to be holding, not getting much worse, and in fact we had the current with us and were actually making very good time.

Leaving the dinghy behind would be a great disappointment. We wanted it for the fun of sailing it when we reached Block Island. Remembering all the hundreds of anchored sailboats in the Great Salt Pond, we imagined making little expeditions to shore, exploring up shallow creeks, visiting other yachts, and generally showing off our salty little boat with its long Danish pennant at the masthead.

Half an hour past Port Jefferson we finally decided to duck into Mount Sinai Harbor to leave *Ivan Kolodko* someplace safe, on land. That would be our last dropoff harbor for the rest of the day before reaching Orient Point. We knew there was a boat club just inside the inlet, and we figured they would not mind our leaving little *Ivan* in their dinghy rack.

We continued on, heading east, just the two of us now, uncomfortably aware of the dinghy no longer bravely following in our wake. Above us the skies continued to darken, and I tied a second reef in the mainsail. Even with this reduced sail area we were surfing down the waves and our speed at times touched eight or nine knots. It was getting harder to control the boat. This would have been fun, exhilarating for a day sail. But we were on a long passage, far from home, with only a desolate shore to leeward. I wondered silently to myself, what was it going to be like in another hour or so, when we finally reached Orient Point and turned around to face these same waves? I kept my worries to myself. Down below Kevin was inhaling a joint he had rolled. That was one of his ways of getting through these ordeals.

The last third of Long Island's North Fork is a very lonely place. Nothing but cliffs and one more high bluff after another. From the deck of a small boat each new headland appears to be the final one, but as we got closer we saw jutting out farther ahead another outcropping of barren hills. Of course, eventually we would reach the bitter end of the Long Island peninsula. Here, almost as an anticlimax, the whole great landmass from Brooklyn to Orient Point peters down to a long spine of submerged rocks. At the end is the plump Orient Point Lighthouse, one of those black and white iron contraptions looking like a spark plug.

The passage is known as Plum Gut, because nearby Plum Island forms a very narrow slot, or gut, through which all of Long Island Sound must squeeze. The currents and sea conditions in the narrow passage that day were truly frightening. Before I came up on deck again, I turned on all our running lights. Just seeing them illuminating our bow and stern helped to sustain my feeling of confidence in our little boat.

We headed for the flashing green beacon atop the lighthouse. We eventually hoped to find refuge for the night in a marina just a few miles back inside Gardiner's Bay. Now, as we began to work around Orient Point, all the water we had been riding along with, the eastbound ebbing current, we now had to head directly back into. All of the sea between the two forks, all of Gardiner's Bay, Moriches and Peconic Bays, all that water was now rushing outbound toward us.

The Tanzer 22 was sturdy enough and down below everything stayed dry and secure. But the seas that day rose up short and steep. We plowed into waves five and six feet high and spaced so close together that our twenty-two-foot boat hobby-horsed up and down. It seemed, in fact, that we were trying to sail uphill. This was impossible, I thought. Kevin and I stood in the cockpit, stiff, silent, and stupefied.

The conditions were too wild and confused to try to sail. "I'm going to drop the jib now," I told him. "We have to get around using the motor." He nodded his head.

"Let me know when you want to head up," he said, now ready at the helm. Behind him the outboard seemed to be running well enough to keep us moving. It started on the second try, thankfully. I crawled up to the bow, pulled down the headsail and lashed it to the railing.

"Hurry up, Gener, I think the motor is having trouble," Kevin called to me. There was a frightened edge to his voice. We both hated depending upon this motor. I could already hear the motor laboring through the rough seas. I left the mainsail set, which was already reduced to the second reef. If we lost our motor we would need the sail up to handle the boat. Of course, if we had to sail, we would be forced to turn around and bear off onto a reach. In these seas we could never make progress upwind, and this was not a night to be heading out into open water, out into the wild blackness of Block Island Sound.

I crouched behind Kevin and worked the outboard's throttle. I knew that the motor's drive shaft was too short; the propeller was not submerged deep enough into the water. When our bow pitched down a wave the stern rose up so sharply that the propeller would fly out of the water. Spinning in just the froth at the surface, with no resistance, the motor would begin racing madly. Then, in the next instant, the stern would plunge deep into solid black water. With the sudden increase of load the motor would almost stall unless I could immediately throttle up again to keep us moving. If we were even moving at all, I wondered.

"This is awful," Kevin said as he surveyed a sea of whitecaps and one phalanx of heaped-up waves after another bearing down on us. But there was no escape now; we were committed to rounding Orient Point. Kevin was steering between the waves, determined to keep us away from the rocks behind the lighthouse. He was standing up, with both hands gripping the long tiller.

"Don't let the motor die, Gener," he called over to me, trying to be encouraging. He did not need to say this. Did he even realize that at times the waves behind us were almost coming above the motor's cover?

"I had no idea it was going to be like this," I said right into Kevin's ear. Should we have stayed in Mount Sinai with the dinghy earlier that afternoon? This was exactly what I had been dreading all during the day's passage. But at least to talk to each other made it bearable.

Amid all the whitecaps we could see the lighthouse and the various buoys scattered around the Gut. The foghorn atop the spark plug was groaning its own low warning, just one more noise in the background out there that kept emphasizing this was a dreadful place to be. Closer to us a green bell buoy clanged away in the confused seas. Hardly a mile astern of us was Plum Island, with its sinister water tank mounted on stilts atop a high bluff. Everything that would have looked normal and innocuous during a summer day took on an evil and threatening aspect that dark and stormy afternoon. Beyond Plum Island was wide open Block Island Sound, miles of pitching and dark ocean.

I looked toward the lighthouse, off to our starboard. It never seemed to change position. I was sure we were not making any progress. We were barely even staying in the same spot. The baleful green light seemed to be flashing right over our heads, as if the light itself had some irresistible power to draw us closer and closer to the very rocks that the iron tower was warning us against. I was gunning the motor into an outpouring ebb tide with waves much too steep for this small a boat. We would never make it into a safe harbor; we would probably run out of gas soon. I was starting to go crazy.

"I'm really getting scared out here," I finally yelled up to Kevin. "I don't think were going to make it!"

"Don't worry, Gener," he shouted back to me, "we *are* making it, just real slowly. Just keep the motor going." We were both suited up in our foul-weather gear, with the rain hoods pulled over our heads. Water was dripping from his moustache and down the tip of his nose. His glasses were so wet I could hardly see his face. Until that night, I never thought I could need him so much. I dreaded having to take the helm just then. He weaved us up and over and around the worst seas. His whole body would twist and duck when a wave sent spray over the cockpit. I could see that he was into it. All we needed was to maintain power to keep the bow pointed right.

It did not seem so at first but after another agonizing five minutes I could see that the lighthouse had actually come abeam of us. We *were* moving. Yes, slowly we were making progress toward a cluster of lights and buildings hardly a couple of miles away on shore. Some of those lights had to be the government ferry dock for Plum Island. But there were more lights, and lights meant people and indoors and safety.

"You're right; you're right," I called out to Kevin. We were past the spine of rocks behind the lighthouse. We were making progress. We might make it tonight. The farther away we got from the lighthouse the calmer the water around us became. Were we through the worst of it?

"Where do we go in?" Kevin asked me. He could handle the boat, but he needed my directions now. We no longer needed to shout. The sound of the engine was again a steady grumble through the water. It pushed the boat along without faltering.

"Go for those three green lights," I told him. I saw the dock for the ferries that go to New London. Next to that was a line of tall pilings marking the channel into an invisible little harbor. That was our destination, our safe haven for the night. I only knew what the chart showed, a long narrow basin protected by a seawall.

I went up to the mast and let go the mainsail halyard. There was no turning back. We were aimed right for the seawall and already past the green light atop the second piling. I had to rely blindly on what the chart showed. And then, miraculously, incredibly, a narrow opening, more of a slit, appeared in the glistening dark seawall, the entrance to the harbor.

The sound of our outboard echoed back to us against the tall boards of the seawall. It was eerily quiet as we slipped through what felt like a short tunnel, hardly fifty feet wide. Once inside we glided, swanlike, atop the stillest water I had even seen. How could anyone find this place? All that had just happened behind us felt like a bad dream. Yet, there above us on shore glowed the big illuminated sign for the Orient-by-the-Sea Marina and Restaurant.

It was just after dusk in August but it looked like nighttime with rain clouds still pressing down. I never before felt so happy to tie my boat up to something fixed and solid. Everything in the marina was silent. Drops of water hung motionless from the underside of all the handrails. The dock's planks were damp, and the air held the pleasant warmth of summer and smelled salty, fresh, and lush.

Still wearing my foul-weather suit and tall seaboots, I clomped into the restaurant to find out about paying for a slip. The place was charming, with all the tables set, and candles flickering. I kept expecting someone to leap up and congratulate me.

Back on the boat Kevin had poured a strong drink for both of us and set the two tumblers on the table. I pulled out one of his cigarettes, lit it, and took a long inhale. *It was all over,* I told myself, slowly exhaling the smoke and immediately inhaling again. I did not care about the smell in the small cabin. I was used to that from Kevin.

"I guess I got pretty panicky out there?" I said as I blew out the warm smoke, noticing how it did calm me. At least just going through the motions of smoking focused me for the instant on something easy and immediate.

"I thought I was going to have to slap you," Kevin answered. I think he meant it. We sat opposite each other at the dinette table. We could not get used to the total stillness all around us. Then he looked toward me with a big smile and added, "I'm glad it was you dealing with that fucking motor. I could never handle that kind of anxiety out there." I felt redeemed, and rewarded for having faced a truly harrowing situation.

"I couldn't believe how long it was taking us to get around," I admitted to him. "It really freaked me."

"I could see you were getting confused and panicky, but I just wasn't going to get any closer to those rocks. I wanted to turn real wide and slow." Yes, I realized, he knew what he was doing. After a while we trudged up the dock to the restaurant. We indulged ourselves with a rich meal. It was mediocre, but we were still much too wound up to taste anything. Aside from the waiter and bartender, we were their only customers, and it might have been more romantic had we not been so tired. I didn't say anything to Kevin, but in truth I was not sure I wanted to continue our trip.

In the morning the sea was flat calm with a little fog. I walked around the marina and discovered another boat, a sailboat much bigger than ours, about thirty-two feet. It must have come in later that night, since it had not been docked there when we arrived. Her hatches were closed but not locked. It was still early, and I assumed the crew was aboard, all sleeping.

The boat looked like a disaster scene. Torn cushions were lying in the floor of the cockpit. The lifelines were loose and stretched out of shape, as if someone had fallen heavily against them. There were wet towels and clothes tossed over the cabin roof. The towels were probably used to sop up water that leaked into the cabin. The mainsail was hanging from the boom in great sagging folds, as if it had been dropped in a frantic hurry. Even the halyard was still shackled to the head of the sail, now lying slack in the windless foggy air.

Her crew had apparently been in a state of exhaustion when they arrived late last night. The general look of the boat was that she had been through hell and had barely survived. *This is a big boat,* I thought enviously, with an inboard engine, probably a diesel. Then I realized that our boat did not look at all like this, and we had been through the very same conditions out there. We were half her size, and surely more vulnerable. Just the two of us and we had handled everything out there. We had no mishaps, no injuries, no leaks, no near disasters. We had been wet and afraid, but we knew and trusted our little boat—and each other—totally.

By mid-morning we were ready to head out for Block Island. The sea was flat, with just the beginning of a long ocean swell starting to slide gently under the boat's hull. Later that afternoon we pulled into Block Island and anchored within sight of Payne's Dock and all the other tacky tourist shops. We had made it at last, and were ready to go ashore in our dinghy.

We pumped up the fourteen-dollar Norwood Charger that would once again be our yacht tender. We clambered into it, and with our feet tangled together like puppies we rowed ashore. We were careful to get out before we scraped against the sharp rocks and glass along the water's edge. Who gave a flying fuck how appropriately nautical we looked anymore to the spectators at the dinghy dock? *Ivan* was safe, and so were we.

# 9

## THE NAME GAME

*Long Island Sound, 1978 and 1983*

If anything linked all my boats' names, it was that they were meant to memorialize someone that I loved and felt grateful to have known. My very first boat, a brand new fourteen-footer, I had named *Lucy Brown,* and there was both a story and a real person behind that name. The next boat, the little Rhodes 19, I christened *David Lange*. David and I had learned to sail together. That was my first visit to City Island. We also took scuba diving classes together. We did everything except sleep together. I called the Tanzer 22 *Normand Gagnier,* not just because this French Canadian was my first boyfriend, but because of how much I loved to kiss him.

Lucy Brown was the super of my first New York City apartment. It was a five-floor walk-up along the Hudson River, on the edge of the Village. I lived on the top floor with my dog, Auggie. The rent was ninety-two dollars, and the landlord was a member of one of the more prestigious Mafia families in New York City. They were always nice people to deal with.

Life was not easy for Mrs. Brown. One son, her oldest, was in and out of prison most of his life and he was not yet twenty-five. Her daughter had a good job as a bookkeeper in one of my landlord's many "family" businesses. Emily Brown came by often on Sundays to bring a gift, usually a cake, to her mother. They would sit around the little apartment and laugh and chat.

Then there was her other son. A good for nothing, she always called him, a petty thief. But a good-looking boy of nineteen. Tall, always dressed in sharp clothes, never jeans or T-shirts, and like Lucy he too had high cheekbones and smooth skin like milk chocolate. Unlike her daughter, whenever he came around the whole building could hear a big fight down there. He would plead insistently, "Mama, you gotta help me. It ain't a lot this time." Lucy would howl up and down the hallways, call him every kind of worthless nigger, and then sit him down and make him lunch.

No one in the building knew anything about any Mr. Brown. Lucy made her own way in life, and once in a while, when she was not drunk or angry or chasing some wino peeing in the hallway, she might smile. Her cheeks would rise up and crease, her black eyes would shine and she looked like she was probably quite pretty as a young woman, I used to think.

Lucy Brown had a daytime job with the City of New York Department of Marine and Aviation. She went to work every day on the Staten Island ferry as a matron in the ladies' room. Why there was a matron I never understood; probably some holdover sinecure written into the civil service books from a more genteel era. A few times I ran into Lucy when I took the ferry to go bike riding on Staten Island. Spying me in my cut-off jeans and bike shoes with their noisy cleats, she would fold her arms and demand, "Ain't you got no job to do?"

Then she would shoo me away with her folded newspaper, raising it up as if to swat my behind with it. "Get your skinny ass back to work," she would yell at me, her voice dropping half an octave to sound disapproving. But it was only an act.

I lived on the fifth floor of our narrow tenement. She lived far below me, so all I knew of her life was what I figured out while rounding the landing in front of her open door. More often than not some kind of trouble, some bad news or unexpected visitor bedeviled her and sent her into a fit of anger at the world. Those were the nights she would get drunk and work off her frustration by mopping the hallways.

First she lugged her galvanized bucket up three flights of stairs. She would start outside my door and slosh water all over the linoleum floor. Down the steps she would slam her mop back and forth across each tread, banging it against the metal stringers of the stairs.

By the second landing the water was filthy. I don't think she even used soap. She would work her way down the stairwell, dropping her pail and letting the handle rattle. By the time she reached the street level the floors were streaked with dried mud from her old mop. All the while she worked, she talked to herself. Or rather she would finish conversations the way she should have with some person earlier.

"'Goddamned mother fucker' . . . I told him, 'You ain't comin into this place with that there shit.' So he says to me, 'I come in whenever I wants to come in.' So I says to him, 'You better get your ass outta here before Mister Ponte comes back.' 'You tell Mister Ponte he can suck my fat dick.' That's just what he said, that useless trash. So I told him, I said, 'Then you can eat out my pussy if you're gonna stay around here all night. That way you be doin' something useful for once in your life.'"

This went on for about two hours. That's how long it took her to do our hallways and have a few cigarettes. Lucy smoked her Camels like a sailor, with the butt always held in the corner of her dark lips. If someone opened an apartment door and called for her to be quiet—it being almost 1:00 a.m.—she would turn on them and yell back, "You can suck my fat dick too, you motherfucker." Then she would go back to her work.

In June 1976 David Lange and I took our first sailing lessons up at City Island. That summer I went up almost every weekend and took out a boat from the sailing school for a few hours. I was intoxicated. The next two seasons I sailed up and down the Hudson River with my friend Robert. Eventually, I wanted my own boat. Learning to sail was the greatest revelation in my life since learning to ride a bike. It opened a whole world to me that I had always assumed was available to only the very rich.

I discovered City Island, Long Island Sound, Eastchester Bay, Hart Island, Little Neck Bay, Manhasset Bay, Execution Rocks, Stepping Stone Light, and so much more. All these wonderful, treacherous, and romantic sites were accessible only by water, and boats did not have to cost a fortune, not anymore.

I bought a brand new fourteen-foot day sailer, an open boat that was a fiberglass copy of a popular class called a Blue Jay. My new boat was bright red, and still with that sweet smell of fresh fiberglass resin. I had worked two months on one job just to save the 1,500 dollars I needed for this boat.

Late one summer night I came home from a wonderful day of sailing around City Island. I had just gotten my first mooring at Grant's Boat Club. I was making friends up there who were just as new to sailing, and were eager to share advice and suggestions. I was becoming a part of a whole new community.

Back in the West Village I looked around and realized how ugly all this was: These endless streets of hot asphalt in every direction, the abandoned and broken-down piers along the waterfront, the junkies filling every city park and street corner. *What kind of life is this?* I thought. Nothing but filth everywhere. No, this wasn't my life anymore, I realized with a bright revelation. Now I had my own escape, my little boat and the wonderful waters up there beyond the Bronx. Back then a whole season at Grant's cost 230 dollars. I could even afford it while I was collecting unemployment insurance. Yes, I was living like the rich, the skipper of my own sailboat, I joked to myself.

"Where you been all day?" Lucy Brown scowled at me as I walked past her open door on the first landing. It was hot inside the hallway, and would be even warmer up on the top floor.

"Oh, I was out sailing. I just got a little boat," I told her without a thought to sounding like a rich brat living a privileged life of leisure.

"You was out doin' what?" she challenged me as I started climbing. Lucy stood in her doorway with her small hands on her solid hips.

"When you gonna take your mama out on your new boat, eh?" she asked me as I smiled down at her from the next landing. I asked her what she was doing the next weekend, and she only started laughing. I heard her go back into her own apartment where she had company. She was still laughing and said something that sounded like, "Hey, Emily. We're going sailing next week." Then there was more laughing.

By the fourth floor I realized it was not very likely that Lucy Brown was ever going out with me. We were neighbors, but our worlds were too different. I could never change that, I realized. By the time I reached the fifth floor I still felt a burden about my life of leisure and privilege, compared to the difficult life of my super. I felt guilty and helpless.

By the next morning I decided to name the little boat after Lucy Brown. That would be my tribute. I glued on the name the next weekend using big white letters. Of course, nobody at the boat club had the slightest idea who this person was, but the name stuck. It sounded cute and lovable, maybe like an unconscious contraction of Charlie Brown and his perennial foe, Lucy. Or maybe it resonated with the Unsinkable Molly Brown. Whatever the reason, it looked good on the transom.

I never told her I had appropriated her name for my little boat. But I felt I had captured some of the spunky and more lovable parts of her personality that could still shine through that caustic and disappointed exterior.

I decided on the name of my fourth boat before I bought it, before I even knew I was going to buy a new boat. The name *Blue Shorts* spoke to everything that was important to me, everything that I loved. As always, there was a story to the name. I needed to compress into one word many of my hopes—both known and secret.

It was time for a new boat. Kevin and I had sailed the Tanzer 22 for four seasons. I was ready for something bigger now. I could afford it; I had become accustomed to paying a boat mortgage every month. The business was getting better, so several hundred dollars more a month was not such a burden. We started shopping. Mostly we wanted something that could stand up better to the ocean and stronger winds. We were tired of being afraid whenever it got a little breezy.

Just as important, I was fed up with outboard motors. I had gone through three on this boat, and now I wanted a more reliable inboard, a serious power plant deep inside the hull with a propeller well down below the waterline, where it had maximum effect.

Then there was the problem of the head. The Tanzer was so nice down below, so cozy, as long as you did not try to stand up or go to the bathroom. The head was a portable camp toilet that was hidden under the v-berth, with just a curtain for privacy. I wanted a real head, a separate cabin with its own door, and no more having to sneak ashore every couple of weeks to empty the cumbersome Port-A-Potti.

The new boat was a twenty-eight-foot C&C with a dark blue hull that made her look much bigger. The space inside left me breathless. The galley was the whole width of the boat just inside the main companionway. Up forward was a real cabin for the owner with its own door. It felt like there were actual rooms for eating, cooking, sleeping, and shitting.

I had confidence in this boat; it was well built and sailed fast. She steered with a wheel, a real twenty-eight-inch destroyer wheel that I soon covered in soft elkhide leather. It was a big serious boat, not a weekend camper.

I got the new boat late in the season of 1985. I had already sold the Tanzer. I broke with tradition and did not name the C&C for someone special in my life, not exactly. Instead I named it for an entire class of people, or, more precisely, for what this group wore. The name was accepted without question by the literal-minded types at my yacht club. The boat's deep blue hull and the fact that sailing was a summertime sport when almost everyone wore shorts removed any erotic shading to the boat's name. *Blue Shorts,* they must have thought. Why not? Indeed, if they only knew.

Across Eastchester Bay from City Island at Kings Point was the U.S. Merchant Marine Academy. A government-run service school to train officers for the merchant marine, it was a specialized college for young men (and now women) in their teens and twenties. One summer afternoon we sailed past the academy in the old Tanzer 22. It must have been late June, the beginning of real summer weather, shorts weather.

The academy had various vessels for the midshipmen's use and training: A fleet of ten-foot dinghies that they raced during the school season, several large sailboats donated by private patrons, all kinds of small working craft tied up in their basin. For serious training their main vessel was a 175-foot motor ship called the *Kings Pointer*. She looked something like a converted deep-sea trawler. She carried a large superstructure of several decks, a broad navigation bridge and heavy towing gear on the stern deck, or fantail. Above her pilothouse was a complete array of radar, SatNav, GPS, and all the other electronic aids the young sailors would have to learn about. The academy used the ship regularly along the East Coast for training skills in ship handling and piloting. But this hot day, as we spied on them from a distance, they were obviously out for a pleasure cruise, maybe an end-of-term celebration. In fact, it looked more like Splash Day in Austin, Texas.

All up and down the decks of the ship young men clambered around from the bow to stern, coming in and out of cabins, leaning over the railings, everywhere. All of them were dressed simply in their clean white academy T-shirts with blue piping, and their no-nonsense, square-cut, standard Navy-issue blue shorts. There were so many of them, all so lean and supple. None had long hair, just regulation crew cuts.

We held our position from about 300 yards away, slowly sailing around in circles, observing their maneuvers through binoculars. A puff of diesel smoke would come from her stack and the vessel would gather headway. Then from the stern we could hear loud hoots of laughter, young men's cheering and shouting. This was no speedboat, no insolent Donzi, yet the young cadets were using this huge vessel for waterskiing.

Trailing astern was a four-by-eight sheet of plywood attached to the ship with a long rope bridle. Trying for all he was worth to stay upright on top of the plywood was a gutsy midshipman dressed in his blue shorts that were now—along with his T-shirt—soaking wet.

They were taking turns to see who could stay up longer. It was an exercise in balance, nerve, and ship handling. Reports from the fantail were relayed up to the bridge by barefoot young sailors. It took a while to get moving and even longer to come to a stop.

We began easing the *Normand Gagnier* a little closer. How I envied them all this fun and camaraderie, their careless lanky young bodies and clear-eyed hopes for careers on the ocean.

The day ended with me a blithering idiot stammering, "Blue shorts." "Blue shorts," repeated like someone who had seen a vision. Just like Mr. Toad after his first near-fatal encounter with a motor car. "Blue shorts," I mumbled, like a mantra. The search was over, my destiny had become manifest, my ship had come in. I had been to the mountain and at least I knew what they were all wearing. Forget faded Levi's, I told myself. Forget loose khakis. Forget cute underwear. It was all clear now and I knew what I wanted. One way or another I could not live a life without "blue shorts."

The name looked appropriate across the transom of the C&C that September. Once again it seemed to fit somehow. It was more lighthearted and spirited than the former names that were all burdened with history and memories. A new chapter in my sailing life had begun, and I felt more confident and adventuresome.

# 10

## THE VOICE IN THE FOG

*Vineyard Sound, July 1986*

By now Kevin and I had been sailing together nearly seven years, and while we had the boat routines well organized, like any couple, we were getting a bit bored with each other's company at times. We both considered sailing a social sport, like going to the movies or Broadway. We found a third or even fourth person made the trip more pleasant, provided more combinations of crew on deck, and also allowed someone to rest while we sailed on all day or late into the night on long passages. I placed a notice in the *New York Native,* a gay tabloid, and that's how we met Howard.

He was not the greatest sailor, but he was funny and could be very campy once he forgot about his career of selling antidepressant drugs to physicians. He insisted it was called "detailing" rather than selling, and he was making loads of money doing it. He exceeded his sales quotas and his pharmaceutical company kept promoting him. He was as tall as Kevin but much more square shouldered and poised. Dressed in his well-cut suit he presented a formidable figure no doctor could resist.

The *Native* ad did bring in a few respondents who thought the ad was a tongue-in-cheek request for a "mate" to have a three-way with us. We did not entertain those answers. An arrangement had evolved that seemed to work for Kevin and me. We were married, after a fashion, and totally dedicated to each other. We were building a life together, and the business, the woodworking shop in downtown Manhattan, was doing better. We were meeting our payroll most of the time. We had good jobs coming in. We had a lovely, though very small, apartment in a great location. From time to time we had sex with each other. For both of us it was not the best sex in our lives, but it was not what the relationship was about anyway.

We loved each other, and cherished each other every night. We slept close, usually with an arm around the other, and we felt comforted by each other's presence. He was mostly oral; I was more anal. We never talked about any rules; there was never any agreement about having sex with other men outside. Kevin often met cute guys his age and his type down on the Jersey Shore, or on the trips he took on his motorcycle. When he came home I would ask him and he would tell me all about them, especially what they wore. He wanted to keep up with what the current "look" was; what the surfer types were wearing from Belmar, New Jersey, to Delray Beach, Florida. He saw himself as a part of that scene, or at least able to fit in.

My own self-image was pretty shabby. I felt lucky to have him living with me. But it was more than that. I also felt he needed me very deeply. In truth, I knew how afraid he was of losing me, of losing a world of stability and consistency that was based upon unconditional love for him. He was one of those people who did not think he was worth that kind of love. But I did. On the surface, he was for me the blond in the convertible. A real catch. I knew I held all his emotional cards, that he had placed this terrible trust in me. He never tried to stop me from meeting other men—and there were certainly many opportunities—but I never did.

I just could not do that to him. I did not envision a fifty-fifty situation. I wanted him to screw around with other guys and then share these hot escapades with me, tell me what they looked like, how they dressed. That was the best way to hold onto him. When I imagined finding others to sleep with, to make great love with, I shuddered when I thought what that would do to Kevin. It broke my heart; I felt inside of him at times. I felt his fear and defensiveness, his quickness to shout "fuck you" when I hurt him, as if he was ready to blow the whole relationship at any instant. I was not. I knew it would take a lot of time and work to prove that to him. That mattered more to me, for those thirteen years, than getting a good fuck now and then.

Howard joined us early in July at Block Island. He arrived by small plane during a short break in the fog. I remember how he hopped out of the little plane, full of smiles, carrying a bottle of champagne in one hand and four new blue boat cushions in the other. The plane kept its motor idling and took off for the Rhode Island mainland immediately, hoping to stay ahead of the next incoming fog bank.

The next day we sailed for Martha's Vineyard. We spent a few days on the Vineyard and then planned to sail down to Newport on the return leg. We had done this trip before; it was about forty miles, a day's sail. The previous night, as was my practice, I stayed up alone in the main cabin doing the navigation work: I carefully marked out all our courses on the charts. If things got rough, it was a relief not to have to do such precise work while under pressure or heeled over.

In the morning I was nervous. We had a long trip, the visibility was not great, and the wind was pretty strong and already blowing from the wrong direction. I wanted to get to our destination. I awoke early and filled a thermos with fresh coffee for Kevin and Howard, who were still asleep. The sleep of the innocent, I thought jealously. I had an inkling we were in for a difficult passage.

It was cloudy, overcast, and not very promising when *Blue Shorts* slipped the mooring at Oak Bluffs. The popular little harbor had been so crowded that July weekend that each available public mooring had to be shared by three boats, all rafted against each other. It felt something like visiting relatives and having to sleep on the living room couch.

We did not bother with a fancy breakfast, just some bread and jam. There would be plenty of time to fix a meal once we were underway, I assured Kevin and Howard. They would have preferred a leisurely sit-down meal at a café ashore, but they understood how we needed to leave with a fair tide. They trusted my decisions.

After we rounded the northwest corner of Martha's Vineyard, we headed down Vineyard Sound, going west-by-south. Unfortunately that was the same direction of the wind, nearly in our face. We could not sail the ideal course I had planned. I was eager to make distance, rather than tack back and forth all day and waste the morning's favorable tide toward our destination.

Nor did I not want to use the motor the whole way. The boat would be slowed considerably by thrashing into headseas. That would be a tiresome and tedious trip. But with the motor running about half-throttle I could cheat a little and point closer to the wind—and maybe our course.

This worked for a while. The boat's engine had plenty of power to move us along. But this same old workhorse Atomic Four had the exasperating habit of overheating whenever I tried to use power and sail together. It had something to do with a poorly designed cooling system, a lack of back-pressure to the upper part of the engine block.

As we pushed our way down Vineyard Sound I sat at the helm watching the temperature gauge. Slowly, inexorably, it was creeping past the safe 175° reading, where the needle pointed contentedly straight up. Inside the boat I could feel the confident rumble of the twenty-five-horsepower motor chugging away under my feet. I continued to watch the water temperature climb up to 180 and then 185 degrees.

I developed this special relationship with the needle on the temperature dial. I thought I could will it back to the left, just a little. How I wished I did not know as much as I did. If we continued to let the water temperature run over 185 degrees the engine would eventually overheat. Sea water running through the block would start to cook and the engine would get hot, causing the lubricating oil to break down. The pistons would develop too much friction; the rings would drag and start to bind inside the cylinders. Most of the fuel mixture would go unburned, sending black smoke out of the exhaust. The salt in the circulating seawater would begin to precipitate out, like in any high school science experiment. The salt deposits would scale up on the walls of the cooling jackets surrounding the hot combustion chambers. The engine temperature would continue to get even hotter, and eventually the reliable old Atomic Four would lose compression, have trouble firing, slow down, and stop.

There is an old skipper's game in sailing called "What If?" When things are going along just fine, you're at the helm, the boat feels great, the sky is clear, and you ask yourself, What if the mast were to fall down? Or, What if a person were to fall overboard? Or, What if there was a fire in the galley? What if a steering cable broke? What if we were holed by a floating log? On and on went the scenarios of near disaster. It's your job to be ready for any of them. You can always do something, if you are ready. And you should be ready. You make the trade-off of losing the relaxed and naive pleasure of being out on the water in exchange for the informed peace of mind in knowing that serious calamity is less likely to happen because you have some defensive plan ready. You're not stupid.

The plan now was obvious. We would use our sails to reach Newport. I told Kevin and Howard that the engine was overheating and to hoist the working jib. I tensioned the backstay some more and pulled in the mainsheet. The two of them were not very distressed by this change of plan, since they preferred sailing anyway. *Blue Shorts* heeled over and dug in for an exhilarating sail toward Newport. Suddenly we were making close to seven knots. The boat sailed much better than she motored. Of course now we were no longer on our direct rhumb line through the water, but rather tacking back and forth. Each tack would bring us no closer than twenty-five degrees to either side of that imaginary ideal course. I had not figured for that last night when I plotted the day's passage. Everything was different now, more challenging and difficult, and would soon get much worse.

As we sailed along the coast of the Elizabeth Islands, I was attempting to keep an accurate account of our journey on the chart. When we came in close to Naushon Island near Robinson's Hole we tacked away at Red Bell Buoy 28. That would be an easily identifiable spot from which to show our new course, since that was on the chart. We went over to starboard tack and headed across toward the Vineyard side of the Sound. That was when the fog set in all around us.

I came up on deck with my hand-bearing compass to take a compass bearing on Red 28, to be certain of its position as we left it astern. I had seen it half a minute before and now it was gone. I knew it had to be back there, less than 300 feet away.

"Where did that buoy go?" I asked Kevin at the wheel. I stood in the cockpit holding the small compass to my eye, but with nothing to take a sight on.

"Oh, it's back there someplace," Kevin said with a casual wave, as if hailing a taxicab on Seventh Avenue. "We saw it just a while ago. Not to worry, it'll still be there when we come back." Kevin seemed very jaunty this morning. Indeed, the boat was sailing beautifully, slipping through the water at good speed, cutting nicely between the incoming waves and sending up a light spray across the foredeck. She was driving fast, and handling it well. This is what my boat was built to do, to sail fast to windward.

I, however, felt nothing but a sinking heart. I knew that I had just seen the last solid object that I was likely to see for many, many hours. This I was certain of, just as I understood why the engine had to be shut off. I knew that the coast of Martha's Vineyard lay only several miles off to our portside. On this course we were five miles from the end of the Vineyard, heading toward Gay Head and a ledge of rocks just off the coast called Devil's Bridge. At this speed we would be there in forty-two minutes, but we would go back over to port tack long before we got that close. We needed to stay closer to the other side of Vineyard Sound, closer to Nashawena and Cuttyhunk Islands. That was the only course that would get us toward our destination.

Getting out of Vineyard Sound was not going to be as easy as it had seemed looking at the chart the previous night. The same off-lying rocks, with buoys all around them, were all now invisible in this fog.

Before we were out of Vineyard Sound we would have to clear Cuttyhunk Island. Beyond that was the single major danger out here, Sow and Pigs Reef. It would probably take two more tacks at least to get safely past that huge field of submerged rocks, larger than the island itself.

After sixteen minutes we tacked back over. That should have carried us just two miles on the first course. I plotted this off on the chart, lightly in pencil, then laid off our new heading back toward Cuttyhunk Island, which I assumed was three and a half miles farther. We had at best a quarter-mile visibility, maybe less. In front of us was just a wall of white, and waves coming down at us from the ocean. The waves were getting bigger, I noticed. Our speed was down a little, to six knots. How close could we get to the unseen island?

One moment when I was up at the bow I thought I heard something out there. Somewhere out in the fog I could pick up the thump-thump-thump-thump of a slow-running diesel engine. Probably a lobsterman looking for his traps. Soon the engine died away and we saw nothing.

The next time I went up on deck I was sure it was windier and a little rougher. The waves seemed bigger. If we were indeed at the opening of Vineyard Sound, I rationalized, then yes the seas would be getting bigger. We were out of the lee of Gay Head by now, beyond the protection of Martha's Vineyard. That was when the radar reflector went overboard. This was a lightweight set of metal plates, about the size of a soccer ball. The line up the mast parted from being buffeted around in the breeze. There wasn't even a splash. I watched it as it disappeared astern of us in seconds. Gone. Just swallowed up in the waves and fog. Nothing. *My God,* I could not help thinking, *what if that had been one of us?*

Howard also watched it go overboard, and called to me, "I hope we didn't need that thing. It was the wrong color, anyway. Shouldn't it have been blue to match the boat?"

"The spare one I have is even worse," I yelled back to him as I came into the cockpit. "It's a phony gold color, and very tacky." From inside the lazarette locker behind Howard, I pulled out the cheap one I had never liked. It would now come in handy. I sent it up alongside the mast on a heavier line this time. I felt I had kept the forces of chaos momentarily away from our little vessel. Hopefully any ships out there with a radar set would see a small blip on their screens, the echo produced by our reflector. I was scared but at least not helpless. I looked at my watch and went below to update our position.

Where were we? Where the hell were we, really? I kept wondering as I looked at our penciled track. Did it bear any relationship to reality? How accurate was our compass? It had not been calibrated by a professional in years. Nor did it ever exactly match the hand-bearing compass. We could be totally turned around, maybe miles off from where I thought. The waves looked the same no matter which way we turned. Would we even see the island in this fog? Would I see trees and beach or just a shoreline scattered with boulders?

Back up on deck again, Howard still had the helm. I needed to check his steering. "What time is the hot bullion served?" he asked. "I do hope the steward has my deck chair set up for me." He was living out some kind of Edwardian fantasy of life at sea. "This fog, oh, it's just so very . . . wet, and it is ruining my set," he added, and tried to fluff up an imaginary Jackie O. bouffant hairdo.

I looked down at the compass. "Hey, bimbo," I told Howard, "you're off course. You've got to try to hold us at three-hundred degrees, if at all possible. We need to make as much ground to windward as we can now." Howard glanced down and frowned at my finger on the compass dial as if he had just noticed the device. He leaned toward Kevin and hissed, "I knew we should have booked a later sailing. There was a Greek liner leaving after lunch. They're a lot more fun."

"It's all those U-boat movies he used to watch," Kevin explained sagely. "He still thinks he's on patrol in the North Atlantic. Don't be surprised if he starts giving us orders in German soon."

"Du bist ein Schweinehund," I told both of them and stepped back as the sub's periscope slid with an oily hiss down into its well. I dove again through the companionway into the cabin. I realized that I would know by the bottom contour how close we were to Cuttyhunk. *When we cross the twenty-four-foot ledge we will tack the hell away again,* I thought, studying the chart very differently than I had before. That would get us close in, but with enough margin to avoid running aground.

Fifty minutes later we were again on starboard tack. Hopefully, we had already passed Cuttyhunk Island. This time we should be able to clear the Sow and Pigs Reef. In this fog, which seemed to be getting denser now, there would be no way of knowing where the island was. We might still run up on the rocks off Cuttyhunk before we even saw the shoreline if my dead reckoning was wrong. Only the depth would be our clue. The digital depth sounder was now our most critical tool for safe navigation. I went up and down, like a jack-in-the-box, between the cockpit and the dinette table where the chart was spread out, each time comparing the depth reading to the data on the chart.

"Oh my God. This is awful," I heard Kevin shout from the cockpit. My heart froze. *What was wrong now?* I thought. What had he seen? I climbed back up on deck.

"What did you put in here, iron filings and seawater? Did you even taste this stuff? Don't you ever measure when you make coffee?" With a grand gesture Kevin heaved his cup of coffee off to leeward, adding a dramatic "P'yech," and spit out what was still in his mouth.

"Maybe it just needs more sugar," I suggested. I had in fact not measured anything that morning. I was too nervous and just wanted to get up and go. "Do you want me to make you guys another fresh pot?"

"Just navigate. Stay away from the galley today." Kevin told me in no uncertain terms. Howard was leaning over the rail with a finger in his throat, and making retching noises.

"Do you want some juice instead?" I asked solicitously.

"Forget it," Kevin answered me. "The only way you can redeem yourself is if you get us to Newport in time for tea dance."

"Me?" I answered stupidly. "I only work here. You must want the captain for that."

In unison, both Howard and Kevin bellowed back at me, "You are the captain!"

"Go back to your chart table and do something useful, dummy," Kevin added. So that's what I did. Apparently they did not need me on deck, and I was thankful that Howard was here to provide some company for Kevin. Together they could share the tedium of steering a compass course with no landmarks on the horizon to look toward.

Yes, the chart, I told myself. Everything you need is on the chart. But beyond the chart was our pilot book, the dog-eared copy of *Eldridge,* the biblelike almanac with the yellow cover that had all the tide and current tables for the entire eastern U. S. coastline.

While reading the tide tables the night before, I had come across a reproduction of an archival letter. It is included in every edition of *Eldridge,* a letter by the founder and namesake of the almanac, the senior George W. Eldridge. He is writing to a sea captain in the late nineteenth century about a peculiar feature of Vineyard Sound. He describes the shore that lay to leeward of us as "the graveyard." I had read the letter with detached fascination, a curious bit of nautical history, something from olden days, when shipwrecks were all too common in Cape Cod as in all these poorly marked coastal waters.

"Many a good craft has laid her bones there, and many a captain has lost his reputation, also," he warned, and explained why. Regardless of whether one was riding on a flood or ebbing tide, the current would always set a vessel transiting Vineyard Sound closer to the shoreline of the Elizabeth Islands. The ebb and flood were not in directly opposite directions, as one would normally expect. Thus a vessel sailing blind in the "thick weather" of fog was unaware that she was constantly getting closer to the shoreline on the northern side of Vineyard Sound. Of course in good visibility this was no problem. But fog changed all that: ". . . hundreds of them have been piled upon the Graveyard." His little sketch had helpful arrows showing the northerly set to both cycles of the tidal flow.

I began to break into a cold sweat. My boat was in exactly this same situation. I had no more information than did a captain 111 years ago; I knew my compass course, my speed, and the depth below my keel. Was I now also inviting disaster as I sailed through "the graveyard"?

Far more experienced captains, with well-found vessels, had come to grief on the very same rocks that lay to leeward. Was I any smarter? Did I have any advantage? I had no sophisticated electronics. Only the digital depth sounder, and if that failed I could dig out the same time-honored sounding lead and marked line. I imagined what an ordeal that would be, heaving the eight-pound lead weight over and over, each time waiting for the bottom to start coming up closer. That's what they used to do, but perhaps the ones who did not do it were on the ships that came to grief.

By my dead reckoning we should have been slipping well past the Sow and Pig Reef pretty soon. I had reshaped our course from last night's plan, taking a much more conservative approach. I put us farther out to sea, a full mile off the end of the reef as we passed it. Originally I had planned to pass at less than half that distance. It was out there, someplace. I had to believe in something. But I was falling apart.

Up on deck there was nothing to see, and I stared hard into the fog, imagining things coming out of the mist. I watched the depth meter intently. It flashed numbers all the time; sometimes they seemed to be random and unrelated figures instead of a natural bottom contour. We were heeled over hard and the boat was bouncing around a lot. The waves were at least five feet, sometimes more, sometimes less. The depths were getting shallower. We were in the forties mostly. A few fifties, then more forties, then the high thirties, then the mid to low thirties. We were definitely approaching the shore. Which shore? Now into the twenties, again the thirties. Kevin and Howard were quiet too, watching the red LED numbers on the little screen on the forward bulkhead of the cockpit. More twenties, then just one reading in the teens, fifteen, then the screen went blank. We rolled up and dove through a steep wave. Gray water scudded astern of us. The boat heaved up and down through the trough of another wave. Still the screen remained obstinately blank.

"We're just heeled over too hard," Kevin said, trying to calm me. He knew exactly what I was thinking. "It never reads well when we're going to windward and it's rough like this. You're making yourself crazy. Of course we'll see something on the shore if we get too close in."

I was not buying anything today. "Head up, hard," I said flatly, and not as a polite request. I didn't need this kind of anxiety. "Bring her almost head-to-wind. Let her stand up so we can get a good reading."

Kevin spun the wheel up to midships and we slowed down and came up on an even keel. The jib began flapping around, then the mainsail above us was flogging. He bore off a little to keep some way on the boat. The depth gauge read back into the mid thirties.

"Happy now?" Kevin said, sympathetically.

"Me? All I need is just a little information about the real world and I'm happy. Know what I mean?" He brought the helm back down and we bore off again onto our course. The sails filled, and we heeled over and started to charge through the seas again. I left the cockpit with Kevin and Howard looking quiet and nervous for the first time.

Staring down at the chart, I felt like crying, I was so consumed with fear. A weight pressed on my chest, making it hard to breathe. I felt small and helpless, humbled by everything out there on deck. I was losing it, I thought. The boat kept pushing onward into the nothingness that was everywhere. I could not face this alone anymore.

I glanced aft to see Kevin and Howard once again joking around at the wheel. Now they were sharing a joint. Howard was telling some kind of long story, probably about a doctor he had detailed half to death. I slipped up forward, into the privacy of the v-berth. Behind the forward bulkhead I covered my eyes and whispered, "Help me. Please help me get through this. Help us find a safe port. They depend upon me. I'm so afraid." I tried to take a deep breath but instead almost started to cry again. My job was to be up on deck. Just once again, I squeezed my eyes closed and added one word, "Please." All the while I kept thinking, what did these words mean after all? I strode aft through the main cabin and back up on deck.

"Who's this?" Howard asked, turning to Kevin.

"Oh him," said Kevin, looking at me and smiling. "He came on board last night. The union sent him over, but he only speaks German."

I wondered if I looked as spaced out as I felt.

"Hast du einen grossen Wiener, Herr Kapitan?" Howard managed to stumble with his German, before the two of them broke down completely in marijuana giggles. They fell against each other, and I envied then their freedom from my terrors. They were having a great time while I had been going through my few minutes in extremis, up there in the sanctuary of the forepeak. How could they feel so chipper when I was so crazy with fear and doubts?

I told Kevin and Howard that they could find me up on the bow if they ran out of things to talk about. In my mind I saw the chart again. I remembered that beyond the reef there was an important buoy and it had a whistle. Maybe we would be able to hear it. The sea motion felt smoother now. The waves felt more regular—just as steep, but not so confused. We were still moving fast, almost seven knots most of the time.

Then I heard something. A faint tone, far off to my right. Then again, low and slow, like an animal breathing. A tone, definitely something man-made. Maybe that was it, the Vineyard Sound whistle buoy. *Maybe,* I thought, *just maybe.* I automatically looked down at my watch and thought, *I know that kind of whistle.* It was operated passively by a simple bellows action, sucking in air each time the buoy rose up in a rolling wave, then blowing it out again on the downward heave and pumping through the foghorn's trumpet. Its sound was eerily alive, with an almost metabolic rhythm.

"What's our depth now?" I called to the cockpit.

"Very deep. In the eighties all the time. Sometimes even deeper." Kevin yelled back to me in a clear, no-nonsense voice.

"Is that good?" Howard asked me, leaning against the cabin top.

"Oh yes, Howard, that's very good," I said, leaning toward him. Then I added with more emotion than I intended to show, "Deep water is always good. It's what all sailors want." I looked back at my watch. Six minutes had passed so far. I listened again out there. Nothing. Again nothing. Someone dropped a plastic plate down below on the cabin floor. Howard was looking for something to eat. I felt a little guilty. I had not made any kind of lunch yet. I was hungry myself, and surprised, too, since I was also so nervous. *You can't fool Mother Nature,* I thought, with a little smile. You had to eat and sleep, feed your body and rest. We were not machines.

Then I heard it. Another tone, off to the starboard again. Far off, and ahead somewhere. Then again, and this tone was different from the first. Eight minutes had passed now. No, we were not sailing around in circles, a ghost ship trapped in time, doomed in the fog. Then again, that same sound. It was clearer already. This one sounded more like someone blowing over the neck of a soda bottle. This could only be Buzzards Bay Tower. It carried a powerful horn, and this tone was definitely more mechanical sounding. We should be several miles downrange of it and it was where it should be, very roughly.

All that mattered was that both these markers were on our starboard side, where the reef also lay. Had they turned up on our left, or in front of us, it would mean we had drifted dangerously too close, and all of my dead reckoning was wrong. But now I knew that we were finally beyond all the rocks, even though we still could see nothing. I wanted to look at my chart again, to see where we might be, maybe to vector the two sounds and plot an estimated position.

I climbed off the deck and went below, saying only as I passed Howard and Kevin, "I hear some foghorns way off out there. I want to figure them out."

I put a small mark where I thought we were. No matter how crude this position might be, it put us in safe water for many hours ahead.

Suddenly, the pencil slipped from my fingers. I looked at the chart, realizing we were no longer in danger. I thought again of how wonderful was the sound of those two distant fog signals, and I understood that what I had just heard out there that sounded like a soda bottle had literally been the answer to my prayer. Had I just experienced a divine intervention or was I just a good navigator? Is that what God's voice sounded like, an empty Coke bottle?

While Howard made some kind of lunch, I took the wheel for a while. Kevin lay down on the settee for a short nap. Up ahead the fog seemed to be lifting. Then I could see the Rhode Island shore, faintly off to the north. Soon, Brenton Reef Tower appeared, along with a line of other sailboats, much closer to the Rhode Island shore, also making for Newport harbor.

There was nothing like decent visibility to change the mood on the boat. With land in sight and the sky starting to clear, Howard felt the tension on board ease well enough that he put on his favorite Tina Turner album. He cranked up the volume of the outside speakers. We rolled along the incoming swells with the stereo blasting, "What's love got to do, got to do with it? What's love but a secondhand emotion?"

Howard came up on deck—who could blame him now—two bulky socks balled up under his shirt like boobs, and a bath towel pulled tightly around his hips. Standing at the rail he stuck out his chin, then tossed his head off to one side in a gesture of defiance. The boat's narrow decks were transformed into mean city streets as he began to storm around, voguing the incomparable Tina Turner in her triumph over men and all the pain they had brought her. He seemed so good at it. His mouth spoke Tina's words, "Who needs a heart when a heart can be broken?"

An hour or so later we were motoring around Fort Adams, at the entrance to Newport. I had kept my promise to get there by late afternoon. Down below, with just the two of us by ourselves for the first time all day, I admitted to Kevin how afraid I had been earlier, because of the fog. I told him that I had been praying. He looked baffled. I started to feel a little silly for having told him.

"What were you so worried about? Just because of some fog? You know what you're doing. Maybe you should have a drink sometimes, or smoke some dope. That's what we were doing all day. You make it all sound so dramatic, like we were in grave danger. And what is all this nonsense about the 'graveyard of the Atlantic'? That's history. Lighten up, okay? We're supposed to be enjoying ourselves, you know. It's okay to have fun sometimes. Don't worry so much about running into all these rocks. You know what you're doing. Don't you think we trust you by now?"

I felt so mixed up. I felt like a little kid who had lost his mom in the supermarket. But I also told myself that through the whole morning's ordeal my nav work had in fact been flawless. I knew every moment what I was doing, and had built in enough of a margin of error that we were never really in any danger. But I had been so afraid and I still felt like crying. Even more now.

"I'm sorry. Yes, I was really scared. I can't be so relaxed like you guys. I feel all this responsibility. Don't you understand?" Kevin looked at me and his eyes began to sparkle.

"My poor little Gener, such a big baby." He stood over me and draped his arms around me. "He was so fwightened by the fwog. My li'l skipper-boy." As he held me I pressed my cheek against his shirt. Mixed with the damp cotton flannel I could smell him, his cigarette smoke, and, of course, the sea. I held onto him. Then I let one hand slide down to his back pocket. I slipped my hand inside and squeezed him. He gave a sigh and pressed his hips against me. Almost by habit, our legs drew closer together. Gently at first, I felt through his pants. He drew in a quick breath. I unzipped his pants and reached inside. He pushed his hips against me, allowing me to extract his dick from his snug pants. It was so warm, and grew stiff and straight inside the grip of my palm. I felt his fingers between my shoulder blades. He brought his face closer to me. "Suck it," he said to me in a pleading whisper. His lips just grazed the edge of my ear and sent a little shiver through me. Then he asked me again, "Please."

# 11

## INTO THE SKY

*South Carolina, October 1986*

"Do it."

"You're crazy. Does your mother know that?" Kevin looked away from the road and faced me for a second. The instruments in the dash reflected dimly against his eyeglasses.

"Do it," I repeated. "You can see the road's perfectly straight. There are no other cars."

Kevin looked ahead at the road, then quickly glanced into his rear-view mirror.

"Come on, do it," I nagged him again.

We crested the top of a gentle hill and could see down into the next hollow and then up to the rise of the following hill. No other traffic. Nothing ahead and nothing behind us, only road and night.

"It's too weird," he said, his resistance weakening.

"Do it," I dared him again.

We were driving along a two-lane blacktop road out of Columbia, South Carolina, heading southwest. It was a clear October night and we were going about fifty. Finally, he pushed in the light switch on the dash and we were plunged into blackness.

"Oh wow," Kevin gasped, his voice low, quivering just a little. I too was mesmerized and fell silent. There was no longer any road, only night and our car catapulting down this hill. Suddenly the road noise seemed like a roar, as if we were doing ninety. Our senses instantly sharpened; we were still too stunned to panic.

In a few seconds our eyes adjusted and the blindness passed. Now we could see the terrain in its entirety, much more than merely an asphalt road with a dotted line. The landscape was peaceful and whole, and we forgot what the road had even looked like. We were driving by starlight and we remained silent.

Trees rushed by us, dark shapes standing out against the night, stoic, yet full of wisdom. Even the Cherokee knew that they could talk among themselves. The oaks and maples remembered the history of the land and wept when the white lumbermen came with saws to harvest the forest.

I craned my neck upward trying to locate the Big Dipper and Polaris, the north star. At this latitude I expected to find it lower on the horizon than in New York. Our car continued to roar through space and time on the unseen highway.

Trees? How could I worship something that could be cut down with a chainsaw in ten minutes? No, I needed a faith that could endure time and terror. Something not rooted in the tangible, something illusive and immanent, unattainable and yet everywhere.

In the darkness, houses and barns stood out in the open farmland. This was so crazy. I could not believe Kevin was really doing this with me.

"I'm still here, Kiki," I said quietly.

"Uh-huh," he answered back and concentrated on guiding our spaceship down the road by guesswork. Without looking he clicked off the heater fan and it grew quieter inside. Of course we couldn't do this much longer.

"You can tell when you're about to run off the road," I said calmly. "You can tell by the sound of the tires hitting the shoulder."

"Thanks. Then what?" Kevin talked without bothering to look at me, but even from the side I could see his pupils were jet black and wide open.

"Then it will get kind of quiet again as we hit the grass, but it will feel real bumpy." I tried to contain myself.

"Yeah, then what?" Kevin said as he eased us gently to the left, where he thought the center line was.

"Then we hit a ditch and the car rolls over and explodes into flames, just like in the movies," I finished in one giddy burst.

"You're an idiot," he said, frowning and twisting his lips in a sneer of exasperation.

"You're making me crazy," Kevin said finally. He was the one driving and I was intoxicated with the danger and the rush of our speed. His face was profiled against the sky outside. Through a corner of one of his eyeglass lenses I could even see an enlarged speck of sky, like something on a microscope slide. But he looked tense, or rather I could feel his tension. We were sharing the thrill, of course, but I also felt a mad desire to give him this trust, as long as we stayed on the highway.

We started to climb a hill, and it felt like we were driving into the stars. For an instant the sound of the tires became quiet and I felt a stab of terror. Kevin instinctively craned his head to see more of the road over the hood. Then the gravelly road noise returned. We were still on the pavement but must have drifted across the center line.

"Okay, turkey, that's it," he said and turned on the lights. There was a blinding flash as the highway reappeared, with the asphalt looking white at first, and the familiar dotted line came rushing toward us once again. Yet I was surprised to find that this sight of normalcy did not make me feel any safer. I think I liked it better the other way, but I did not tell him that. Then I realized that the broken line was on our right and that we had been driving on the wrong side of the highway.

"You and your asshole ideas," Kevin complained as he nudged the car back over to the right. This time he faced me for a second so I could see both the furrows of tension in his brow and a little wiseguy smirk around his lips. We were still alone on the highway in the South Carolina night.

"I wasn't scared. Were you?" I asked.

In our eight years together, I knew that despite his outward confidence, he needed me to catch him whenever he drifted into feelings of failure and inadequacy. That was my role. His job was to stay alive long enough to find out how much I loved him. I wanted to tamper with Nature, to enter him in some way not sexual but metaphysical, to alter something about him, his destiny or his karma; maybe just to slow down what seemed like a heedless rush to find out what his life was going to add up to. I worried that he did not stop enough to evaluate his life, to reward himself for his passage into adulthood and for making a home for us both. "It's all yours," I wanted to say to him in some way that he would believe. "The moon and stars, take whatever you want. You have all the time you need."

# 12

## AN UNWANTED VISITOR

*Brooklyn, June 1987*

We became carpenters to the rich and famous, for a while. Our shop was busy building fancy display fixtures for a new chain of food stores. It was all part of the booming mid-1980s economy. Expansion and ostentation everywhere: the Laura Ashley store up on Madison Avenue with two floors of oak cabinets, and the Hess apartment on Park Avenue, with so many rooms we had to plan where to meet each other for lunch. Then of course, all the Burke & Burke stores, one right after the other. Lush interiors with curved cabinets, Rosso Levanto marble tops, miles of mahogany shelving. We called it "the groaning board" psychology of marketing, and it seemed to be working. Fill the shelves to near bursting with tempting imported foods, crown the cash desk with goodies, like Valrhona chocolates stacked high, and customers would yearn to be a part of the atmosphere of plenitude.

By 1986 we were building two stores a year and already remodeling stores less than a year old. Everyone was spending money. Kevin was no longer a helper. In the wood shop he had finally found a secure place for himself, a trade, a métier, an identity. I provided the framework, got the new jobs, dealt with the clients and business problems. He ran the shop, doled out projects among the different carpenters and helpers. In addition, he kept the books, did the payroll, gave out the checks. Kevin supervised the daily goings-on in the shop while I ran around meeting clients and getting supplies. Like everyone else in New York City, most of the time I was stuck in traffic.

It was close to Christmastime of 1986 and the city was glittering with holiday lights. There was an upbeat atmosphere all over. Everyone was giving parties. We sometimes went out together to soirees wearing our tuxedos. People were impressed. Carpenters! That was around the time we were building closet interiors in a sprawling Park Avenue apartment for the famous oil executive.

How could people spend so much money on their closets? we wondered as we pored over the architect's drawings back at the shop. Shirt drawers with clear Plexi fronts. Shoe racks that would have delighted Imelda Marcos. Enough chrome hangrod to open a Seventh Avenue showroom. All for the lady's coats and dresses; her fur coats were in storage elsewhere, the designer let us know. The cedar closet needed to be relined; the aromatic wood had lost its pungency.

We worked together at times, but we each had our own responsibilities. I reorganized the company with Kevin as an officer so that he would have more than just check-signing authority. He could legally replace me. He didn't want the power; he wanted a sign of my trust in him—of his commitment to the business and to me, really.

We started to look at houses. It was time to move out of our tiny cubbyhole above Canal Street. I had come into an inheritance and wanted to secure the money into real estate before the business inevitably sucked up more cash. Moreover, we were both getting sick of the dog-shit ambience of Canal Street as well as the ceaseless noise of our nearest neighbor, the Holland Tunnel.

The place had been lots of fun. Our friends visited us constantly. We were halfway between Greenwich Village and TriBeCa and even the World Trade Center. We had converted the sloping tar-covered roof into a meandering garden of potted plants and picnic tables. There was even a barbecue. We gave silly parties and served blueberry daiquiris. The roof was reached with a beautiful clear pine ladder we built after cutting open the landlord's roof hatch that was falling apart anyway. We added a bulletproof Plexiglas insert that allowed sunlight, for the first time in 120 years, into the interior hallway of the little building. With all that sunshine, Kevin started hanging plants in the stairwell. We salvaged a huge mirror from a showroom and anchored it to the wall that rose upward from the first-floor landing. The mirror bounced back so much sunlight that what was originally a dreary flight of stairs took on a striking elegance. The materials were cheap, but anyone could see style and cleverness in their use, and professional skill in the installation. We were two carpenters living together, so we just kept building things. When we ran out of room to build we were ready to move. We found a two-family row house in Brooklyn, close to Prospect Park.

With the new house looming closer that spring, I realized I would never have time to both renovate a seventy-five-year-old house and spend the weekends on *Blue Shorts*. I sold the boat two weeks before we closed on the house and it was a huge relief.

We were moving from the virtual anonymity of a Manhattan warehouse district to a long-established Irish neighborhood. This was a genuine worry for us. Would we be accepted? Would someone spray-paint BURN FAGS on our lovely front door? The house was one of a group of identical brick homes joined with common masonry walls. All had deep lintels and blocky front stoops made of pink limestone. They were hardly the grand brownstones of nearby Park Slope, but they were built as respectable homes for second-generation Irish and Italian immigrants. Probably their first private homes after leaving the tougher neighborhoods of cramped and airless tenements along the Brooklyn waterfront or infamous Lower East Side.

But two queers? How would that play at Farrell's, the raucous saloon that catered to cops and Teamsters on one corner or among the parishioners of Holy Name, the block-square Catholic edifice on the opposite end of Prospect Park West? Still, it was an area in transition and not lily-white anymore. It seemed to attract many young couples and just did not have a constricting Archie Bunker mentality. At least we never detected any scornful looks during the several inspections we made the winter before we moved in.

It was mostly middle management, middle class—homeowners, cops, and firemen. The church and the saloon grounded the neighborhood but no longer seemed to dominate the lives of the younger residents. I told myself that homeowners are fairly predictable in their anxieties. Property values always come first. What would be more reassuring, I posited, than the sight of two good-looking guys pulling up with a huge station wagon? At the time I drove an Oldsmobile Custom Cruiser wagon, a nine-passenger behemoth that virtually screamed out, "I buy American!" Then, I imagined watching us in fearful anticipation, our future neighbors would see emerge from the cavernous bay of the wagon a big black setter dog followed by bags and bags of groceries from Pathmark, along with a twenty-five-pound sack of Alpo and another bag of No Frills cat litter. What could look more normal, unthreatening, and utterly bourgeois? Or so I kept hoping as our moving day approached.

In June we moved into our house in Brooklyn and immediately plunged into the renovation work necessary to get the first-floor apartment into rentable shape. We knew we could not afford the mortgage on the place without the income from downstairs. Kevin stripped paint and wallpaper, pulled up old linoleum, and hired a guy to refinish the floors. I rehung every door, took each lock apart and found the original skeleton keys again so they all closed with a businesslike snap. We were so busy that summer that we did not miss having a boat.

We had six rooms upstairs for ourselves, all of them now filled with boxes from Canal Street. The place was a rabbit warren of odd little rooms and doors seemingly everywhere. We changed our minds frequently about how to use these rooms, how to settle into this place where even the smallest room had two doors leading off in opposite directions. You just had to like the house to tolerate its irrational layout, and we did.

As the heat of summer overwhelmed Brooklyn, we thought it a clever idea to move our bed, for now just a mattress, into the smallest upstairs room. Its single window faced the pleasant street outside. Measuring hardly five by nine feet, it was perhaps intended as a nursery or a sewing room, our broker had suggested. It became virtually wall-to-wall mattress. We did not even bother stripping off the peeling wall paper. It was just a place for sleeping where it would be easy to cool down with a small air conditioner. As before, Kevin slept pressed against the wall, and I took the outside. There was barely room to walk next to the bed.

By the second week in the new house we were already jacking up the sagging floors with posts and two-by-tens down in the basement. On the first floor we had pulled off the tacky red wallpaper that was appropriate only for a San Francisco bordello. The kitchen we stripped bare of the cheap metal cabinets. Paint cans and plastering tools were everywhere.

We were still sleeping in the little front room when very late one night the phone rang and no one was on the other end of the line. I hung up, feeling uneasy. Were we being checked out, stalked, watched, I wondered? Much later that night while in bed, I heard Kasha give out one short bark and I awoke. Just a single nervous-sounding "woof." I knew all her barks by now and I felt anxious. The house still seemed so big to us, with an entire empty apartment below us and then an unfinished basement below that. We felt like children huddled together into the most remote corner of the house.

I fell back asleep and went into an unsettling dream: The country had been taken over by a paramilitary regime, with broad powers to walk into people's homes and make searches. It was all very arbitrary. One morning we were visited by soldiers; at least, they had uniforms and weapons and they were not friendly. They came in to investigate something about us. It was like a scene from Sinclair Lewis's *It Can't Happen Here*. I remember trying to act normal and being very afraid. This was dangerous and real.

I woke again feeling extremely afraid. It was now 4:00 a.m. I knew what those soldiers were looking for. I was still harboring fears of exposure about Kevin and me living together here in this old neighborhood. Up all these streets were rows of identical houses with bay windows. American flags came out on holidays, and elderly white-haired grandmothers attended mass each morning. I still feared that our lives could be made awful if intolerant fanatics saw us as a threat and an abomination. Eventually, I drifted back to sleep.

That was when the room changed around me. I woke this time with a very powerful sense of a presence near me. Kevin was certainly asleep, breathing slowly. I felt a swirling light next to me, like a whirling of blue nascent gasses. I had a weird feeling that some kind of entity was trying to contact me, a something that could not quite come together into solid form. I felt a presence in motion, and it was very near. As if still in a dream, I was totally paralyzed with fear.

Something was happening. I knew I was in my house lying next to Kevin and this was still Brooklyn. I turned my head to the wall, fourteen inches away. I had measured it before we brought in the mattress. In the darkness all the blue spots were glowing—fluorescing, it looked to me. My eyes were having difficulty focusing. The wall became translucent, a kind of veil, no longer made of plaster, lath, and studs. Even the wallpaper pattern was throbbing with some kind of force.

I looked at one of the little flower patterns closest to my face on the wall. It too was changing. What I saw emerge from within the sepulchral depth of the wall was a human skull. Its mouth was open and it was screaming, but I heard nothing. It rushed toward me but did not reach me. I was frozen and then closed my eyes and immediately the skull was gone.

I sat up. I felt something was trying to make its presence known to me, but did not mean to harm me. It was just looking for a window, some outlet from a place of unrest. Whatever this thing was had found in me a pathway for a very brief visit into reality. Something about me allowed this entity to emerge.

I sat there too afraid to move. Where could I run? This thing could go through walls, after all. The bedroom door was open, and in a little while I felt calm again and could refocus on the nearby wall. The faded blue paper was there, of course, with the fussy little cornflowers. Even the peeling seams of the dry paper were visible in the light from outside the window. I clicked my tongue and heard Kasha's jittery paws on the wood floor from the other room. The dog came in with her tail wagging nervously. She was panting and her eyes flashed in the darkness. I rubbed her thick fur and she pushed her snout into my lap. She folded her legs and nestled her body against me. I could feel her heart throbbing against her breastbone. After a few minutes she got up from the cramped space next to me and went back to her own blanket in the other room.

I lay there, my fingers laced behind my head, staring out of the window as the first changes of daylight came to the new day. *What the fuck had I just seen?* I kept thinking. The street light outside had gone off by now. *Had this been a dream? Did it have something to do with death,* I wondered? Did I believe in "restless spirits"? Why did this happen so soon after we moved in here? Was there something our real estate broker had neglected to tell us before the closing? And what about the odd phone call? Should I tell Kevin or would he think we had made a terrible mistake and had moved into a haunted house?

Maybe it was all just homophobic anxiety, like the visit from the armed fascists in my dream? Or was I having some kind of prescient episode? Did I even believe in that stuff? The house felt quiet now, safe and pleasant. I began to hear the birds outside. They called to one another from the roofs and trees. Soon I could hear the footsteps of people heading for the subway, eager to get to work before 8:00 a.m. It felt like a normal summer morning again.

Whatever this vision meant, I would understand when it was necessary. I still liked our house and was sure we had made a good move. I stoically resigned myself that this visitor had some reason for being in this house, as legitimate as my reason. I could do nothing about some past tragedy. I still felt no evil humors wafting over me. All my instincts indicated we were in a happy place. Still, I did not tell Kevin that morning.

That evening I gave him a watered-down version of an uncomfortable night's sleep, a creepy claustrophobic attack that made me insist we move out of that room and use any other instead as a bedroom. We argued again about how to best divide up our living space. I did not want to go back in there and I would never sleep in there again.

We grew friendly with the family next door. The mother was an attractive young woman who had grown up in the same house and now was raising her own family. Three generations lived together. Her Irish mother remembered when the huge horse chestnut tree in our backyard had been first planted—Woodrow Wilson had recently been elected the President. This tree now towered over the building, and its branches mingled in the sunlight with the lovely catalpa tree in my neighbor's yard. Our chestnut would blossom in May and just as the little towers of white flowers fell off, the orchidlike flowers of their tree would start to open up.

One of the previous owners of my own house, a decade earlier, had been the godparents to my neighbor Cathy's first son. Bonds of family and history were all around us. Births and baptisms, weddings and funerals, all had passed through the oak doors of Holy Name Church up the block.

"I'm so glad you guys moved in here," she said to me one morning during our first month. We often chatted over the common backyard fence. Cathy had broken the staunch Irish Catholic canons of the neighborhood and had married a black man, a thoughtful and gentle man from the West Indies, a psychologist. It had not been easy for them at first, she told me. They were snubbed by some of the old timers, people in whose kitchens she had eaten and played as a girl. She made me feel that with our arrival in some way our fates were already intertwined, like the honeysuckle bush whose roots sprang from her side of the fence but whose vines rambled far into my own garden.

"At least now we're not the only ones," she joked with me, with a cup of coffee in her hand, her hair still damp from the shower. I knew what she meant. They had broken the color barrier and now we were cruising through another old rampart of prejudice.

"You know, Gene, if these old walls could talk," she added in a wistful way as she began to get ready to go to work. "These little houses . . ." she started to say, then paused. "They've seen so much life come and go, so much love and tragedy has passed through them. We'll just never really know, but we go on and try to make our lives inside them, just the same." She tossed me a quick smile and ducked back into her own house.

Later that day her husband, Peter, asked me if I could help him carry an air conditioner upstairs from his basement. I told him I'd be glad to help.

Amid the thousands of projects that the house required and the excitement of getting to know the new neighborhood, I tried to forget about that one disquieting night and the unwanted visitor. Whatever it portended, I would learn when I had to.

# 13

## DEEP WATER PASSAGE

*Bequia Island, March 1988*

When we came back from our test sail, Hans said to us, in his terse Norwegian manner, "Take it easy out there, when you make the passage over to Saint Vincent. Just take it easy, okay?" *What was that supposed to mean,* I wondered? Obviously, it was some kind of warning about what to expect when we left the coast of Saint Lucia and made the ocean trip down the Windward Islands chain to Bequia. For all six of us, coastal sailors really, this would be a challenging deep water passage.

Our charter was to start from Saint Lucia, in the lower Caribbean. We planned to sail past Saint Vincent and reach the little island called Bequia. From there we would continue down to visit the islands of the Grenadines group.

We were three couples: Kevin and I; my friend David Lange and his longtime girlfriend Laura; Laura's younger sister Jenny and her boyfriend Steven. David had made all the arrangements and would be the skipper. I would be the navigator.

Bequia intrigued us because it was still one of the very few islands in the Caribbean that had no airfield. It could be reached only by boat. This gave the place an exotic appeal; we would have to get to the island on "our own bottom," as the old-timers used to say.

Before we sailed off, the charter agency wanted to see if we were ready to handle their boat in ocean conditions. They called it a "demo" sail, but in this case it was us, the crew, rather than the boat, that was being observed and tested. This part of the Caribbean demanded more skillful sailing than the Virgin Islands, where everything was within easy reach and protected from heavy ocean swells. Unlike other more popular cruising areas, if we ran into a problem the charter operators could not come out and rescue us in twenty minutes with their speedboat. We would be on our own once we left Saint Lucia.

We were given a serious ocean sailing boat, a factory-new, forty-three-foot Beneteau Oceanis, and it was spectacular. None of us had ever been on anything quite so luxurious and seaworthy. There were four separate staterooms, two heads, and an immense main cabin with a galley along one side with a double sink. On the opposite side was a navigation station with plenty of room to work on big charts. Painted across her stern was the name *Split Vision.* We never learned just what that meant.

Hans met us at the dock near Rodney Bay, where our boat was berthed and from where we would soon depart. He was there to watch us and evaluate our skill in handling a large and unfamiliar sailboat. Hans, the big Norwegian, was a genuine Viking. About six-two, bearded and blond haired, he padded about the decks in his old sandals with the confidence of someone who has been on boats all his life. In fact, he had sailed the Beneteau over from France just two weeks before. The ship's log was still in the nav table, half of it unreadable in his finicky Norwegian handwriting.

Hans pulled on his red foul-weather suit and then helped David a little with the engine controls as he got the boat underway and backed out of the slip. Kevin and I cast off the dock lines and David throttled up gently as we motored out of the protection of the yacht basin into Rodney Bay. As we cleared the breakwater Kevin and I hoisted the mainsail and got the huge genoa sail set. Steven too, lent a hand. The sails filled and the boat came alive. The speed and power were awesome. We all just looked at each other, wide eyed, as the water began rushing past the hull.

Not five minutes out we were hit with a squall. Perhaps the charter agency, or Hans himself, had made some special arrangement for a rainstorm to descend from the sky at this moment. A perfect way to test a green crew, to see how we handled a situation so typical out here that it was hardly even an emergency.

In two minutes there was driving rain and wind already blowing over twenty knots. The boat dug in and heeled over into the whipped-up surface of the ocean. David gripped the huge steering wheel and looked nervously up at the darkening sky. The boat was racing along like a downhill freight train. Laura moved next to David, ready to lend encouragement, or maybe just take over. Jenny and Steven looked around anxiously, not sure of what to do next.

*Split Vision* was vastly bigger than any boat I ever owned, but I knew she was overpowered now with full sail up. Kevin and I looked at each other from opposite sides of the deck. David had his hands full and seemed to be waiting for something to happen next. I jumped onto the cabin top, near the mast, and called to Kevin, "Let's get this monster reefed down." He sprang up and joined me as we sorted through all the coiled-up lines looking for the mainsail halyard and the control lines for the first reef. Everything here was so big that you needed a winch just to release a line under tension. All the important lines led through locking devices called stoppers. They were lined up on the cabin top in ranks of four, with all the different lines color-coded. But boats all work the same way, big and small. We hauled up the topping lift on the mainsail boom, eased off the sheet and released the halyard. The big sail went slack and I called to David to come up.

David feathered the boat up into the wind as we dropped about two feet of the mainsail. Steven figured out what was going on and helped us tie down the flapping sail along the boom. The headsail was a roller furler, so all we had to do was wind in a few feet to make the jib smaller. Unlike my own little boats, the Beneteau could jog along a lot longer even when overpowered. She was not going to lay over on her beam ends so easily. With less sail up the boat was easier to control, and Hans was clearly impressed by our confidence and teamwork. We returned to the dock feeling a little less intimidated by the boat. In two days we would sail for Bequia.

Kevin and I were the oldsters in the crew, meaning we were together as a couple the longest. We had been sailing and living together for ten years. Being on a boat felt normal to us—cooking, navigating, piloting, reefing, anchoring, getting ice and fuel were all a normal part of our domestic routines. The novelty of sleeping together down below was not as important as the chance to do some serious ocean sailing, to explore the islands and maybe even get in some scuba diving.

During our first night on *Split Vision* Kevin and I shared the port side quarter cabin, located in the stern, underneath the cockpit. That lasted about forty minutes before I became claustrophobic. The ceiling was too low. I was the one stuck sleeping on the inside, where the footwell of the cockpit above us left hardly room even to sit upright in the bunk. Besides, Kevin tended to drop off early while I often stayed up for hours studying the charts of the next day's run.

So I moved to the forward cabin, portside, where I actually preferred the narrow upper and lower bunks. It felt more like being on a real ship, up in the fo'c'sle. I had only the spare linen in the bunk above me and a few hundred cans of orange juice in the locker below me for company. I liked being able to move about all night and not disturb the others.

Also up forward, Jenny and Steven bunked in the starboard cabin. They were the "kids" among us, and it was a test of their compatibility with each other, this living and eating and sleeping together in such close quarters.

Jenny, at twenty-three, was younger and prettier than Laura, but she lacked her older sister's confidence. She and Steven were living in East Los Angeles. It was cheap and he thought it more appropriate for them to live in a Chicano neighborhood. Steven was in filmmaking school, and somehow, someday, he hoped to make a statement about the world around him that he felt needed changing. Talk about skinny! He was small, rather cute and intelligent-looking. With all his ribs sticking out, Jenny made a mission of feeding her boyfriend anytime he looked hungry, or even tired. Nothing fancy, she fed him mainly peanut butter and jelly sandwiches or whatever leftovers were handy—anything to fill in between all those bones. As a pair they acted so considerate and polite with each other one might guess that it was their first long trip together.

Laura was crazy about David. They had been together off and on for almost twelve years. Their relationship seemed to run hot and cold. They would spend entire summers sailing together and then break off and date others for some months.

David and Laura had been seeing each other throughout Laura's residency at Yale Medical School. David even kept his boat in New Haven Harbor for two seasons, just so they could sail together on weekends. Much of the time they spent pushing David's boat free of the many sandbars in the broad and shallow harbor.

Laura was building her own career as a doctor and had moved away from New York City to establish a surgical practice. David preferred to remain in his East Village apartment. Still, they were close and it appeared likely they would eventually marry. As a couple they looked good together. They were both ambitious, focused on their careers, but had not seen each other so often in recent months. This cruise would be a chance for them to play at living together, like a real couple. Much to Kevin's annoyance, I had known David long before I had met Kevin. We had an abiding friendship and affection for each other. David had come to New York fresh out of high school. He wanted out of Lockport, New York, a suburb of Buffalo. That was the same time I was living in the Village, near the Hudson River.

As he filled out some more in his twenties, David looked even better, and was doing well at graphics work. He was very popular. With his long blond hair and easy loping walk, he caused both men and women to stop and stare at him as he walked by, as if seeing a bundle of sunlight and daffodils that one day decided to grow legs and coalesce into a young man.

I never did anything with David in bed, but we did a lot of "guy" things together. We rode our bikes around the city, played Frisbee, and sometimes he would drive me around on the back of his motorcycle. I trusted him totally, with my arms around his waist, as he ran the red lights crossing Seventh Avenue in the Village.

One day he suggested we check out an offer of sailing lessons given up at City Island, in the Bronx. I had never even heard of the place.

Two weekends of sailing in early June for sixty-five dollars. What could we lose? The school even provided rain gear. That changed both our lives, mine certainly. My second boat, the Rhodes 19, I named after David Lange.

Kevin, David, and Laura were all about the same age. I was the oldest, leaving Jenny and Steven as the kids.

Two days after our demo sail we pulled out of the marina again, this time on our way. For our first day we headed south to the end of Saint Lucia. That would keep us close to shore and protected from the easterly trade winds and the heavy ocean swells.

We put in the first afternoon at an open roadstead in the shadow of the two huge volcanic peaks known as The Pitons. They both rise up 2,500 feet, like two sharks' teeth. They stand close to the shore and form the principal landmark of the island, visible from miles away. We anchored off the beach by Soufrière Bay. Nobody got much sleep that first night, what with nervous anticipation and the raucous "jump up" party going on all night on shore.

Alone in the main salon, I studied the ocean chart long after our crew had turned in. I had with me the elegant British Admiralty charts for the area. Printed on heavy stock, with their fine black lines they felt more like antique etchings. The chart for the island of Saint Vincent was originally published in 1908, and that chart was based upon soundings first taken in 1861 by the English navy surveyors aboard HMS *Sparrowhawk.*

Sitting alone in the dark cabin, I tried to imagine the square-rigged mother ship *Sparrowhawk,* lying cautiously off the coast while her seamen rowed in closer to shore to take soundings. They probably used an eight-pound weight with a hollow cavity on its bottom, the same kind of lead line I kept on my own boat, just in case the electronic sounder failed. The concave hollow on the bottom could be smeared with tallow to help in pulling up a small sample of the bottom material, and that information, along with the depth readings, would be carefully noted. The fathoms I was now reading were the very soundings those sailors from *Sparrowhawk* had taken. It was tedious but important work. They were surveying these coasts in the hopes of finding a safe harbor for the English fleet.

That was in Queen Victoria's time, when the English fleet all but dominated the oceans. Accurate soundings could mean finding a safe haven for warships and merchantmen seeking shelter from hurricanes or enemies. It was precious knowledge then, and still is today. Looking at the big chart spread out on the nav table, I felt a connection with those men on *Sparrowhawk*. They were on their own and had only the skill of their officers to rely upon if they hoped to see England again. On our little ship I was the navigator, and this crew would likewise rely upon me tomorrow.

I marked out the course I expected our own vessel would follow. David was our easygoing skipper, but I was driven by this neurotic fear that I had to worry for everyone, that the moment I relaxed and just enjoyed myself something catastrophic would befall us.

I looked at the thin line I had drawn on the chart connecting the islands of Saint Lucia and Bequia: twenty-eight miles to Saint Vincent, then twenty-five more miles to Admiralty Bay. How simple, I thought to myself, almost a straight line. What would be out there tomorrow? How long would we be out of sight of any land? Which way would we be set by the ocean currents coming through the passage between the two islands? To the east of the Windward Islands lay nothing but open ocean all the way to the coast of North Africa, 3,100 miles away. The ocean built up waves and then squeezed through the slot between Saint Lucia and neighboring Saint Vincent. What would those seas be like?

This was the real ocean, big, empty, and deep, very deep. I followed our course and noticed that at times we would be sailing over water measured by the English at 1,082 fathoms, almost 6,500 feet deep. Nearly a mile and a quarter of salt water would be below us. The image made me shudder. I thought of all that water with our boat just suspended above it, a mere six feet of our hull precariously floating there. It seemed to defy logic. How could there be so much water under us?

I was making myself crazy. Deep water is exactly what sailors want—that's where it is safest. Ships are in their greatest peril when close to shore, close to rocks and shoals and foul currents. In storms, big ships always put out to sea to avoid being battered helplessly against the land. Why then did it so unnerve me, these staggering ocean depths?

That one haunting thought—like death itself—of a ship, maybe our ship, falling and falling, tumbling, rolling, breaking apart just like the doomed *Titanic*. How long would it take to reach the bottom? So many other luckless ships had made that awful one-way passage. Did the ocean even care? Was it a sinister force that hungered for captives, needed to humble those who dared to venture abroad on its thin uppermost membrane? How wonderfully safe we felt up there in the sunshine and spray. This was no way to begin a vacation in the Caribbean, I told myself.

No, the ocean is not evil, and has no dragons waiting to eat us up. It is a force to reckon with; like playing checkers with a gorilla, like the raging furnace of the sun, it can be both benign and terrible. Yes, we are incredibly small compared to all that surrounds us, but that does not stop us. The ocean does support us, happily or not. Our boat is both solid and buoyant, and with moderate care from her crew she will rise up and float no matter what is out there. There are six of us, together, and *we matter to each other*. That is the answer, I finally realized, and began folding up the chart.

It's not just me, alone, like some burdened Gulliver pulling our vessel through these gargantuan obstacles. We would do it as a crew: Kevin, David, Laura, Jenny, Steven, and I. "Take it easy out there," Hans had cautioned us. It was a warning, certainly, but it also carried the assurance that among us we had the means to stay out of trouble.

In the morning David ran the engine just to charge the batteries and get everyone awake. This would be the only time David was awake so early. Laura pulled out boxes of cereal. Kevin made a pot of coffee. No one had slept well, but we were all eager to get under way. With help from the local boat boys, we retrieved our stern line from the beach. That left the anchor still down with more than 240 feet of chain out. We quickly gave up on the manual anchor windlass, and all the men on board took turns hauling up the crusty anchor chain, hand over hand.

We cleared Soufrière Bay and turned south for open water. The sea was flat and sparkling and there was even a rainbow, the epitome of good omens for any voyage. We passed close ashore to Beaumont Point, with one of the Pitons towering above the water's edge. Our vessel would still be in the lee of Saint Lucia for another six miles.

That first day on the ocean it was Steven, all 120 pounds of him, who handled *Split Vision* for most of the morning. He hardly resembled a character from Jack London, but there were qualities of steadiness and confidence that were not at first visible if you just looked at his droopy shorts and skimpy T-shirt. Behind his small wire-rim glasses he was handsome. I did not envy those pipe-thin arms, but I admired his sense of himself and I understood why Jenny depended upon him.

Three hours into the trip Saint Lucia was just a smudge on the horizon. Now I could feel the sea conditions definitely building and I began to understand what the laconic Norwegian meant. The seas grew steeper, and the wind steadied at about sixteen to twenty knots. Perfect trade wind sailing.

"I think it's time to reef down," I suggested quietly to David. He readily agreed and once again Kevin and I hauled down the mainsail. Forty-three feet no longer seemed quite so huge out there. Even with the reefed main, we still made 7.5 knots, only now we felt a better sense of control over our vessel.

The trip settled into a routine. There really was not much to do; it was a passage to get someplace. All of us were enjoying the balmy tropical air thirteen degrees above the equator. A malaise settled over Laura and Jenny, a queasiness as the boat rose and fell on ever steeper waves. Unlike Steven, Jenny was not ready to take a turn at the wheel. I did not blame her. I fretted below at the nav table forever, studying the charts of Saint Lucia and the entire lower Caribbean. We should reach Saint Vincent in little more than two hours.

In truth, it felt great to be on our way, going somewhere, putting sea miles behind us at last. With all the shopping and stowage of gear, the excitement of the demo sail and the departure, only now I had time to think about all that I had seen on Saint Lucia.

"Hey, David, what's going on up there?" Laura called out to our skipper. She looked up from her half-nap to scan the horizon and had noticed something.

"What's up?" David poked his head out from the main hatch; in his mouth was still a hunk of a sandwich.

"David, I think something up forward is shaking, maybe the anchor needs to be pulled in tighter." Laura was no novice. Jenny lifted up her head a little for just a peek, but did not bother to get up. David and Kevin looked forward as we climbed another wave. The bow pointed toward the sky for a few seconds and then pitched over the crest and started the familiar plunge into the trough. At the bottom the boat gave a quick shake, shrugging off the water sloshing over her bow, and then started up the face of the next wave. That was when we all saw how the anchor was shaking from side to side.

"Are we losing our anchor already?" I asked as I joined the others in the cockpit.

"The CQR is definitely getting loose up there, watch," David replied, pointing forward. Steven was at the wheel keeping *Split Vision* steady, already learning to pinch up just a little to try to take the biggest waves just off our bow, and then bear away again on the down turn. Each maneuver another wiggle of five to ten degrees off our intended course, I fretted to myself.

"Oh, what's the big deal? I can fix that." Kevin put down his drink and headed along the side deck toward the bow. He seemed so far away up there.

I watched him hanging onto the bow pulpit as we heaved and pitched up and down. Each wave would lift us eight or ten feet as we came up to the crest. Each time, again and again, the boat would rise up, heavy as she was, yet astonishingly buoyant in the foamy Caribbean water. Each succeeding crest rolled beneath us, then continued curling and foaming away on its rush toward the coast of Central America, 1,400 miles to leeward.

"What's the story?" I yelled up to Kevin.

"I need some rope, something to tie it down." Kevin called back. We should have removed that heavy piece of gear right at the start, I thought. I longed to be the source of security and confidence on board, still slightly resenting David's authority. He was already digging into a locker, looking for some light line. Kevin half-stumbled and half-walked back to the cockpit, not yet timing his steps to the rolling motion of our decks.

"Yeah, this should do okay." He snatched several short pieces of rope from David and once again walked back awkwardly toward the bow. I watched his slender figure, dressed only in a skimpy Speedo bathing suit. From this distance he looked reedy, like a leek.

Laura took over the helm from Steven. She caught my expression and registered my anxiety. Kevin looked so vulnerable up there at the bow, at the end point of a forty-three-foot fulcrum arm. Even the cockpit farther aft was far more stable, its motion less extreme than where Kevin was working to wrestle down the anchor. The possibility of the damn thing coming loose was too dangerous. Dangling over our bow the thick plow-shaped thing would batter against the hull and eventually gouge a hole up there. Even worse, if the anchor chain let go from the capstan the anchor would plunge straight to the bottom, taking along all 600 feet of chain shackled to it. This was not a situation we could ignore.

Kevin, in just that Speedo, now looked like a bunch of sticks that could be tossed around by the sea's will. What would we do if he slipped and went overboard? I watched him trying to thread a rope around the crown of the anchor and then lash it to the bow pulpit. No longer holding onto the railing, Kevin bent down to fasten his knot securely with both hands. "Get back here, already," I wanted to yell up to him. He gave the anchor another shake to test it. "That's good enough," I told him through closed teeth.

Laura glanced over at me from behind the wheel. She had done this kind of ocean sailing before. I felt a little better. Right now, she was in control, she could dodge a rogue wave, softening the blow against the hull. She smiled at me, almost by habit, then narrowed her vision as Kevin persisted in testing his handiwork and tightening the safety line on the anchor again. All I kept imagining was Kevin being tossed overboard, just a blur of blond hair and a flash of red from his Speedo, and he would be gone.

We rose up the crest of another ten-foot wave. Surrounding us was an immense panorama of empty ocean. Wave upon wave rolled toward us from the east. They lifted us and then continued on their unstoppable way, like a force of nature at full tilt. Laura stretched her neck and stood up on her toes to see the bow a little better. Her hands remained supple on the big wheel, not a frightened death grip. Through her open shirt she could just rest her breasts on the spokes. Her hands looked strong, a surgeon's hands. They were not especially pretty hands, but they looked confident as she gave the wheel a quick nudge to leeward.

Kevin was coming back to the stern. He was smiling, and drops of seawater dotted his mustache. "Well, that's all done. Now let's have a drink," he said, and he tossed the extra line back into the cockpit. My skinny cowboy, I thought with relief, just in from roping those ornery anchors. His back was already starting to get tan and freckly.

Was I the only one so dogged with fears? I looked again at Laura. She smiled at me, then closed her eyes and gave a slow and silent puff with her lips, a sigh of relief we both shared. Kevin came back from the galley with a beer, and as he flexed his arm to twist off the cap I noticed, as if for the first time, how muscular and fit he looked. He was not at all the spindly rag doll I had imagined while he was up at the bow, nor did he see himself as a scrawny thing tossed around by the wind. Why then did I fear so much for him whenever he was far from my grasp?

As we closed with Saint Vincent the waves and wind began to shift aft. From the chart I guessed we should be about halfway across the channel by now. On deck above me I heard the slow creaking of the lines being eased off the winch drums, a comforting sound. We were easing off to a beam reach; our boat would no longer be taking the waves hard on the bow. We were making progress for sure.

I stuck my head up on deck and announced that I was going to take a short nap. Laura said that was a good idea because I looked tired. "Sure, go to sleep," Kevin said to me. "We'll wake you up when we get to Bequia." Clearly I was not needed, so I stretched out in the main cabin, close to the nav area. I tried to doze but began to think about Saint Lucia again.

We had a few days before getting on the boat. One night our group wandered down to the beach looking for a local bar called the A-Frame. It was a typical outdoor bar, with a shack serving burgers and fish nearby. Everyone ate outside at the picnic benches in the sand. There were other tourists, some local boat types, English and scruffy looking, and a group of young Germans, all of them tall and earnest. Off by themselves at another table were sly-looking locals wearing dark glasses, quietly watching everyone else. Under our feet the powdery sand felt good, and the surf was only a few dozen yards away. We could hear it in the darkness. A few rowboats were tipped upside down with their bow lines tied to palm trees. Three local guys were playing softly on their steel drums. I tuned out all the conversation and heard that they were playing a sentimental version of "Blue Moon." Around us smoky torches filled the air with soot and an oily smell that was supposed to keep the bugs away.

We sat with our drinks, excitedly wondering what our boat would look like and how difficult it was going to be to buy a week's provisions. Had we made the right choice to get all the food ourselves rather than let the charter agency do all the provisioning? Kevin, with his culinary background, wouldn't hear of that, and we were all so picky about food that we opted to do a major shopping orgy the next day.

Closer to the beach an older couple on vacation were off by themselves, just dancing. Probably they came from one of the chartered sailboats anchored out in Rodney Bay. Their dinghy must have been the one just at the edge of the surf. I watched as it rocked a little whenever a wave rolled in, and wondered if it should be pulled up higher.

The man was well into his sixties, heavyset, with a graying beard and thin hair. With his glasses, he looked very much an academic type or an executive. His wife was perhaps a little younger and nearly as tall, with a better figure than he, but the folds around her eyes and neck revealed her age.

She wore a colorful one-piece wrap of batiked cotton gathered under her shoulders. It hung down in soft folds to her knees. The light fabric moved easily around her, lifting softly like a curtain in an open window. She had attractive legs, shapely for her age. His movements were stiffer than hers; maybe he was starting to have a little arthritis trouble. But as they swayed together she seemed comfortable letting him lead in his desultory way.

The man wore khaki shorts, faded, a size too big. His shirt, untucked, had a red monogram and was probably expensive. He had a lumpy build and would have looked more at home in a business suit. He was not particularly handsome, but he projected an authority, a confidence that showed in his shoulders and forehead.

The couple hardly danced, but just shuffled their feet around in the sand. At times they merely held each other and only swayed their hips to the music. Maybe they remembered listening to this song long ago. I first heard it as a teenager and could still hear Elvis murmuring the words: "Blue moon, you saw me standing alone, without a dream in my heart, without a love of my own."

As they danced to the velvety music, I looked down at their feet. His were thick and blistered on the tops from the sun. He probably was not used to going barefoot. In the torchlight there were flashes of red polish from the woman's toes. She wore a thin gold chain around her ankle and now and then it sparkled, symbolically, like a wedding band. Their feet looked so different yet moved so easily together.

For a while they closed their eyes. She rested her head on his chest and he embraced her lightly with one hand on the corner of her hip. He still carried a drink in his other hand, as if they had started dancing offhandedly, and the man was just too housebroken to dump out his drink into the sand. A flashlight protruded from his back pocket. They would need it later when they rowed back to their boat.

*Split Vision* rolled along majestically as I lay on the starboard settee. Above me I could see the sky arching back and forth through the curved windows in the cabin roof. But I was still remembering the couple in the sand, as they danced, back in Saint Lucia. I was glad not to be so old and lethargic, not yet. Yet I admired their familiarity, how comfortably they fit around each other. There was a gracefulness not so much in their dancing as in their attitude toward each other. They had already stepped over the threshold from youth into middle age. Soon would come the first stages of frailty, which led to infirmity and the inevitability of loss.

In their frumpy way, they were cool, and apparently still in love. They had a look of constancy with each other, of surviving together. They knew what mattered and what was just silly. And I envied them, just a little. As I heard all the laughter around me from the bar and the Germans shouting, I realized that what they had was not such a bad thing to want. Then I turned back toward Kevin across our picnic table. He was a little drunk already from the bar's rum punch. He was planning a foray later with Steven to try to find some local ganja. Another adventure. I told him I did not think he had to look very far, and nodded toward our neighbors in the conspicuous dark glasses. I wondered if he and I would ever become like that couple dancing in the sand, so used to each other and still in love. I imagined a moment of future déjà vu, years from now, and I wondered, in advance, what will have changed when eventually I look back at this night.

"Oh Gene, I think you'd better come up here." It was Laura calling me from up on deck. There was an odd mixture in her voice, concern and mischief.

"Gene! Get your fat ass up here." That was Kevin. I climbed up the companionway thinking, *What now; what new problem have they come up with for me?* Out on deck nothing seemed to have changed; we were rolling along and still doing over seven knots on a course of 210 degrees. I could see at least one, maybe two other sailboats far astern on a similar course. We were no longer alone. "Not back there, jerk. There!" said Kevin, pointing forward. Laura and David said nothing, but I thought they had odd smiles. I looked forward and saw only ocean.

Finally I saw it and my mouth dropped. "Holy shit," was all I could manage at first. There, miles and miles away, in the haze above the horizon, was an apparition I was not prepared for. The island of Saint Vincent, our first landfall, rose up so high and so steep it did not seem possible. Yet there it was. I had never considered what a 4,000-foot mountain looked like from fifteen miles away. Indeed, the volcanic mountain was ghostly, looming up at an altitude where one would normally scan for aircraft. Immense and brooding, it towered like a Chinese hat faintly traced into the clouds. Henceforth, my navigation would be irrelevant with that kind of landmark in front of us.

"Where did that come from?" was my feeble attempt to save some dignity. *What an incredible relief,* I thought, still staring up at the mountain and the sharp slope of its sides.

The mood on board noticeably lightened. Each of us, in his or her own quiet way, was obviously awed by this vision. But more importantly, we were impressed with our own audacity to be out here comfortably closing with this great God of a volcano. Laura got Jenny to come below and help her make something for a light snack. Farther ahead we could see another sailboat, and we were catching up to it.

Our euphoria was tempered half an hour later when Kevin noticed that the anchor was again shaking around up at the bow. This time David inspected things up forward.

"The whole roller fitting is falling apart up there. We've got to take the anchor off completely this time." The bow was rising and falling with the long waves, at least ten feet high, and as much as 200 feet between the crests. These were real ocean swells.

This time David and I went up to the bow to deal with the unruly anchor. We put on safety harnesses, something that really should have been done before. I was nervous, but I was not going to put anyone else through the same anxiety I had endured as a spectator when Kevin was up there.

"Be careful, you guys," Laura called to us. "No heroics today, okay?" Steven looked a little worried; I probably made everyone nervous. Except for Kevin. I knew how much he trusted me at these times. He took the wheel from David and propped one leg up on the cockpit coaming, the same way he often did at home. It was good to see him at the helm, as if we were on our own boat once again.

Up at the bow, David and I clipped our safety tethers to the nearest stanchion base. We saw immediately that the entire roller fitting that supported the anchor was falling apart. All we had to do was unshackle the anchor and hand it back over the bow railing and then stow it in its locker on deck.

I crouched into the anchor well and eased off several feet of chain while David moved forward to the very edge of the bowsprit and carefully muscled the CQR over the railing. Everything was done in slow motion. We had to time our moves with the heaving of the boat up there. Each time the bow plunged downward the acceleration was astonishing, making us dizzy. David unscrewed the shackle and I took the anchor from him and finally dropped it into the well beneath me.

We were frequently buried in water to our knees. Warm seawater foamed and bubbled all around us then ran back off the deck. When we got the big anchor safely away I stood up and noticed rivulets of red streaming from my feet. Somehow I must have cut myself, I thought, and had been too occupied or frightened to have felt anything. David looked down too. The sight of all that watery blood started to make me feel queasy and lightheaded.

"It's your shoes, Gene," he said. "They're running." The shoes I bought for this trip were losing their dye right there in the seawater.

"But they're *boat* shoes," I said to David, trying not to sound too stupid.

"They're cheap shit," he answered back as I looked down to see the very lifeblood of my moccasins staining the foredeck.

We came back aft to get out of the harnesses. We had both swallowed some seawater and now felt a little sick and surprisingly tired.

"You guys were really great." Laura gave David a long kiss and then turned to hug me. I felt her wet hair cool against my forehead. Then she hugged me a second time, a little harder, and I sensed that this time it meant she was relieved to see me back in the cockpit and safe again. Were we the real grown-ups, who did the worrying for everyone else? David downed a soda and then went to rest, stretched out on a cockpit seat, looking pale.

"Good boy," was all Kevin needed to say to me, and he gave my nose a little squeeze. "Yech, you're all wet and snotty," he said, and shook from his hand the water and mucus that were dripping down my face. "And look at your feet. What did David do to you up there?" Brownish red stain formed a puddle around my shoes. "You're a disaster area. Ask Laura to see what's wrong with your feet."

"It's my shoes," I told him. "The dye is running."

"You bought those cheap-shit Fila shoes, didn't you? You never learn. That's why David is the skipper and not you. He has real Top-Siders." Kevin looked over at Laura for support.

"I'd sail anywhere with him, even with his cheap shoes." Laura grabbed me from behind and affectionately pressed her wet hair between my shoulder blades. "Don't listen to Kevin," she added. We stood there, in front of Kevin at the wheel, and he reached through the spokes and grabbed the harness still cinched across my chest. He pulled me up to him, with Laura still hanging on, and kissed me by sticking his tongue into my ear and making it all wet in there. He liked to do that even though he knew I could not stand getting my ears all gooey.

On the cabin top, Steven and Jenny were lying in the sun, only half watching the three of us in the cockpit. Steven turned around to face Jenny as she lay on her back with a towel under her. He kissed her lightly, and she reached up to stroke the back of his head. I freed myself from Kevin and Laura and went below to get out of the shoes and safety harness.

Ahead of us now the towering shadow of Saint Vincent filled most of the horizon. With the seas coming from the port quarter we eased out our sails some more for a broad reach. We were quickly catching up to the other sailboat, and the crew waved over to us. The sea around us sparkled like silver in the midday sunlight. The island was green and densely wooded. The sea air formed a mist that still shrouded the bottom of Saint Vincent in mystery as it brooded over us in the distance.

The other boat surged ahead with the seas. At their stern a perfect quarter wave rolled along with them. We were slowly passing them, and we could almost see their faces as they watched our boat. *We must look just as good to them,* I thought, as I filled with emotion. For the first time in this whole trip I felt really glad to be out there. *This is where I belong,* I thought. It was all worth it.

We passed the length of Saint Vincent's fifteen miles in barely three hours. Now we could see our destination, the neighboring island of Bequia, eight miles away across another open channel.

We spent three days on Bequia. We all bought colorful model boats along with a big bunch of green bananas, what the locals called a full hand. We hung them from the boat's backstay until they eventually ripened. We hoped it would make us look very native.

Out on the reefs, we made a dive to ninety-seven feet to see a wrecked sailboat lying on her side looking strangely peaceful, as if asleep. I had never gone so deep before. We all went down very slowly, but had a limit of only six minutes to explore on the bottom. On the way back up we had to make a decompression stop of five minutes at thirty feet. It was a precaution to prevent nitrogen sickness, what Lloyd Bridges used to call the bends.

What a long time five minutes seemed, just hanging on the diveboat's anchor line, doing nothing but breathing. Yet it was good for me, just hanging there, neutrally buoyant, merely breathing in and out. Occasionally I would check the air gauge on my console. I no longer needed to take such deep and panicky breaths from the regulator. Below me were the bubbles of David and Laura as they, too, slowly inched their way up from the bottom. Far above me was the surface of the ocean and the shadow of the diveboat's hull.

*It was all up to me,* I thought. I could panic and thrash my way up to regain the air and sunlight at the surface. Then I would burst my brains out with an embolism of compressed air in my blood. I looked down and saw Kevin, just below me, also hanging onto the rope and waiting. His bubbles rose and trickled up through my legs. I watched them mix with my own and then continue up and up to the surface where they finally popped open. Looking up at me, his face was compressed inside the lens of his mask. He looked funny. Kevin shrugged his shoulders. I knew what he meant.

Bob, the dive master, came floating slowly past me. He looked at his watch and signaled with his fingers that I had two more minutes to wait.

"Everything's okay," I said, giving him the diver's hand signal.

David and Laura were finally married on the last day we were together on the boat. The two of them would continue sailing for another week by themselves. The rest of us were to fly home, catching a series of small inter-island commuter planes.

We were sailing to Mayreau, an island even smaller than Bequia, which had nothing there but a restaurant and a shallow reef for snorkeling. Jenny had the helm and seemed pretty much in control of things. Steven reminded her every time she was off course. Since the island was right in front of us, four miles away, she told him she did not need to bother with the compass anymore.

David and Laura were both in the cockpit. He wore a shirt to keep from getting any more sun on his fair skin. She was shirtless, trying to get an even tan on her breasts. Jenny, too, was shirtless. They looked more like sisters that way. Laura's dark hair was a total tangle from constant salt spray. It hung around her face in long spiral curls. Suddenly, Kevin stood on the cockpit seat and held up both his arms, very Solomon-like. *Now what's going on?* I wondered.

"Come before me, my children, and receive the sacrament." Kevin said this in a very authoritative voice from high above us all.

"Does that mean you're going to give us all blow jobs?" I asked him, and began getting myself ready.

Kevin scowled at me. He looked down at David and Laura and motioned to each of them with his outstretched palms to move closer together. "Let us begin the ceremony," Kevin announced.

"David. Oh my God! This is it. We're getting married," Laura said, giggling with anticipation. "Jenny, how does my hair look?" she asked and began arranging herself.

"Leave it alone, Laura. You're only making it worse," Jenny told her sister. She added, "It's okay, you look perfect." They smiled at each other, sharing the joke. Then Jenny suddenly became very silly and blurted out, "Oh Laura, I'm so happy for you." She let go of the wheel and hugged Laura. Steven reached over and steadied the helm. The women kissed and Jenny sat down next to her older sister. David slid closer to Laura on the other side. They were smiling, and very agitated.

Standing high above us all, Kevin intoned like a priest, "If any among you object to this holy union, speak now or forever hold your peace." Laura fidgeted a little, squeezing David's hand. Jenny looked at Steven, steering the boat, and put her finger to her lips. David seemed embarrassed, not sure how to react. Laura took both his hands in hers, and brought them to her chest, between her breasts. They looked at each other affectionately.

"Can I just hold my piece and speak later?" I asked after a pause.

"Cast that one from the temple!" Kevin bellowed, pointing a scornful finger in my direction.

"Oh, let him stay," Laura pleaded and looked up at Kevin, adding, "He's my other sister." Laura looked at me with a conspiratorial smile.

In his normal voice, Kevin looked down at the couple and asked, "You guys ready?"

"What do you think, David? Are we ready?"

"Well, since they're all leaving tomorrow, we better do it now. Okay." Laura hugged David and they giggled again.

Kevin stood up and held in each hand a petal from two different flowers, one pink and the other yellow. They came from a bunch on the cabin table, below. Jenny had picked them before we left Bequia.

"By the power granted to me by mighty Neptune I now join these two forever, in love." He put the two petals together between his fingers and held them high above us all. We all looked at his right hand. Kevin glanced down and in an urgent voice whispered to David, "Kiss her; kiss her."

David bent closer to kiss Laura, and their sunglasses clicked together at first. We all laughed and shouted, "Kiss her; kiss her." Then he wrapped both his arms around Laura and they embraced, each turning their head sideways this time. Kevin stepped close to the rail of the boat and intoned, "Let no man cast asunder what great Neptune has now bound together." Then he tossed the two petals high up into the air. We all turned to watch as they started to fall toward the sea. They landed and at first seemed to stay pressed together. Almost in unison everyone sighed, "Ahhhh."

The two petals quickly drifted toward our stern and then separated as the boat sailed on its course. In just a few seconds they were gone, swallowed up by the waves. For a while it all seemed real.

# 14

## THE VISION
*South Florida, August 1989*

We are driving north on I-95, from Fort Lauderdale to Boca Raton. Eight lanes of people in fast cars searching for a better life, or at least something to distract them from the relentless flatness of south Florida. We are rushing along at better than seventy-five miles per hour, and still other cars pass us in the warm night. In twenty minutes we should be back at my mother's condo.

Kevin is driving. I look over at him, steering with his arms stretched out, his legs extended straight and the seat tilted back to a semi-reclined position. That is the way he likes to drive.

Despite his boyish frame, his arms look capable, covered with curly blond hair, bleached from the sun at the beaches from Delray to Key Biscayne. He looks confident and relaxed at the wheel of our rental car, still with its factory-new smell. It had to be red, and we waited an extra half-hour at Avis while they washed one for him.

Kevin is in his element down here, where the realm of youth and beauty means everything. Where the look of the surfer boy, with torn flip-flops and tousled blond hair, is the stylistic icon of the Florida youth culture. Kevin is still young enough to feel he can be a part of this. I am not, but I follow him on this journey of skin and superficiality.

Inside our car it is exquisitely cool and dry from the air conditioner, on at full blast since we left Fort Lauderdale half an hour ago. After a swim we paid a sentimental visit to the Marlin Beach Hotel, where dusk and tea dance brought the familiar turnout of pretty boys, muscle boys, and all their aging admirers. Were it not for Kevin, would I too be among those same chicken hawks circling between the pool and bar hoping for an encouraging smile from some attractive youth? But I am lucky: I live with someone ten years younger and stay connected to the styles of the current generation. Maybe I could never fit into his skinny Levi's, but we like the same music, and this has prevented the inevitable middle-aged retreat back to The Beatles and The Mamas and the Papas. In rock and roll I have found a cheap elixir for prolonging my youth.

We zoom past the exit to Pompano Beach. Somewhere out to my right, three miles east, the Atlantic Ocean rolls in and the beach is deserted. Earlier, when we left A1A for the interstate, the surf had been flat calm. But now, with the sun down, the breeze had returned and so too the incoming surf out there in the darkness. Once we tried swimming together in the ocean at night, but it was too creepy, the warm surf at once both inviting and malevolent.

Longing for the smell of the ocean, I fumble around for the window control of this sporty new car. I crack open my window about four inches and there is an explosion of inrushing tropical air. At first it's a deafening roar of noise from highway and night, but I had to break this feeling of detachment from the gritty reality of Florida. I needed to remember what is out there that draws us back.

Warm air fills the car. It is alive with the smell of salt and hibiscus. It is humid, and mixed faintly with concrete dust from the latest highway-widening project. The smell of something rotting in the drainage culvert beyond the shoulder, which mixes with the perfume of blossoms and the ever-present car and diesel exhaust. The air complex and alive, insinuates itself into the interior of the car and makes me feel anxious.

Kevin glances at me, annoyed that I destroyed the perfectly controlled environment we have spent the past forty minutes creating with cool air, rock and roll, and the sulfur glow from the instrument panel.

"That's your Florida air out there," I shout to him over the road noise. He looks at me a moment, leans across the console, and yells into my ear.

"You're a turkey. Now close the window!" In the darkness I did not see his right hand leave the steering wheel. I should have been prepared but I never am. His hands are strong and with a thumb and forefinger he reaches up and grabs the tip of my nose, squeezing it until I squeal in pain.

"Oooow," I plead pathetically. I was always such a baby, a sensitive child. Some nights when it was time for us to leave the carpentry shop, I would turn off all the lights and wait for Kevin in the darkness, hiding in a corner. I was supposed to wait for him to find me and then startle him with a sudden "Boo!" I could never pull it off. I scared myself so much waiting to surprise him that I went into a spasm of hysterical anxiety and would burst out of my corner goggle-eyed and shaking as if I had just been touched by a ghost. He would look at me, calmly shaking his head with amusement.

"You scared yourself, didn't you? Right? You're a turkey, aren't you? Don't be ashamed." I would stammer some feeble denial, then get flustered and shake my head first up and down, yes, then side to side, no. "Do you want me to leave you here, in the dark?" he would ask me. Then I would run out of the place screaming, "No. Don't leave me here alone."

Distracted by the highway, Kevin grabs the wheel again and accelerates into the left lane. We ease alongside a pickup truck, crawling along at sixty. I see all kinds of lumber and plywood sticking out of the truck's bed, with a heavy tool box behind the cab. I expect some local redneck types heading back to their trailer park after a sweaty day of building sun decks or tract houses.

My window is still open as we glide past the rusted Ford. To my right I see the forearm and elbow of what is undoubtedly a young man, Caucasian and slim. Through the truck's back window I see the heads of two twenty-year-olds, both with their caps turned backward in that familiar gesture of cockiness. A tangle of skinny arms and elbows drapes along the seat back and out the windows. I can see the forearm and hand of the truck's driver, now only a yard to my right. It is tan and scratched, and the fingers are long, though relaxed while gripping the truck's roof. The two boys seem to be laughing about something with each other.

We are passing them now, and suddenly I'm getting tense, already expecting some kind of predictable nastiness that young punks are so skilled at. Like a "fuck-you" finger held out with no provocation, as if in their predatory instincts they know why I am looking at them.

The two boys, hardly in their twenties, remain for this instant level with me. Kevin watches the road as we pass them. This whole psychodrama on I-95 is all in my hands. We are slipping ahead, and I consider just ignoring them. But I sense their presence, their wiry veins, callused hands, and muddy work boots, even the cans of Coors among the Burger King wrappers on the truck's dirty floor.

*That's stupid,* I think. *I'm not so vulnerable.* Not another frightened Northerner speeding home in his rental car. So I lower the window completely and look right across into the driver's face, thinking, why am I so scared?

His eyes are small, a soft gray, and not at all mean. His nose is red but surprisingly fine. A little gold ring glitters in the lobe of the boy's left ear. And with absolutely no hesitation—as I wait cringing—the kid winks at me, and then gives me this big smile, showing the teeth not of a hillbilly, but probably a college student, working a summer job, having fun getting dirty. And in that wink, with the truck already behind us, I am no longer afraid.

I bring up the window and quiet returns to our spaceship in the humid night. I look again at Kevin's profile as he watches the road ahead, and I think how beautiful he is now at thirty-four. His body is still angular, the outlines of his chin and nose are square and clean. No flab has settled under his jaw or around his eyes. He has filled out from the boy who moved into my life eleven years before. I have watched him become a man. I have seen him grow thicker and more confident.

We cross into Palm Beach County and pass the Hillsboro exit. In five minutes we will get off at Glades Road in Boca Raton. In another twelve minutes we will be back at my mother's apartment, unless we stop to eat at Bennigan's or Friday's. I'll let Kevin make the decision.

I look over at him once again. He is silhouetted by a headlight glare from the left and all his features are blanked out for an instant. Suddenly I know, with a wisdom that I never asked to be given, that I shall outlive him.

I try to pretend I did not have this thought. His face looks normal again as the headlight is passed. It doesn't work. I know I've just been given a vision—wanted or not. *That's how it happens,* I think, nodding my head. Kevin slips into the right lane as the sign for Glades Road zips by in the corner of my eye and, of course, already I am wondering, *When?*

# 15

## NOTHING LEFT TO FEAR

*Mamaroneck, January 1990*

The name of the boat was *Exodus*. "You'll love this one," the yacht broker promised me on the phone. "The icebox is so deep I can't reach the bottom." I attached no particular symbolism to the name, just the usual token to the owner's longing for escape from daily cares, temporal or otherwise. It was December, but the weather was still mild so we agreed to meet him at the yard next weekend to have a look. Of course Kevin would come along. This was not a joint purchase, but it was a joint decision.

Norm liked us. He knew from the way I talked and looked over prospective boats that I knew what I wanted and would be insulted by sales talk and bullshit. Still, he admitted to us that he was very close to losing his job with the McMichael yacht agency, and was eager to close a sale with me. He was determined to find me a boat. I was a hot prospect. Since October I had been thinking about a boat. We needed to be sailing again. We were starting to feel trapped in Brooklyn.

Kevin, too, was pushing for a boat. Sometimes he said he wanted to get out of Brooklyn completely, that he wanted to live in Florida. He had always hated Brooklyn, he said in one of his low moods. It reminded him of his parents—his original parents—and brought up feelings of defeat and hopelessness. He was often depressed, moody, and impatient. "I don't want to die in Brooklyn," he would shout at me when I argued that it was crazy for us to leave New York and the house and business that we had here. We had worked for two years fixing up this house. It had been fun; now the house was a refuge for us and we were proud of how lovely and comfortable it was. But we felt land bound and isolated, especially on the weekends. Our old friends back in Manhattan rarely ventured into Brooklyn.

In September we had gone up to the fall sailboat show in Stamford, Connecticut, just for a change, just for a look around, just for a chance to keep up with the market. A pleasant day's outing. Kevin, Howard, and I. Howard was now a marketing vice president, and the pharmaceutical company had sent him to its head office in the Midwest to plan entire sales campaigns. He was successful, but missed the nightlife in New York and sailing with us. We joked about that wild sail through the fog in Vineyard Sound that we had together in *Blue Shorts*. "You guys belong on a boat again," Howard said to us as we walked among the docks of beautiful yachts for sale.

This was 1989, and although the stock market had crashed in October 1987, people were still buying boats. At the shows brokers looked edgy, sales were off, and customers were cautious. The industry was on the cusp of a downturn. Everyone knew it, but tried to be optimistic.

Some nights I would leave the shop and drive out to the desolate Red Hook waterfront. I needed a way to clear my mind from a day of aggravations, disappointments, and costly mistakes. Out there, beyond the crumbling piers and warehouses, was Upper New York Bay. The water reassured me that somehow I would survive. Better than that, I would sail again, out there in my own harbor. I smiled, standing amid all that rubble, and could feel a big heavy boat under me, the touch of her helm, the magical power of sails pulling her through the seas. So one fall weekend Kevin and I met with a broker in Mamaroneck and told him our needs and price range.

I wanted something substantial for serious cruising, not just weekend trips, and with room enough for four adults to sleep and eat comfortably for as long as two weeks. I wanted a galley where we could really prepare meals, and mostly I required a forward cabin, where Kevin and I could stretch out without fighting over foot room all night long.

All that November our broker would drive us around to inspect boats in the thirty-foot range. Norm would wait in polite silence as the two of us went forward to the v-berth and tossed out all the sailbags and gear stored up there and then lay down as if we were sleeping together, with our coats and shoes still on. We were serious customers, so he kept trying.

*Exodus* was roomy. I saw that immediately from a walk around her hull. At the bow she was more blunt than pointy. She would not knife through the seas like a China tea clipper, nor send solid green water crashing onto her decks. Rather the broad bows gave her enough buoyancy to let her ride up steep waves. The broker called her shape "sea kindly." This boat was perfect for sloppy weather. In rough going, with waves spaced closed together, her decks would stay dry. *It did seem to make sense,* I thought, only slightly suspicious of his motives. He seemed to know boats, and he said he had grown up in a wooden sailboat in Florida back in the 1960s. A real boat brat.

Norm was right about the icebox. Through a hatch on the countertop was an insulated compartment that was deeper than my arm could reach. It was roomy enough for our needs.

With Kevin I had become accustomed to eating well ashore and afloat. He turned up his nose at pedestrian canned stuff for convenience while sailing. No, he felt eating on board should be even more splendid than at home, like a trip on the Orient Express. Cooking was his main creative outlet. He would put as much time into planning menus for a long weekend on the boat as I did in coordinating our departures with the tides. He was no longer the skinny aesthete I had met twelve years before. I myself had gained twenty pounds by then from all the rich sauces and butter-laden deserts. And of course, I loved it.

The closer we inspected the interior the more I realized that this was a good boat, a one-owner yacht that had been well taken care of during the previous ten years. The owner had bought her new and now was using the boat as part of a trade-in deal to move up to a forty-one-footer. His new boat would cost close to $140,000. Norm explained in confidence that this gentleman had grown wealthy in the fish business. He owned a fish company, whose little red trucks delivered lox and whitefish and sablefish to every corner of the city. Kevin dubbed him the lox king.

The only thing holding up the deal for the lox king was to find a buyer for *Exodus*. That put me, the potential purchaser here, in a good bargaining position. "You're our white knight," Norm said to me as I climbed down the ladder to examine the hull and underwater parts. I gave the huge black rudder a shake to test the mounting bearings. She felt solid. "I think this is the perfect boat for you guys," the broker suggested, trying to sound like the three of us could really be candid with each other this time. After a close walk around the hull, he asked if I wanted to inspect the sails, inside the warmth of the carpeted office nearby. Not yet, I told him. I liked the boat, that was apparent, but I was still cautious. He did not push, but he knew we would come back.

What he could not know was another quandary I faced. This boat was not for me alone; it was for both Kevin and me. I knew I was making a decision about a future for the two of us that was very uncertain.

The whole year had been overshadowed with worries about Kevin's health. He had been getting thinner throughout the previous year, and seemed to always be sick with something or other: A cold, a sore throat, sinus infection, ear problems, sometimes diarrhea. We loved the little house we had moved into together. We felt so fortunate to have in our deep backyard a cherry tree, an apple tree, and a grand old horse chestnut tree. We were liked by our neighbors. The house was both cozy and dignified, with much of its original circa 1905 woodworking details still intact.

It felt like a charmed existence, but it was not. All around us there was some awful disease that was making people we knew very sick. All during the early 1980s young men were dying mysteriously and quickly. We had been to at least two or three memorial services already. It had to be sexually transmitted, but unlike syphilis or gonorrhea, this had no cure. No one even knew what the incubation period might be, or if they might have "it" already. Everything from a cold to a skin rash seemed to be a possible symptom.

We tried to distance ourselves from the epicenter of the problem. Neither of us was going out to late-night sex clubs anymore. We stopped buying the *New York Native*. We no longer wanted to read the strident headlines about the latest death count in the gay community.

The previous winter had not been a happy one. Kevin was sick most of the time around Christmas. Nothing very specific, nothing worth calling a doctor about, but he had no energy or interest in parties or presents. We stayed home most of the time and watched videos. I got into the habit of picking up at least two each evening on my way home. By this time Kevin was not coming in to work very much. He seemed to need so much sleep, yet his sleep was not peaceful; he was restless and sweaty and constantly coughing up gooey mucus. Sometimes after breakfast he would have a coughing fit, and finally spit into a tissue. "It's breaking up," he would reassure me. Then he'd examine the mucus for color and consistency.

Two years earlier we had seen a doctor on West Fifty-Seventh Street. Kevin had a sinus infection and I had a peculiar rash. We both left with prescriptions for antibiotics. In the waiting room we asked the secretary if he thought we should be tested for this awful new disease. He shot a wary glance toward his boss's closed door and leaned closer to us.

"If I held the date of your death in my hand," he said, with his small manicured fist clenched in front of us, "would you want me to show it to you?" We said nothing as he shifted his gaze between us. He was trying to be helpful, to save us from terrible and hopeless news.

In time each new problem seemed to pass. Still I worried. We dared not talk about our fears. We dared not name the thing that was becoming a constant unwanted visitor our little house on this quiet street. By January 1989 Kevin looked so thin, his pants sagged down, and his arms, I was certain, were just not as robust as they used to be. What was all this about? I agonized each night and each morning. Did Kevin have AIDS?

By now nearly half the people we knew either had this disease or lived with someone who did. Had we moved to Brooklyn hoping to escape the plague? It hurt me to see the strain on Kevin's face. I felt this need to protect him from terrible events, but I could not protect him from fears that no longer seemed so improbable. We had chosen to live in ignorance. What good was it to know? There was no cure, only a terrible death. Maybe living out in Brooklyn gave us this illusion of being out of the mainstream of city life, with all its charms and dangers. What folly.

By May 1989 Kevin was in the hospital. It began when his head was pounding from a rampant sinus blockage. In the months before he finally checked into Lenox Hill Hospital I came to learn a lot about those mysterious chambers inside the human skull. No one seemed to have a good explanation for all those hollow cavities above the mouth and behind the eyes and forehead. But they did collect snot and get infected. They gave our voice resonance, and maybe they kept the skull buoyant. When the immune system was not working, they became unreachable end points for dark and festering infections.

As his health worsened he would see new doctors, and by the time he went into Lenox Hill he had collected a retinue of specialists: An ear-nose-throat doctor with a morose sense of humor, a pulmonary expert with an operatic-sounding Italian name, and a self-confident infectious disease man who seemed to relish a good fight with any new pathogen.

I would pick Kevin up after each doctor visit. He would settle himself into the car and then pass me his latest doctor's business card. "A top man," he would say sarcastically. He wanted to believe that their prestige alone could ensure his recovery from each new infection.

The efforts of all these top men were orchestrated by Kevin's principal doctor, who held the rank of Chief of Medicine at Lenox Hill. Dr. Gerald Bahr liked Kevin. They would spend most of the time during office visits telling jokes, while I waited nervously in the waiting room, hearing odd bursts of laughter behind the doctor's closed door.

I continued all our jobs without Kevin. He was in good spirits even though after several weeks they still had no specific diagnosis for what was wrong with him and why he was not getting better. They pumped him with intravenous antibiotics. I came up every day, even brought up the payroll books and general ledger for him to update and make out the paychecks. I hated to admit that he was not around to work along with me.

After two weeks they moved him into an isolation room. They were running tests, was all I heard. The red barrel for infectious waste stood conspicuously outside his door, an ominous reminder that something was very wrong with the young man inside.

Finally one evening I cornered his doctor, the affable Gerry Bahr, around whom aides, nurses, residents, and technicians seemed to revolve like the planets in Galileo's model of the heavens. It was sometime after 8:00 p.m. and Dr. Bahr was making evening rounds of his own patients. His day had begun on this same floor before 8:00 that morning. By midday he had office hours. This went on seven days a week, and he never looked tired. Adversity seemed to nourish this man, I thought to myself.

"I'm really getting worried about him," I said to the doctor in the corridor outside Kevin's room. He looked troubled himself, as if he needed to share his anxieties with someone.

"You have good reason to be worried," he answered. I asked if we could talk, and he suggested I see him the next day in his office on Park Avenue, a few blocks from the hospital. When I got home I called Kevin's family in New Jersey, and his mother Sue said of course she would be there with me the next afternoon.

Bahr wanted to break the news to us in the most personal manner, as if to show that his taking this time to meet Kevin's mother and lover was a sign of the importance he placed on the case. Of course we all knew he had AIDS. Bahr was a good doctor, and we felt very lucky that Kevin had the benefit of such a team of specialists now. We thanked him and stepped out into the glaring June sunlight. We held hands but did not talk as we walked back to my car.

We could not talk, not there on the sidewalk, but we knew we were linked through our bond to Kevin. Each of us had taken turns shepherding him through life, like marathon runners passing a torch and carefully sheltering the flame. I felt I had moved into the place she had once occupied in his life.

Over the years I had ferreted out of Kevin how he had come to live with Sue and Jules in Brooklyn. He liked to play a game of confusing everyone whenever he referred to his "parents." Sometimes it meant Marqueritte and Kurt, his birth parents. Other times he meant Sue and Jules, who had adopted him in his teens. Maybe the ambiguity was on purpose, as if he had never fully given up on the original set, even after their deaths.

Sue and Jules were neighbors to Kevin in Fort Greene, Brooklyn, where he was living, sometimes, with his father. The parents had separated. Kurt was often away working on ships, or else there was a woman in the apartment and Kevin had to wait around on the street.

So an insistent-looking boy with blue eyes and a sweet little mouth came to visit Sue, hoping to play with her adolescent daughter Leslie. She did feel sorry for him and knew the family situation was terrible. Sue was a social worker and had helped Kevin's father at times. But with Kevin, she held back at first. She was still reluctant to expose both herself and especially Jules to this child who was so full of needs. Their life felt comfortable and settled. They had put behind them the loss, just a few years earlier, of an infant daughter. Stephanie's death had been an ordeal for Sue that remained as a wound inside her, and it had crushed Jules in ways he still could not talk about. And they did not try.

Kevin was shuttled between his father's apartment down the block from Sue, on Washington Park, and Hicks Street, in the Heights, where his alcoholic mother lived. This was no life for a little kid, no matter how precocious he acted. So grudgingly she let him in, most of the time, knowing she was taking a chance that she felt she could not afford again, a chance to grow close to another youngster, give of herself, and risk the unknown consequences of loving again. She tried not to at first, for Jules's sake, she told herself. But as the months passed she knew all too well that Kevin needed a family.

I opened the car door for Sue and then got in on the driver's side. We sat next to each other saying nothing. Did we always know that this moment would happen, that we were to be bound to each other like this? For a long time we just held each other. There was nothing else to do.

"He's my whole life . . ." was all I could stammer.

"Yes, I know. I know what this is doing to you," she answered. "I know what he means to you." Then she added cryptically, "You take a chance . . . you just have to try . . . and to love."

As she said this I realized that I had not made the emotional wager that she had with her life. This was so unfair to her. She has given, and given, this tiny woman, hardly five feet tall. How do you measure someone's feelings? I felt she was trying to sum up her whole life, to come through this tragedy and not feel embittered, cheated, broken. In the equation of things I felt she had now suffered far worse than I. Probably she thought the same for me. For that moment, in the car, we were both naked and defenseless.

Kevin was barely sixteen when he moved in with them, and in a couple of years they became his legal parents. He admired Jules like a father. For a while he was safe. And now after growing accustomed to watching him become a man Sue learned that Kevin had AIDS and would probably die soon. Did she really need to do this to herself?

Yes, her tears told me, as I drove cautiously through traffic to see Kevin. We knew that he must also have learned from his doctor the news of the diagnosis. Yes. Whatever happened, she had chosen to be his mother.

When I saw Kevin at the hospital he seemed smaller already, needing me, annoyed at why I had been so late. Yes, Dr. Bahr had told him earlier, and he said he had been crying a lot. Then he looked up from his bed and with a little smirk admitted that he had cried so hard all afternoon that his sinuses finally opened up. I could hear it in his voice, too, and he did not look like he was about to die. For the first time in months I slept peacefully that night. There was nothing left to be afraid of. I could stop worrying.

He came home a month later and immediately got to work on the house again. He wanted to add a back porch. He worked with the determination of someone who has only one chance to accomplish something. We slept together once again, and I could reach my arm over him and feel his warmth against me. I would whisper in his ear, just his name, at night and hold him. Soon he gained his weight back. Occasionally we would have sex, but he seemed detached. I did not care that much. I felt so thankful to have him back.

Two weeks after Kevin came home I was tested and to no one's surprise learned that I was harboring the same virus in my own blood. The lab report came back with a T4 helper count of 220 cells per cc of blood. Normal is at least 800. We each saw different doctors. Dr. Bahr preferred to deal with only one of us. Kevin was not happy about my HIV status, but a camplike atmosphere pervaded the house, with each of us counting out our daily dosages of AZT and Bactrim, and whatever else, each morning. Sometimes we had pill fights, or would torment the cats with them, and for a while we toyed with the idea of naming our next boat AZT. The three letters would be shaped like the familiar blue and white capsules from Burroughs-Welcome. But would they shun us at the yacht club?

Despite the steady ninety-degree heat of August, we constructed the new back porch. We did the job together, working shirtless and taking breaks for iced tea. He wore his old panama hat, and ignored all the familiar warnings to avoid the sun as immuno-supressive. He wanted to be tan again. Later that year he built a new bed for us. Things were happening again around the house.

By January 1990 the deal on the boat went through. A few months later the broker lost his job anyway, another casualty of the decline in the boating industry. As soon as the weather was warm enough we began going up to the yard in Mamaroneck to work on the new boat. As usual I had my interminable lists of changes. The name, of course, would be one of them.

One sunny day in March, Kevin scraped *Exodus* off the transom and we renamed our boat *Bevel*. The name had grown out of the exasperating experience that past winter with a job that called for dozens of different-sized doors all with beveled edges.

That entire winter we were overwhelmed with two jobs from a contractor in downtown Manhattan. They hired us to supply all the doors to a loft job in lower Manhattan. The artist client was successful enough to buy and renovate an entire building in TriBeCa. The company also hired us to provide all the doors for a new gallery on Prince Street, in Soho. Every door was different, and I cannot remember how many nights we stayed late at the shop with complex charts, or "door schedules" as they are called, making changes and corrections. We were way over our heads, and the contractor made the situation worse by sending us another change order each morning along with a reiteration of the penalties we were in for if we did not meet the contract deadlines.

The relationship become totally adversarial, and both Kevin and I were in a constant state of tension over all the fucking doors. We made mistakes, and the construction company made mistakes, and each time I had to dash over to my subcontractor who was making the doors. Gerry Schlemowitz's shop was close to the fetid Gowanus Canal in Brooklyn. I would burst into the shop screaming, "Stop everything!" Mercifully, Gerry was always behind schedule, and I would usually find him sitting around yakking on the phone.

The two jobs moved along, and doors were slowly getting installed at both sites. Then one day I reread the plans for the Soho art gallery and my knees began to fail. I had specified the two eight-foot-high entrance doors, already made up in custom matched anigre veneer, with their edges beveled in the wrong direction. I had misread which way they were to swing. This time Gerry threw a fit and kicked me out of his shop for good. The doors could be salvaged but he would only deal directly with the contractor after that.

The contractor agreed to release me from both job obligations provided that I deliver all the expensive bronze lock sets. They handed me a check to cover only my net costs and I gave them several heavy boxes with the 4,000 dollars worth of hardware. The next day they stopped the check. We had been tricked.

For weeks I seethed with anger and resentment. I longed for revenge, to hurt them, damage them, somehow. I plotted new schemes each time I drove past their second floor picture windows.

When I realized that the whole experience was poisoning my heart, and that those lowlifes were not worth it, I walked away and began making lists of things to improve on our new sailboat, our *Exodus.*

The job had been a disaster, yet what pulled us through that winter was the anticipation of getting the new boat—and the hope for our future together that it implied. All that spring we escaped to Mamaroneck whenever the sun was out and together we worked to get the boat ready to launch.

I told people that "bevel" was a common woodworking term that sounded slightly feminine and was easy to hear on a ship-to-shore radio. But I could not explain to them that for Kevin and myself the name had really become a code word for faith. The incorrect bevel on the doors was just the culminating disaster in a series of problems that challenged both of us to find something to look forward to each day. The boat was not simply a toy or a place of escape, but a tangible metaphor for what we meant to each other, and the certainty that no one could ever take that from us.

# 16

## THE TOWER

*Little Calf Island, June 1992*

How did he get so fat? I wondered again as I looked back at Jeffrey standing at the wheel. What happened to that scrawny collection of elbows and knees who taught me how to ride a bike back in Brooklyn?

"Are you ready up there?" Jeff called to me from the helm.

"Yeah, let's head out that way," I yelled back, pointing to open water and away from the dense crowd of anchored boats close to City Island. "Try backing the main," I suggested.

Jeffrey stepped up on the cockpit seat and heaved his weight against the boom, pushing it into the breeze and just for a moment keeping it out on the wrong side. "So, are we off yet?" he asked again.

Finally, as the bow swung over I tossed the mooring lines and pickup buoy overboard and shouted, "You're off!" With his foot Jeff nudged the wheel over a few spokes and the boat gathered headway. Then I heard a big thud resounding against the cockpit floor. That was Jeffrey, all 205 pounds, jumping behind the wheel. I went back to help him with the mainsail.

*My God,* I thought as I slipped past the port side shrouds, *it has been thirty years now, that long ago since he taught me how to ride a bike.* Our lives now were separate, and involved with our own commitments. But out here on the Sound we could be together and find the sense of adventure and goofiness that was such a part of our adolescence.

Jeff tried to pull in all the mainsheet but was getting the sleeve of his bulky jacket tangled in the ropes. "Can you straighten out this mess while I steer?" He asked me, and moved aside.

"Yeah, yeah. Look out. Just head for Rodman's Neck," I said, pointing west.

"Thanks, cap'n, except we're going to have to tack pretty soon. Who's that right in front of us?" Jeffrey pointed to a buxom old ketch, my neighbor out here.

"Oh, that's *Carmella*. She never goes anywhere. The owner uses it just to get away from his family. She only leaves the mooring to get more fuel." Black streaks from acid rain ran down her topsides.

"Anyone on board now?"

I ducked around Jeffrey for a better look. "No engine exhaust coming out of her stern. She looks all closed up. Let's get a little more speed on."

"Ramming speed!" Jeffrey yelled out as *Carmella's* unsuspecting flanks drew closer. I would not do this if her owner were on board. I also knew how Jeff liked to cut things close. It was not that long ago when we sailed small boats, fourteen and nineteen footers, through this same mooring field. We would tack among anchored yachts as if they were obstacles on a miniature golf course. It had been good practice for maneuvering this thirty-foot cruising boat.

"Uh . . . Jeffrey?"

"I know, I know," he answered as we plowed steadily closer to *Carmella*. The words "collision" and "responsibility" kept seeping into my mind along with a courtroom scenario: I am sitting upright in the witness seat, nervous and fidgety, like Humphrey Bogart in *The Caine Mutiny*. Yes, I was the skipper, I answer to the lawyer's question. I was responsible even if not actually at the helm. She was *my* vessel and under *my* command, nonetheless. Above me the admiralty judge, in black robe and powdered wig, scowls at me. Then he leans over and intones, "It was all your fault."

"Helm's alee," Jeffrey bellowed and put the wheel over. *Bevel* swung away from the ketch, hardly four yards away. The mainsail slammed across over our heads. We would have to make several short tacks like this to get free of the moored sailboats.

At the same moment we both realized that the dinghy we were towing behind us, *Ivan Kolodko,* still had not followed us around the turn. Instead, the intrepid little boat seemed to have an impudent will of its own and continued poking along toward the ketch. When the bow painter came up short, the dinghy jerked to a stop, paused a second, and then obediently followed its mother ship. Still, the edge of our rowboat scraped along *Carmella's* waterline and we could hear the clear thump of contact.

"I'll pull *Ivan* up closer," I said, reaching behind Jeff for the stern cleat where the painter was attached. He knew he had cut too close. All these maneuvers were a routine part of getting out of Eastchester Bay. Every trip began and ended this way.

"Good idea," he said flatly.

I used to wonder if he liked cutting so close for sport, or if he was just accident prone and intemperate. In high school, when we met, he had the exasperating ability to learn and retain information very quickly. At the piano he could sight read well enough to pull off a dazzling performance of a Bach Invention, playing fast enough to cover all his mistakes. I would plod along for weeks learning the same piece, phrase by phrase.

From the beginning I think we were drawn to each other as similar misfits in the unforgiving milieu of high school. Over the years I had always gravitated to tall, skinny boys. Back then Jeffrey was the definition of skinny.

We passed *Carmella,* but had to tack over again in front of her to avoid more anchored bats. Jeffrey did it by himself this time, allowing more room for the dinghy. When we were finally out in clear water he asked, "Ready for the genoa, cap'n?"

I cast off the furling line and Jeffrey pulled out a few yards on the jib sheet. When the wind caught the loosened sail, the whole thing completely unwound itself with a loud whoosh. Jeffrey winched in the rest of the jib sheet, and all the while he kept his hip pressed against the steering wheel to hold our course. Pretty cute, I thought to myself, and I wondered if despite the immense gut hanging over his belt, he still felt like that gangly seventeen-year-old perched on top of his bicycle.

It began one afternoon after school. I do not remember what we first talked about. Classical music, probably. We both played the piano. Maybe he was impressed to find someone else who was learning Bach. He knew some of the two-part Inventions, and I was already learning the more difficult three-part Inventions. Apart from music, we both felt like dorks, and were sexually naive at sixteen. We hung around with neither the jocks, the bullies, nor the smart science boys. Yet, we seemed to have so much to talk about, so much in common.

Except when he learned that I did not know how to ride a bike. He lent me his indestructible Schwinn one-speed. I took the heavy bike home and tried a few wobbly runs in my basement, where I felt safe leaning against the walls next to the boiler room. Then one day after school we found a quiet tree-lined street to practice. He did not hold me up like a little kid, but I did need him there for encouragement. This was the first time anyone had patiently taught me a sport. The sycamore trees on Schenectady Avenue were spaced fifty feet apart, so my progress was easy to measure by how many trees I could pass before I fell over. I never actually fell over. When I lost my balance, or my nerve, I would totter along just far enough until I reached the next tree and would lunge for it. Like the nimble squirrel that I was then, I would clamp onto the tree while the Schwinn fell from under me. It proved a useful skill in later years.

That first year with Jeffrey had been breathtaking. I was transformed from a shy, sulky, almost misanthropic boy into a jittery teenager with boundless energy and confidence. All because of the bike. A gutsy and competitive side of me emerged. I had spent my early adolescence carefully avoiding confrontations with other boys. I dreaded passing a ball field, lest a fly ball land at my feet and an impatient knot of snotty Flatbush kids start yelling, "Hey, jerk-off, let's see da bawl, awready!" Now, at last, I too could now actually do something athletic.

With the pavement rushing under my wheels, and the winds of Brooklyn in my face, I could revel in the exuberance of boyhood. That year I became first a bicycle fanatic and eventually an aficionado.

Within a year we both had expensive ten-speed bikes. Jeffrey's twenty-five-inch Raleigh towered menacingly over my gleaming gold Atala, a pure racing machine. With their sinister drop handlebars and narrow leather saddles, they must have been vehicles for our nascent and unfocused sexual energies. We laughed disdainfully at the clunky bikes boys in the neighborhood still rode. White boys were already thinking about cars; only the black kids, hanging out on street corners, knew anything about fancy racing bikes. How many times had I shot through the "bad neighborhoods" at top speed, feeling their envy as they called out, "Hey man, gimme that bike!" My speed was my defense and I knew no one could touch me as I streaked past.

In the evening after school the two of us would often sit together on Jeff's unmade bed and compare our two bikes. His was made in Coventry, England, and mine came from Turino, Italy. All the while we would listen to music, usually Bach, usually Glenn Gould playing the Goldberg Variations. Other times he would put on Wanda Landowska at the harpsichord, playing Bach of course. To us it made perfect sense, the music and the machines. Both were the products of long aesthetic traditions from Europe, both built with care and excruciating attention to detail, both works of consummate loveliness. You can still feel such platonic passions when you are seventeen.

Like country boys with their first ponies, we went everywhere on our bikes. We rode into Manhattan, "the city," as our parents forebodingly called it. We might spin around Wall Street on a summer night when the streets were empty. Uptown, we would circumnavigate the fountain at Lincoln Center a few times before heading down to Eighth Street in the Village. There was no stopping us. The bikes were our escape from Brooklyn. We ate ravenously, never got fat, and never gave any thought to danger or accidents. Instead of helmets we wore cute little bike hats that Italian racers wore, with the brim bent up showing the name CINELLI or BIANCHI or ATALA. Anything Italian.

We both took some falls, but Jeffrey was the one who really got hurt. He was taller, with a higher center of gravity, and when he fell all those spindly arms and legs were more likely to get bruised. Jeffrey had his worst crash one day on Ocean Parkway, and from the way he landed I knew he would need help. I guess we found out that day what we meant to each other.

Jeffrey was ahead of me, going very fast on the bike path. We never went anywhere slowly. He tried to maneuver around a car blocking an intersection, attempting an "S" turn at an impossible speed. His bike skidded sideways. The big Raleigh with its ungainly frame spun out from beneath him and catapulted him helplessly onto the concrete sidewalk.

I dropped my own bike and ran over to him. He was dazed and trying to stand up and find his bike. He did not realize that his elbow had been ripped open. I saw from the bloody sleeve that it was much worse than a scrape. The knuckle of his humerus bone glistened a sickening white through all the torn skin. It was the first time I had ever seen a human bone, and for an instant I was afraid I might faint.

We had to find a doctor for him right away. He had not even noticed all the ripped-open skin at his knee, visible through the torn leg of his jeans. When he finally looked down at his arm he just groaned and turned pale.

I grabbed my own bike, took his in the other hand, and hustled Jeffrey across the six lanes of Ocean Parkway. We found a private doctor's office in the lobby of a nearby apartment house that looked like a Tudor castle. The doctor's receptionist gave us a hard time at first. We had no idea what a gastroenterologist did, but the sign outside said MD, and that was what we needed. The doctor came out of his office and saw two frightened boys, one of them a bloody mess. While I watched our bikes out in the hallway the doctor put a temporary dressing on Jeff's arm and leg. Back outside we pooled our money to pay for a taxicab back to his building. My biggest fear was that his parents would blame it all on me, the bad influence on Jeffrey. But as far as he was concerned, I had been there when he needed help.

*Bevel* quickly accelerated with both sails up now. We were making 5.5 knots, sailing parallel with the shoreline of City Island. Jeffrey lit a cigarette, using the flaps of his jacket to make a little tent. He smoked only when he sailed. He looked good that way. Overweight as he was, I could see women being attracted to him, with his odd mixture of adult bulk and that silly mop of hair, still black with a little gray at the temples.

Jeffrey's parents did not particularly like me. I think they tolerated this friendship because I could play Bach, Mozart, and even some Bartok. It was the Bartok, the discordant *Mikrokosmos,* that most impressed them. In his house it was assumed that a youngster would appreciate and study classical music on both piano and violin. At fifteen, my parents worried about the time I spent practicing so intently, rather than playing stickball outside with other boys.

Jeff needed me to help him escape the silent walls of repression and hysteria that his watchful parents lived behind. His mother fussed over him as if he were a little kid, making sure he finished his food and sat up properly in his chair, the kind of nonsense no teenager would tolerate. Nor was he especially encouraged to be independent. My own mother knew early on that her baby would eventually grow up, break her heart, and run away. To Jeff, I was the worldly one: I had access to cars and tools, was already accustomed to being out late on my own, and had even wandered the streets of Greenwich Village. Even then, at 16 or 17, the West Village had a special appeal to me. Although I was clueless about what all those slim young men in white Levi's did with each other, I knew they were different in some important way. I was afraid of them and also wanted to be around them. They noticed me walking alone and would smile. Many years passed before I realized that this was called cruising.

While I saw myself as a borderline sissy, to Jeffrey's mother I was a mischievous influence who might lure him into danger and adventures beyond our quiet, Sabbath-observing neighborhood. Exactly what Jeffrey hoped for.

"So, where to, cap'n?" Jeff asked, standing at the helm. The boat heeled over, and Jeff braced one leg against the cockpit seat. He watched his cigarette smoke drift backward as the wind increased.

We were making 6.4 knots. The boat's bottom was still clean. The June air was mild and filled with promise and optimism, and the sun felt good.

"Ever visit Calf Island?" I asked.

"Maybe. Where is it?"

"Just before Greenwich, inside Captain Island. You've passed it plenty of times."

"What's there to see?" Jeffrey asked.

"The Tower," I answered in an ominous voice.

"Sounds too scary. Do we have time? It's almost noon." Jeff squinted up at the sun, already past its zenith.

"Easy sail with this wind, maybe two hours each way. We can eat lunch as we sail," I said, trying to be encouraging.

He steered toward a fuzzy spot on the Connecticut shore in the distance, well past Larchmont. The boat felt nicely balanced, zipping along and heeled over a comfortable twelve degrees. She was in a groove, and for a while we felt no need to talk. Jeffrey steered with just two fingers on the helm.

"So what are the kids up to today? I thought they wanted to come along?" I asked as I poured him a cup of coffee from a thermos.

"Sara's class is going on a nature trip someplace and Ann has a violin lesson. She's really getting good, considering she's ten and a half. She's even working on some Scarlatti."

I climbed onto the cabin top, pressed my head against the mast, and sighted straight up the sail track to see if there was much sag in the rigging. Only the top third seemed to bend away to leeward. I fussed with the leech line on the trailing edge of the jib, tightening it in to stop it from fluttering.

We were coming abeam of Execution Light on our portside, and on starboard was the broad opening to Hempstead Harbor.

"What about Susan? What's she up to? I thought she wanted to sail today. That's what she said to me on the phone yesterday."

Jeffrey was peering under the mainsail. "She said she wanted to last night but this morning she had a lot of pain. It's in her legs this time, the MS again. We might see her specialist again on Thursday."

"Can he do anything for her?" I asked.

"You know what they do: They put her up on the lift and poke around under the chassis looking for something dripping. Then they send a bill."

That was his way of saying no. I thought of Jeffrey's wife and how awful she had looked six years earlier, all thin and craggy, so wobbly on her feet she needed two canes just to stand upright. Her speech was almost unintelligible back then, another one of the capricious effects of multiple sclerosis.

"I thought she had been doing well in the last couple of years. Her speech is practically normal again."

"Right. They're always trying new drugs. Remember the hyperbaric chamber experiment? Basically she's been in remission, and the Prednisone helped her put weight back on, finally."

"She does look good lately," I said, and meant it. "So she doesn't mind your being out sailing today?"

"No. She's glad you asked me. She doesn't want me around feeling sorry for her; it makes her even more pissed off. Anyway, she's got a friend she talks to on the Internet. This woman also has MS."

"Good, I won't feel guilty about how nice it turned out today," I told Jeffrey and leaned back to study the clouds.

Jeff altered our course away from a tugboat pushing an oil barge that was heading toward us from the opposite direction. The barge was empty, riding conspicuously high up in the water, what tug skippers laconically call "an oil can riding light." He could be reckless at times, but neither of us wanted to be the kind of asshole who confused commercial skippers with erratic or indecisive movements. We knew the tugs and ships had no room to maneuver in this part of the Sound, and it was good seamanship to avoid close calls early on. He steered a little more to port.

Maybe he still remembered that night long ago when we were sailing the Rhodes 19, and had as close a call as we would ever like. The night was dark, even though it was summer and warm. We were crossing the Sound on a broad reach, with no particular destination, just sailing around really fast. At least it always felt a lot faster at night. The boat was low to the water so that you could drop a hand over and feel the water rushing past. In the blackness to our left I noticed some lights and wondered if they meant anything special: two whites and beneath them a green. Just lights, no shapes or outlines in the darkness. I reassembled from my knowledge of running lights that the whites had to be masthead beacons, the lower one being forward, and of course the green meant a starboard sidelight. I realized that I was looking at a huge freighter steaming directly in front of us, and the whole picture became horrifyingly simple.

"Oh, shit," I yelled out. "Tack! Now!" There was no time for discussions.

"Huh? What's up?" he asked, dreamily fondling the tiller and looking at the stars.

"Big ship! Tack!" was all I could get out. I could already discern an immense shadow looming in front of us.

"Helm's alee!" he called and put the tiller over.

The Rhodes came about in its own length. I looked over my right shoulder to see the silhouette of a cargo ship towering over us, at least 400 feet long, and moving ghostlike as it obliterated our view of Manhasset Bay. She proceeded inexorably through what would have been our own wake in another minute or two. All we ever heard was the hissing sound from her bow wave.

"Good tack," Jeffrey announced, a bit nonplussed, but appreciative nonetheless for saving our lives.

"So what about your Kevin? Didn't he want to come out today?" Jeffrey glanced over at me, as he kept an eye on the barge getting closer.

"He doesn't like it unless it's warm enough to wear a bathing suit. He thinks of sailing as a tropical sport," I answered jokingly.

"How's he doing?" Jeff asked in a more serious tone.

The barge was almost abeam of us. The tug pushing from astern had the familiar red and tan colors of the Turecamo Line.

"So-so," I said, rocking my hand from side to side. "He sleeps a lot lately."

"Is he actually sick with anything, again?"

"I'm never sure. He's been staying home most of the time. He came up only once this whole spring to help with the boat. You were here too that weekend."

"He looked okay then; he was doing everything with us."

"He's much too thin. Couldn't you tell?" I did not want to tell Jeff that I was starting to get paranoid whenever Kevin went out in public, afraid people would know he was suffering from a wasting syndrome.

"He was in a good mood that time. He painted the waterline stripe," Jeffrey said hopefully.

"That was almost a month ago," I answered. "He's tired a lot more lately and getting depressed."

I gave a wave toward the pilothouse of the tug and got a perfunctory wave back, a token salute from the skipper, meaning, "Thanks, buddy, for staying out of my way. If only more of you fucking sailboats would do the same I might enjoy my work out here." On the deck below him, a fat crewman wearing a dirty T-shirt and apron gave us a friendly high five. Obviously the cook, taking a break from chopping onions or frying bacon.

"He's starting to get that hollowed-out look of fear. Know what I mean? I've seen it too many times already."

"Sure. There was a time when Susan was pretty thin," Jeff replied.

"Yes, I remember back at my big fortieth party; she looked like a scarecrow. Sorry," I said, with a sheepish smile.

"No, her own doctor is amazed. But that's how MS is; she's been pretty lucky so far. Can you take the helm? I need to piss really bad."

I slid over to take the wheel. Jeff perched himself on the edge of the transom, opened his jacket and fumbled with his pants. He still had the cigarette in his mouth. Kind of butch, I thought, and wondered if I would be able to hear his stream hit the water four feet below the boat's deck. I usually discouraged less experienced crew from peeing over the stern, natural as the act seemed. I showed everyone how to operate the toilet down below in the dollhouse-sized head. I thought of times Kevin and I would return home and rush upstairs to the toilet. How solid and prodigious his own young stream was, making me feel rather pathetic. He would never fail to call attention to what he called my "geriatric piddle," sometimes tickling me so that I would miss the bowl and dribble onto my pants.

"Did you piss all over the transom?" I asked as Jeff finished.

"No, most of it's in the dinghy now," he answered, stepping back behind the steering wheel with a bit of swagger. We towed the rowboat about eight or ten feet astern.

"Doesn't he still work with you at the shop?" Jeffrey continued.

"He tries to come in sometimes. But he gets tired by the afternoon, so he leaves. I really need him there. Some days I come home, come into the house downstairs when it's dark outside and I find the mail just lying there and the hall light off. Then I realize that he's never gone out of the house since I left that morning."

"How often is that?" Jeffrey asked.

"More and more lately." I told him, and then admitted that I really didn't look forward to sleeping with him. I would lie there, afraid. "Ever hear of night sweats?" I asked.

"Is it from fever or an infection?" Jeffrey replied.

Just another peculiar symptom, I told him, and related how some nights I would feel him and find his back and neck soaked and clammy. I would move away, not wanting to wake him, or I might put a towel over him. Sometimes he might get up to put on a dry T-shirt. Standing there, alone in the dark, I could tell how scared he was, knowing how skinny he was getting. I sensed his fear. When he lay down again I might give him a little pat just to let him know that I was there. Eventually, when I knew he had fallen asleep again, I might touch him to see if he was sweating anymore.

Jeffrey looked out on the water and was silent for a moment. Then he asked, "What's that buoy up ahead? Anything we need to worry about?"

"It's probably Red 36 marking the channel into Mamaroneck. I'll check the chart."

"But he did so well, two years ago when he was in Lenox Hill. He never even looked very sick." Jeffrey spoke to me as I studied the chart in the cabin. Yes, two years ago, I remembered—those visits from Jeffrey and the girls during the first time in the hospital. Like a big party, both kids sat with Kevin in the hospital lobby and we all played Trivial Pursuit. All around us people watched, trying to figure out which one was the patient.

Kevin refused to wear a hospital gown, and Doctor Bahr agreed that it was probably better for his morale. One time he even snuck outside. He slipped on his jacket, pulling the sleeve over his ID band, and went for a walk along Lexington Avenue, just like real people. He came back with some pastry.

"It's different now," I continued, as I sat back in the cockpit. "He's wearing out, and getting hollow in the face. It's more than just losing weight; it's a look of fear and hopelessness. It's a gaunt look, and I've seen it before. It's the look of death." Jeffrey had no answer.

"Look," I said, pointing, "there's Great Captain Island, the larger of the dark bumps on the shore, at about eleven o'clock. Can you see the stone lighthouse on top?"

"What do you think? About another half an hour?"

"Maybe a little more than that," I answered.

"Good. I'm going below." Jeffrey started down into the cabin. "Want a sandwich? I've got ham or turkey."

"Turkey. And something to drink, also, pretty please?" I said, puckering my lips.

"Just steer da boat, mahn," Jeffrey shouted up while unwrapping things in the galley below.

Thirty years, I thought to myself. Almost as long as Kevin's total life. Practically as long as Susan's, too. We're still friends. Still able to find that dopiness that has always held us together. Now we had money, homes, families, careers, and something else in common. Kevin and Susan were about the same age.

Susan had good days and bad. By now she needed a little electric scooter to get around any distance out of their house. Their home had to be a ranch style, to avoid steps she could not manage. Back in college she had been a writer and poet, but her hands did not work very well now. Still, she could work on a computer keyboard well enough to keep writing, and they were managing to bring up two girls. The older one was my godchild and had been sailing on my boats since she was barely four months old. Both kids were very smart and confident and felt completely at home on board a boat.

I was happy for Jeffrey. I felt no sense of contention over whose spouse was doing better. But I was sure that Kevin was running out of luck by now. I could no longer imagine his continuing in terms of years, but rather months. Susan's condition seemed strangely reversible. I knew it was different for Kevin.

"Here's yours. Gimme the helm for a while." Jeffrey put down a plate with a fat sandwich oozing mustard, along with a bag of Ruffles. I was hungry, but not ready to eat. I needed to talk to someone about Kevin's letter.

"The most painful part of what's happening to Kevin," I continued, "is my fear that he knows I want to get away from him sometimes. He even asked once—he was in a really discouraged mood—how I could still want to make love. I almost cried. I miss being around healthy guys, a lot. I ache just to hear laughter and feel the solidness of someone's body."

"Wow. Makes me feel lucky about Susan, at least for now," Jeffrey said, with a mouthful of food. "She can still get me off—know what I mean? When do we start heading toward your enchanted island?"

"Head straight for Captain Island. When you see a red nun off the tip, give it plenty of room. There's a day mark on a short tower to port. Turn in front of that and follow Big Calf Island, keeping a few hundred yards off. There's also a huge field of rocks without any marker, so it's a little tricky."

"You expect me to remember all that shit? Let me see the fuckin' chart before we run aground."

"It's not as difficult as it sounds," I assured him. "We should be able to see the top of the tower pretty soon."

"Do you ever worry that he might want to kill himself, if he got really sick or depressed?" Jeffrey asked quietly.

"That's a funny question," I answered, adding, "Yes, in fact, just once." Ignoring my lunch, I told Jeffrey how two months earlier Kevin had worked all day with me at the shop. It was for a job that had to be delivered the next day. He did this for the whole day. Yet, when I was ready to go home, he did not want to leave. I knew something was bothering him, but he would not talk about it. He seemed placid and unemotional, just sitting at his desk writing something. I told him I did not like leaving him there alone. But he gave me a peculiar look and said, "Don't look so worried," and I left him there.

"Then what?" Jeff asked, slowly finishing his sandwich and steering the boat with his knees.

"I came home, still worried. An hour later he showed up, but very tired. The next day I found his letter on my desk at the shop. It was overwhelming. I can't even begin to tell you all he said."

This letter had been a painful turning point for Kevin. He must have felt he was running out of time. Six pages, I told Jeffrey, handwritten and single spaced, filled with his feelings of regret and failure and guilt. He blamed himself for infecting me. He saw himself as basically nothing, a zero, a dilettante who had accomplished little with his life. A pretty boy with no brains or substance or skills.

I sat there, alone in my office, and took both telephones off the hook for an hour. His whole personality was disintegrating. I felt my heart would break for him. Then I swore that I would not let him die believing all this about himself. I vowed to redeem his soul from such despair and guilt.

"Jesus, Gene." Jeffrey sighed and shook his head. This was not the kind of stuff we usually talked about. He looked at me again and swallowed. "Can I ask you something very personal?"

"No, but go ahead," I answered.

"Did he infect you?"

"Maybe. Maybe you want to call in the CDC in Atlanta and have them study our behavior for the last ten years?"

"But he was the one who was always fooling around. That's what you said."

"Yes, and so did I, during our first couple of years together. I could just as likely have infected him back then. It's irrelevant to me anyway. It's an epidemic; it's out there. We were all vulnerable."

"I guess it was a stupid question," Jeffrey said apologetically.

"No, it's a very obvious one. But the answer is useless to me. We're in this together, Kevin and I."

Jeffrey looked at me with his astigmatic blue eyes, and asked, "'Till death do us part'?"

"Yes, it looks that way," I said and then added, "Want to talk about something else for a while?"

"I only hope I never get a letter like that from Susan someday," Jeffrey said, obviously still affected.

"I don't think she has such difficult things to resolve as Kevin. But then, who knows? Everyone's got buried secrets and regrets. We're supposed to be talking about something else, I thought?"

"Where's that copy of *Paradise Lost* you keep on board? Maybe we can take turns reading Milton to each other." I looked at him and smiled. He knew, and I knew, what the joke was.

Years ago he had worked as an aide in the main reading room of the New York Public Library on Fifth Avenue. I would meet him there during the summer and wait around until he had his break. We would saunter down the marble stairs gawking at the paintings on the walls towering above us. The most prominent one was titled *Blind Milton Dictating* Paradise Lost *to His Daughter.* As we fell in step on the broad landing beneath it, Jeffrey would often thrust out his arm and grab my shoulder. In a stentorian voice he would exclaim, "Help me, daughter, a new chapter has just come to me."

"Sorry, but I left it home," I told him. "Anyway, we're getting close to Captain Island already. Let's get the sails down."

Jeffrey feathered the boat close to the wind, and the jib started flapping around. He pulled in the furling line and the sail disappeared as it rolled itself snugly around the forestay.

"Look, there's the tower." I pointed to shore. "See the green peak just above the trees? That's on Little Calf Island. Better start the engine; I'll douse the main."

Jeff shoved the engine into neutral and started to crank the little two-cylinder diesel. From below we heard several lethargic bangs as the sleepy pistons slammed up and down. After a few more attempts, the little monster growled to life with a puff of black smoke. In a minute the diesel settled down to a steady clackaty-clackaty-clackaty sound. "The Yanmar sounds good," Jeff said, and shifted into forward gear. We both had seen all the same wartime movies about German U-boats and recognized the hypnotic clatter of valves and lifters on a slow-reving diesel engine.

We got the anchor set and we lay a few hundred yards from shore. We climbed over the stern, dropped into the little green dinghy, and rowed to the beach on Little Calf Island.

There was a fairy-tale aspect to this place, this little uninhabited island, a few hundred yards from the prissy Connecticut shore. Standing above the trees was a round tower made of a pale stone, probably granite, about four stories tall. Its peaked roof was copper, oxidized a soft and mottled green.

Tramping single file, Jeffrey followed me up the path from the beach until we reached a clearing at the base of the tower. *All this seems so familiar,* I thought. Of course, I had been here with Kevin eight years ago. We were always making landfalls in those days. Everything was new, every cove and harbor, and we felt like Columbus when we first discovered this island.

"Bring the flag; bring the flag," I shouted back to Kevin as he followed me up from the beach. He was wearing surfer-boy shorts with the extra long legs and a broad red stripe across the butt. He reached into the dinghy and brought out the triangular pennant with the silhouette of a penguin sewn on both sides. That was Burgess, our mascot, and we thought he looked very gallant and stalwart. The flag was attached to a slender bamboo stick. Kevin trotted up next to me and jammed the flag into the sand until it stood by itself.

"What are we going to call this place?" he asked me.

"How about Calf Island?" I answered stupidly.

"Isn't that what we called the other place?"

"No that was Duck Island, off of Northport, and don't confuse that with Duck Island Roads, near Clinton. Here," I said, bending the flag toward him, "you name it."

He pushed the pole deeper into the sand and said aloud to the beach, "I claim this island in the name of Queen . . . who?" He looked at me with a frown.

"Isabella. Remember, Queen Isabella of Spain?" I prompted him. Although we did this ceremony several times at landfalls along the shores of Long Island Sound, her Serene Majesty had yet to acknowledge our tributes. Still, we felt like such adventurers. We felt so young.

Jeffrey stood next to me and looked up at the tower. Standing in front of it now, up close, we could see it had a brooding quality and was even rather sinister-looking.

The tower was apparently built as a memorial. Cut into the stone above the entrance were the words IN LOVING MEMORY OF AUGUST OTTO EIMER II FROM HIS PARENTS, 1925. For years I had wondered, who was this beloved Otto Eimer and how had he met his fate? Kevin and I used to invent legends, always filled with romance and tragedy.

*One time Otto, on vacation from Yale, tried to swim across the Sound and was run over by a steam launch. Another time a hurricane hit the island and he was swept clear into the maelstrom, never seen again.*

Jeffrey followed me into a damp vestibule. The entry doors were entirely gone. Everything had been vandalized for decades here. Inside was a spiral staircase, made of iron and built right into the stone walls. It was in bad shape, with its railing loose and some steps missing entirely.

"We're supposed to climb up that?" Jeff asked, pointing to all the missing steps. He give the rail a tentative shake and it rattled ominously up its entire height.

"Oh, it's not that bad. Just don't try to bring Susan here. The girls would probably love it, I bet," I said, gingerly shifting my weight from the second to the fourth tread up. We could hear pigeons roosting above us somewhere in the rafters of the peaked roof. Their dropping coated all the treads and gave our footsteps a crunchy sound. It all felt so creepy and haunted. We climbed the rickety stairs past two empty landings until we reached the top level. We gazed out of the missing window at a view of a placid Long Island Sound stretching out across the horizon. In the distance the low hills of Glen Cove and Oyster Bay looked so pristine. This was the very same "fresh, green breast of the new world" that Fitzgerald wrote of.

"Pretty neat, eh?" I nudged Jeffrey as we stood at the window, feeling the warm breeze.

"Amazing. You've been here before?"

"A few times. Almost every summer Kevin and I would anchor here. Sometimes we would swim ashore."

"So who's this Otto or August person? What'd he do to deserve this tower, eh?"

"I'm so glad you asked me that," I responded in my helpful docent's voice. "It's a very tragic story."

"Oy vey, here we go." Jeffrey rolled his eyes to the torn-up boards that used to be a ceiling.

I gave Jeffrey Kevin's favorite version of the legend: "Young Otto, rich, foolish, and impetuous, with his hair slicked back in the style of the twenties, long ago summered on this private island in the family's white cottage. (The ruins of the cottage can be inspected after the tour is over.) With a handsome companion at his side—nobody remembers if this was a man or a woman—he slipped behind the wheel of the gleaming mahogany runabout, probably an Elco. 'Just a dash over to Cold Spring Harbor, Mother,' he called to his parents as the speedboat disappeared in a flume of propeller wake."

"This better be good," Jeffrey interrupted.

"The other version has Otto swept away in a hurricane, if you like," I told him, and smiled.

"That's okay. What about the Elco?"

"On their way back a terrible thunderstorm caught them in mid-Sound. One of those awful storms that can make up late on a summer day, turning the western sky into a wall of black. Soon the storm kicked up steep waves and the little open boat was overwhelmed. Its engine was swamped and there was no radio or even life jackets on board. The companion was lost entirely, but the next day Otto's beautiful body washed up on shore, all bloated and hideous."

Jeffrey was still listening.

"His parents were inconsolable in their grief," I continued, "but they did manage to erect this lovely tower where they could come up and look out to the south," I said and pointed, "silently hoping that the little runabout might appear again."

Jeffrey knew of course that it was all bullshit, yet he was moved and quiet. His eyes grew misty. We were both silent for a while.

"You know . . . we worry about you, Gene," Jeffrey said, still looking out the window to the south. "We know what you're facing. We want you around. Sara needs a real uncle, not one of Susan's dour relatives." I knew it was Jeffrey, of course, who was most worried about my prospects. In the distance another oil barge and tug moved steadily down the Sound.

"No one escapes," was all that I could answer. It was quiet here, the only sound the clucking and cooing of birds somewhere above us, uninterested in our worries.

"Sometimes I wonder myself why I am not sick."

"You're on all kinds of drugs, no?"

"Sure, of course. Sixteen pills a day, I think. But I don't really believe that's the whole story. I've seen plenty of people get even sicker on the same drugs that I'm taking for years. I just think I have to keep myself going like a mental exercise. It's as if I have to reinvent myself each morning in order to go on, otherwise everything will come crashing down, and then I really will get sick."

"Sounds like a lot of work all the time," Jeffrey said. "You can never relax."

"Maybe not. But I decided from the very beginning never to rely on anyone else for my health and survival. I won't accept a life of waiting for 'them' to find an answer, some kind of cure. The 'answer,' whatever that is, has to be within me, somehow. Can you understand that?"

"You don't trust your own doctor, you mean?"

"Up to a point, only. But he goes home at night, and I'm here all the time. Besides, I have to stay okay for Kevin. Right now my short-term goal is for him to outlive my mother. I don't want her to have to go through his loss."

"Well, I hope your plan works. I guess I'm pretty thankful about Susan doing really well lately, and watching the girls grow up getting so independent."

"When are you buying them a boat?" I asked.

"I think they're going to want boyfriends more than a boat soon—at least Sara does."

"Mmmm, me too. Say, talking about staying around, doesn't Susan bug you about not smoking and losing weight?"

"Less than she used to. Women aren't so bothered by guys with a gut. It makes them feel secure, like Daddy's home and they can sit in his lap and feel sexy. I guess it's different with gays."

We had been up there hardly fifteen minutes, yet it seemed the afternoon was already passing. We retraced our steps down the stairs. Scales of rust sloughed off from the weight of our steps. I made sure we were not too close together on the way down.

"Actually, there is a real story to this place," I assured him as we neared the bottom. "The Greenwich Historical Society sent me a long article a few months ago."

"It's not another boy romance ending in tragedy?"

"Don't they all?" I said with a sigh. "No, not really. There was an Otto Eimer, he was forty when he died, and his family did summer here. They all did lots of sailing, in fact. That's their old cottage over here, in ruins."

We left the cold entry lobby and stepped out again into the sunshine. Then I told Jeffrey the real history of the tower:

August Otto Eimer had been on a business trip representing his father's chemical firm. The Eimer-Amend Company was involved in importing radium at the turn of the century, and was also the first manufacturer of glass lightbulbs for Thomas Edison. It had been a very successful business. Otto, or "Uncle Gus," died of pneumonia before he could be brought back home. His parents built this tower to house a local sailing club downstairs, and on the topmost floor there was a showcase of souvenirs from their son's life. Everything had long ago been removed or vandalized.

"I think I liked your first story more. Better ending," Jeff said as we stood outside, once again looking up at the tower. "What's all this about?" he asked, twisting his head around to read something cut into the stone threshold of the entrance. "VIVO VOCO . . . what's it say?"

"Funny you should ask," I said to him, realizing that I had been waiting all day for this moment. I read the inscription in a normal voice. "It says, VIVO VOCOS MORTUOUS PLANGO."

"Sounds like Latin. Know what it means?" Jeffrey asked.

"Yes," I said, holding up a pedagogical finger, "but it's ecclesiastical Latin and it took us six years to find this out. None of my scholarly friends were able to translate it."

As we ambled back toward the beach I told him how Kevin had carried these Latin words scrawled on a paper in his wallet for years, curious though ignorant of the meaning. Then in a bar in San Diego he met a priest, a former priest, who recognized it immediately.

"So what the fuck does it mean, already?"

I turned around and answered him, saying, "LONG LIVE THE VOICE OF THOSE WHO PLEAD FOR MERCY." We were both strangely quiet. I could not talk for a few seconds, and I was surprised. I felt like I was about to cry, and I did not know why. Something about that benediction seemed to have a power to humble me. Maybe Jeffrey too, I wondered. We both looked back at the tower. Then he grunted and turned away. I let him walk on ahead back to the beach where I hoped the dinghy was still waiting for us.

The tower again soared above us. That one big empty window seemed to be a single gaping eye staring down at us, wounded but defiant. A survivor. The tower looked different to me, changed somehow. Not so much friendlier but less threatening, as if I had just heard its plea and sensed its vulnerability. I felt a closeness to it, a shared life, a brotherhood with its stones and sad history, both real and made up.

The afternoon breeze had come up, promising us a brisk sail back to City Island. Jeffrey asked me to repeat the Latin inscription one more time when we got aboard the boat, as if he wanted to be sure to remember it for some later use, the same way Kevin had scribbled it down and kept it so long.

As we went through the routine of getting under way it seemed to settle over both of us, these words, this blessing: VIVO VOCOS MORTUOUS PLANGO. Maybe Uncle Gus was at peace now, his wooden sailing dinghies, trophies, and souvenirs long gone, but the benediction that his death had inspired endured, and could move anyone who heard it again.

In twenty minutes the tower began to disappear astern. To the west we could already make out the tops of the Throgs Neck Bridge. It would be almost dark when we returned to the mooring.

Jeff came back to the cockpit and sat beside me while I steered. "When you feel okay," he started, "when everything's working right, you don't want to be bothered with other people's problems, you know?"

"Like the way I feel sometimes wanting to get away from Kevin with all his medicines and doctors and night sweats? I look at him and it hurts."

"Uh-huh, yeah. Like Susan's tiredness and handicaps, needing a cane just to get around the house. Christ," he drew in his breath, "she's not even thirty-six. Sometimes she can be so moody and bitchy. She must feel so frustrated sometimes seeing this happening to her," Jeffrey added.

"The healthy are always repelled by the sick," I told him. "It's the brutal side of life needing to go on at all costs. We're repelled by infirmity, it frightens us, makes our skin crawl. We don't want to be reminded of what could just as easily happen to us."

"I guess it is like you said back there earlier, at the tower."

"Something about Uncle Gus?"

"No, schmuck," Jeffrey came back, "about how no one escapes."

"Yeah," I said, quietly, "like the sign at my butcher's says, PLEASE TAKE A NUMBER. YOUR TURN WILL COME SOON."

Jeffrey rolled his eyes up to the masthead. I started to go below to retrieve my sandwich. Then I turned back to Jeffrey and asked, "Want to listen to some Bach for a while? What about Glenn Gould playing the Goldbergs?"

"Certainly," he said enthusiastically, "let's have some Bach." He stretched his legs across the cockpit and made himself comfortable.

I came back up with my sandwich. From the cockpit speakers the music began, the long patient string of Bach's variations that began with a heartbreakingly simple theme called The Aria. Contained within the little universe of its disciplined melody was all the emotion I had ever felt. Running through all the variations was a sense of yearning for something good and permanent, something that was perhaps more accessible in Bach's time.

Halfway through the cycle Jeffrey turned to me. "Ach, Johann, these fugues, they are so vunderful," he said, and gently patted his heart. "Look at all this," he added, with a sweep of his arm. In his gesture he linked the music, the boat, the water, and the changing sky.

The Variations filled the space between us as dusk approached and we drew closer to City Island. "Yes, Bach!" Jeffrey added with an expansive gesture of his arm. Then he added, quietly, almost to himself, "Always Bach."

# 17

## THE DONZI

*The Gulf Stream, July 1992*

He died the morning of July 16, 1992, a glorious midsummer day. Thunderstorms of biblical proportions tossed anger and retribution throughout the electrified atmosphere that last terrible night, as Kevin lay dying, motionless in a rented hospital bed in our study. That was the night I realized I could not manage his care anymore. I was falling apart from lack of sleep. I was not trained to provide twenty-four-hour feeding and care and medications for a desperately sick young man. But I had tried. When I saw that I was screwing up his intravenous feeding, with a terrible sense of defeat I admitted my failure. I called Cabrini Hospice at ten-thirty that night and asked for the next available bed for him.

His mother Sue stayed over that night, intending to help me organize a schedule for all the nursing people coming throughout the day to our house. There were three full-time aides each day, and a social worker visited every few days. Sue really came to see how I was holding up. Technicians from the medical supply house provided the infusion pump along with cases of drugs, all of which had to be prepared and dosed in different ways. It was amazing how much I had learned in just a few days. I knew he was going to die, and I wanted more than anything else to allow him to die, quickly and easily. To his family and our friends I know I seemed the very picture of strength and courage, but throughout the entire ordeal, actually spanning four years, I was to find out simply this: I never thought it was possible to care so much for someone and to hurt so much.

Two weeks after his death I joined my old friend Laura in Nantucket to help her sail her boat back to the Hudson River. As I drove to Newark Airport I realized that this would be the first time I would have to park the car in the long-term lot by myself. Where was I supposed to turn? Was it Lot E or D? We had lived as a couple for thirteen years, and in these situations Kevin told me what to do.

The sail with Laura had been a way to open things up inside of me, to deal with her boat problems, to be with Laura and to laugh a lot.

After I returned from Nantucket there was still the business of his ashes to be scattered into the waters of the Atlantic Ocean. This simple request was relayed to me by his brother Richard after he had a very painful visit with Kevin in the hospital one month before he died. Despite his fuzzy brain and failing memory, Kevin made it clear to Richard that he did not want his last resting place to be Eastchester Bay, or any of the waters off City Island. Though we had sailed together out there for so many years, he wanted something better than this polluted estuary in the shadow of the Co-op City apartment complex and a contaminated municipal garbage dump.

He used to speak wistfully of wanting a Viking funeral, with his body incinerated on a pyre aboard a traditional Scandinavian warship. Definitely something to get the attention of the gods that his Danish ancestors worshiped long ago. But while Kevin aspired to grand gestures, he rarely had the determination to finish all his projects. This was one task left for me to complete.

After all I had been through I expected the disposal of his ashes would be a kind of afterthought, a token gesture of farewell. Merely a symbolic postscript after I had held him in my arms and watched him die. Afterward, there had been no doctors or any professionals attending while I had shaved him, trimmed his nails, and finally removed the IV needle. I was determined that he leave this life as unfettered as he had arrived.

All he had wanted from me was to get him out of the hospital and home again. It was to die, of course; we both knew that. Even that required weeks of negotiations between the insurance provider and the private hospice as well as additional arrangements for in-home nursing services and all the supporting vendors for home care supplies. All the while Sue and I knew we were gambling that he would not live beyond the time his limited home-assistance benefits ran out.

He did come home. His doctors watched me wheel him down the hallway of Eight East that day with a look of tight-lipped regret. The young and arrogant infectious disease specialist, like all the others, had finally run out of tricks to save this handsome guy who had so often recovered from fevers and infections during the past four years. He had been their model patient, an ego boost for a staff that faced death several times a week on the same ward.

"What do you believe in, Eugene?" Dr. Michael Tapper had asked me, as I sat across from him at his desk. He used a small office just a few doors down from Kevin's room. He looked tired, but more than tired, he looked defeated and deflated. He was not his usual confident doctor self, always ready to attack the next opportunistic infection in an AIDS patient. "Are you religious?" he asked me. He was too tired to be rhetorical. He really wanted to know, and I wondered who was supposed to be the expert here.

"Are you discouraged?" I asked him frankly. We had been through so many tête-à-têtes regarding what new approach to take with Kevin's treatment. We had talked often, but this was different. He needed someone to absolve him.

"Of course I'm discouraged. This whole disease can be terribly defeating at times." As Tapper answered, he folded his hands and stretched back in his swivel chair. He was a young man still, intense and committed to the alchemic magic of his craft.

"And you like Kevin, too," I said.

"I care a great deal about all my patients," the doctor answered me, sitting up again with his elbows on the desk.

"He just wants to go home now," I said. What I meant was: You have had your chance with him, and now he is mine once again.

"He belongs at home. I'm very glad you are with him." Dr. Tapper slowly closed a file folder on his desk. It was just one of many that belonged in Kevin's huge hospital record. He stood up and reached across the desk to shake my hand, saying, "Good luck, Eugene. He needs you now more than us."

"Thanks for all you have done, Doctor," I answered. "And yes," I added, "I do believe in some kind of God, and I don't blame him, either."

Tapper held my hand, and pressed his lips together as if wanting to say something that was difficult for him. Finally, he added, "You're very lucky, Eugene. I mean that."

Two days after his return, I had the daily routines well enough under control. I needed to return to work for a while to check on the situation at the shop. I had hired a manager to oversee a huge store project that had come in that summer. I needed someone to deal with the client on a daily basis and insulate me from trivial problems. The job was another Burke food store on Fifth Avenue scheduled to open by Christmas. It would be the largest job I ever did.

It was a typical summer morning in Brooklyn, and the traffic was hopeless as usual. Flatbush Avenue, a two-mile stretch with all the lights timed backward, turning red, rather than green, in regular succession. Only in Brooklyn. It was just an ordinary morning while driving down Flatbush Avenue when I was struck by an inspiration and I knew what I had to do: I would bury his ashes in the axis of the Gulf Stream off the coast of south Florida.

I was awed at both the audacity and the appropriateness of this plan. The delays and red lights no longer mattered to me. I understood immediately what I sought to achieve. His ashes would enter the Stream in the southern waters, the flow being northerly up the Atlantic Coast until Cape Hatteras, where the main body bends to the east heading for the Canary Islands, and then once again the current branches apart mostly to Spain; but some of this sumptuous warm water continues to the British Isles—and then, and most important, this same great flow headed farther north to wash onto the shores of—yes—Denmark. That explained the relatively mild though overcast weeks of winter up there.

Could it be that the specks of his dust that remained would now make this epic journey back to the homeland of his father, Kurt? Through Kurt, in spite of abuse and drinking and long months away,

Kevin relished his blood heritage of the Vikings and felt himself a distant heir to those seagoing maniacs, those fearsome blond giants in wooden longboats who long ago struck terror in Christian souls across the coastal hamlets of northern Europe. Although he was raised in Brooklyn Heights and Lakewood, New Jersey, he knew he had Viking blood, and it was in Denmark, not Brooklyn, that he felt his soul belonged.

What more perfect place than Florida for this journey to begin? We both loved it down there, and had played on the beaches of Dade, Broward, Palm Beach, and Duval Counties dozens of times during the previous eight years. My mother had died just that April, three months before Kevin. He had, in the end, managed to outlive her and spare her another tragedy. In her final years of widowhood in Boca Raton, we had visited her nearly every three or four months, until our time in Florida seemed like a parallel life to both of us. Brooklyn was a necessary ugliness to endure until once more our Delta plane thundered down the runway and lifted away toward Fort Lauderdale.

We loved Florida. We loved the caressing heat and the oppressive tropical humidity, the saltiness you breathed, the insanely air-conditioned malls with fountains and skylights, the familiar chain stores with their airhead salesgirls. Above all, we loved the boys. Boys everywhere in shorts with tan and fuzzy legs, eager to look pretty, wear pretty colors, drive their pretty cars with bare feet since there was no broken glass on Boca Raton streets. Boys who rode their surfboards in the heavy winter swells. Boys so lithe that they could twist and ooch every last yard of exhilaration from a dying wave before they finally stopped and carelessly fell over into the foam. Boys in black wet suits with a bright green stripe down the sides and a Body Glove handprint logo between their shoulder blades, their hair wet and stringy, their toes curled with animal deftness around the edge of their boards, their thin ankles tethered with a bungee cord to those fiberglass surfboards with goofy designs. These were not the youths of places like Bushwick or Bay Ridge, where looking ugly and mean were de rigueur, where shorts were cut way below the knees and sickeningly baggy. What was the matter with them? Why was everything in this city so unrelentingly ugly?

Neither of us was ever involved in any organized religious observance, at least none that left a sense of following any prescribed ritual at life's special and terrible moments. I was not at all surprised that Kevin wanted to be cremated and have his ashes find a watery end.

Twelve hours after he died, I was finally alone in the house that beautiful July day. I sat in his usual chair at the dining room table, the walnut table his parents had given us when we moved into this house. I guess it had been a wedding gift, although nobody used those words.

In front of me was a neat array of colored file folders containing all his affairs. Each was titled: INSURANCE, LENOX HILL HOSPITAL, MEDICATIONS, EQUIPMENT/RENTAL, EQUIPMENT/SERVICES, NURSING SCHEDULES, HOSPICE, FUNERAL HOME. I had been entrusted with orchestrating the passing of someone's life, and I had done it. I wondered again who I was to be given this responsibility, this insight, this trust? I had been sitting alone in the house, overwhelmed by the emptiness and finality of his passing. Then, in the familiar room around me, I felt a presence, very subtle, more like a sense of okay-ness that came over me, while I sat at the dining room table.

A sense of calm filled me, almost a presence that reassured me, saying, "I am so glad you could take care of all this crap for me. You know how bad I am at paperwork." I did not hear a voice, but I experienced the relief and gratitude that Kevin felt.

For the first time in months I felt completely peaceful. Actually happy. The house was quiet with just the birds and summer crickets out in the backyard. The two cats were asleep somewhere. Then, just as I got used to it, the mood passed, leaving me to wonder if something extraordinary had just happened.

I didn't expect him to come out of the bedroom with a sheet over his head, hands outstretched like Casper the Friendly Ghost. But I could accept that two people, so merged and committed in life, could reach each other after the clinical status of death. How would we know when we were sought out by the evanescent nothingness of someone we loved as he struggled to coalesce into a something that could whisper to us, "It's okay. I'm happy." No, we are not taught to expect such incorporeal visits in our dining rooms.

Two months later I was in Broward County, driving south on I-95 toward the Hillsborough exit. At the Cove Marina a dive shop ran their boats twice a day for scuba trips. I had gone out with them several times, out to the reefs and wrecks forty and ninety feet deep. Both Kevin and I had earned our certificates for diving in Florida.

In the car, on the backseat, was a cardboard box. Inside that was another, smaller sealed box containing the plastic "urn" of ashes. I had never seen a person's ash remains. In another bag was a small knife, some tools, and latex gloves. A bunch of flowers rested on top of the box.

I wanted everything to go well. I wanted to let go of all that remained of him and not allow one speck to either touch me or stay with me, thus the gloves. Where all this sense of ritual and finality came from I have no idea. I had never even lit a Yahrzeit candle for my father in the eight years since his death. But I knew that all this was necessary. It was part of the trust.

Dave, the dive shop operator, remembered me from previous trips, and explained that it was not legal to dump ashes, or anything, into the protected coastal waters. They were sympathetic and admitted they had done this before. They simply wrote up the bill as a private dive trip. I had not expected this to be so simple.

The boat was waiting for me at the dock with two crewmen. They already knew about my intentions. Everything seemed to be falling into place, and I felt swept along by the sheer power of my own intentions. On the other hand, they were unwilling to send out a huge forty-five-foot, twin diesel dive boat designed for twenty-five customers. Instead they gave me a speedboat, called a Donzi.

It was long, gleaming white, and unashamedly penislike, a hopelessly impractical toy for overly successful garmentos who wanted to get to some place in a big hurry. It was powered by twin 225-horsepower Mercury outboards and capable of making close to forty miles per hour, which is warp speed as boats go. In fact, the dive shop kept it just for those extravagant visitors who had to squeeze in a couple of dives and then rush back ashore, probably to pick up their wives at the

Galleria Mall. Well, it was hardly a sinister black gondola used for funerals in Venice, but, hey, this was South Florida, and why not have some fun along the way to the cemetery?

At the dock I found two men getting the Donzi's engines started. Mike, my captain for the run, was a grizzled old dive-shop type familiar all up and down the Florida Keys. A little watery in the eyes, a few teeth chipped, but basically a reliable boat skipper for at least half a day. He was showing Kimo, the mate for this afternoon, the controls on the Donzi's aircraft-like instrument panel. Most of what I heard concerned watching the two tachometers to bring the engines into synch, and keeping an eye on the oil pressure when running over 6,000 revolutions per minute.

They were friendly and appreciated my help casting off the dock lines and bringing in the fenders. They seemed a little distant, not sure about intruding on my privacy during this mission.

Kimo was obviously Hawaiian and wore a wonderful shirt with parrots and swaying trees. I'm sure I had seen the same one at Hilo Hattie's outlet store five years before on the Big Island. How Kimo had lost his middle finger, I did not ask. It seemed part of the risk of making a life around the waterfront and taking whatever came.

With clouds of smoke and the two engines growling impatiently at low rpm's, we inched out of the marina and steered into the Intracoastal Waterway, heading north for the inlet at Boca Raton. We cleared the stone jetty fifteen minutes later and Mike began to ease the throttles ahead, all the time making slight adjustments to the trim tabs mounted on the stern. The trick, he shouted to me over the roar of the twin Mercs, was to get the boat to ride up its own bow wave and onto a plane. You wanted the hull sitting almost level, just slightly bow up as the boat tore over the tops of the waves.

The power and speed were more exhilarating than I had ever imagined. As the Donzi got up on a true plane, at first I felt the rush deep in the gut. Then, like any good narcotic, it moved with predictable ecstasy further down as I felt my stomach get light and my balls begin to tighten up. In any case, we were headed east toward the Gulf Stream.

I showed photos of Kevin to Mike and Kimo. Pictures of him sailing, building our porch, wearing his tuxedo.

"You guys were, uh, kind of really good friends, I guess?" Mike asked me, with both hands braced against the Donzi's steering wheel.

"No," I answered. "We were lovers. I was crazy about him," I said and smiled broadly at Mike and Kimo. I watched their faces go through the evolving stages of embarrassment, confusion, recognition, acknowledgment, awakening, and finally, relief.

"You were both, like, gay?" Mike said, trying hard to be diplomatic.

"I still am," I yelled into his closer ear.

"I never knew . . . that you kind of guys sailed, you know what I mean?" Mike said slowly.

"We did," I assured him. "We had five boats together. We sailed everywhere."

"Wow, man. That's great, really," Mike said to me, shaking his head, his right hand now gently easing back the twin throttle levers.

"This is it," Mike said to me, significantly. He slowed the Donzi down to almost an idle, and behind me the two big engines rumbled and missed occasionally. "You're in the Stream now."

Moving to the back of the boat, I began neatly cutting open the box. We never made it to the true axis of the Gulf Stream, which lay another ten miles farther out to sea. We were definitely in the Stream, and we came to a stop in very deep water, about a thousand feet deep. We stayed there rolling in the swells four miles off the Boca Raton coast. Wearing the gloves now, I slit open the plastic bag inside the box to find a sack of very coarsely ground ashes with small pieces of dull white bone. It weighed eight pounds. It went into the ocean with one whoosh. That was it. Just a symbolic gesture for closing a life.

Kimo was at the controls, holding the impatient Donzi's bow into the wind, with the engines noisily idling. Mike, without my asking, had written down the latitude and longitude coordinates for me from the boat's Loran set. The time was 3:05 p.m.

I peeled off the gloves like a surgeon and plunged both of them over the side and swished them around in the sea to clean them off. Then I packed them back into the cardboard box and it was over. I tossed my flowers on top of the sinking ashes. Now he was part of the eternal ebb and flow of water and air and I had released him forever.

Nobody cried. We all shook hands. Mike's hand was knobby and strong, as I expected. Kimo, a great big guy with tender hands and stubby fingers, gave me a bear hug, and I was aware of his missing finger as he pressed my back. *It must have hurt so much,* I thought.

On the run back to shore I urged the guys to open up the Donzi a lot more, and we hit twenty-seven miles per hour. The two monster outboards just behind us roared in synchronous unison, making any talk, let alone thought, impossible. We got back to the marina before five o'clock. I helped with the lines and said good-bye. They both wanted to shake my hand again.

"Hey man, I just hope someone does this for me someday," Mike said. He meant it.

"You're okay, guy," Kimo added. "You're a pretty cool dude." He was not much of a talker but I was touched by his admiration. I gave his bull-thick shoulder an affectionate squeeze. He did not mind.

I left the marina and picked up A1A north and then drove to the beach at the Boca Inlet, the same beach where we had played Frisbee and snorkeled dozens of times in the past years. I sat in the sand. It was Friday, and the beach was empty. I looked out to the spot, four miles away, and said good-bye again. He was mine no longer. I had arrived in Florida less than twenty-four hours earlier and it was all over now. I was dazed.

There was no marker, no grave, no stone, no plaque, no memorial tree, no square in the gruesome AIDS quilt. Absolutely nothing. That felt right to me. In my pocket were written these numbers: LATITUDE 26° 22.18' NORTH, LONGITUDE 79° 58.83' WEST. I had no need for anything else.

# 18

## LAURA

*Newport, August 1992*

Lying at the dock in Nantucket her boat looked clean and racy, at least from the outside. The white hull, sharp bow, and crisp lines told me that this was a boat meant to go fast. It was named *Penn Central,* and on the side of each bow was a big graphic of an old steam locomotive, like something from a Monopoly board. At twenty-eight feet overall, she was both shorter and lighter than my own boat, and with someone else as skipper I hoped I'd be able to relax. I also welcomed a reason to get away from the house in Brooklyn.

But from the day I arrived the boat had a smell down below, a kind of piss-sour smell, and there was a suspicious thick green liquid in the boat's bilges.

"Uncle Danny said it was probably antifreeze leaking out," Laura said, going along with a hunch by her uncle with five decades of boating experience.

"But it stinks, Laura," I said suspiciously. I told her I wished she would let me check around on my own.

"I was hoping you would. I think it's kind of gross down here," she added and began inching back up the companionway toward fresher air. I stood by the boat's galley, my fingers dripping with green fluid, and I looked for a paper towel above the sink.

"Any paper towels?" I asked her politely, not wanting to get pushy too soon.

"We ran out on the trip up last week, and I've been staying at Uncle Danny's place since, so I haven't bought any stuff for the boat."

We spent the rest of my first morning in Nantucket at the supermarket, stocking up for the three or four days we would need to get Laura's boat back to Long Island Sound.

Flying up to Nantucket via Boston, my plane cruised low above the Connecticut shore. Through the window I could easily identify every harbor on the north shore of Long Island Sound. In twenty minutes the plane covered my entire sailing area for the past eighteen years and I was left with the eerie feeling that I was being rushed forward, like it or not, into the future.

This trip was supposed to be fun and relaxing, a chance for Laura to decompress after months of performing difficult microsurgery, like reattaching people's smashed fingers in the OR, and for me, my first long sail since all that had happened during the months from May through July.

During those difficult months before Kevin died she had been a source of support. The sprawling house she was living in up in Rockland County had several times become a weekend refuge for me, a short but needed escape from the ordeal of witnessing Kevin's irreversible decline. As a surgeon, death was a given part of her profession. Now, even in silence, we could enjoy each other's company. We both knew that there was a subtext to this voyage from Nantucket to Long Island Sound. She knew that these were familiar waters for me. We did not have to talk about it, not yet at least, but of course for me Kevin was everywhere.

We had a special relationship, more like brother and sister, and that quality freed us to care about each other in a very unencumbered way, without the inevitable sexual tension and competition. Then, too, maybe for her I served as a link to her old boyfriend, David Lange. We both had known him almost as long, and we both still loved him. She knew that she had lost him, despite their shipboard marriage four years before on the voyage to Bequia Island, when Kevin had petitioned Neptune to unite them forever. Though she had a new boyfriend now, I knew she still missed David.

Later that first day, I snooped around the boat's interior until I found the holding tank for the head, a neoprene bladder that was filled to near bursting. The manual discharge pump nearby, buried under the v-berth, was already oozing thick green liquid from around its gasket. Not only was the system under too much pressure, but there were nasty leaks. The mystery was solved: semitreated sewage was leaking back into the cabin. Laura called the dock boy with the portable pump-out cart and I gave the boat a serious cleaning down below with bleach.

Later that evening I suggested Laura rename the boat *Lady Clorox*. She thought about it, appreciating the crisp antiseptic smell wafting up from the cabin. She smiled down at me from the companionway. She looked happy. I knew that she really hated tedious cleaning and repair jobs on the boat. I also felt I had already made myself useful, rather than moping around remembering times with Kevin.

"Sounds too commercial, Gene," she answered after some consideration. "People might think I'm some kind of feminist laundry service and start dropping off bags of underwear to be washed. Why don't you help me put all this food away instead."

The next morning we pulled out of Nantucket, and despite the haze and lack of wind we arrived at Cuttyhunk Island later that August afternoon. As it glided through calm water close to the shore of the Elizabeth Islands, the boat felt light and both of us were glad for the quiet after seven hours of motoring. With sundown still hours away we went ashore and hiked up the rolling lanes to the island's western end. There we found the old lookout tower that had once been used to watch for German U-boats lying in wait off the east coast. Now it was visited mostly by tourists and fire watchers during dry spells.

The view from this peak surveys all of Buzzards Bay as far north as the Cape Cod Canal and down the entire length of Martha's Vineyard. Block Island was just a blur over the southern horizon. I had been on this same platform a year earlier, with Kevin and our City Island friend Rick Valentine. I did not mention any of this to Laura.

As usual, Laura went to bed up forward in the v-berth while I made up one of the settee berths in the main cabin. I was not on my own boat, but it was good to be sleeping on a boat again. I felt a little less anxious now that we were on our way. Still, I could not shake the awareness that I was single now, with no one waiting for me at home.

In my knapsack, along with the tools, electrical tape, shackles, and boat hardware that I had packed for this trip, were two small keepsakes of my time with Kevin. They were the two toy animals that had lived for weeks on his bedside table at Lenox Hill Hospital. They were part of my ongoing game of dropping toys in his luggage whenever he traveled away from me. It was my way of always reassuring him that I would wait for him.

I had no way to hold onto this beautiful but insecure blond boy. He craved adventures out on his own and fresh sexual conquests. So from whatever distance necessary I sought to manipulate him with these little surrogates who could silently attest to my promise that I would never leave him.

I did not want to get sentimental or maudlin about them; they were only toys, finger puppets, hardly two inches tall. One was a little dog with black spots, like a Dalmatian puppy. The other was a yellow monster with saucer eyes and a mouth full of rubber teeth.

In the dark of the cabin Laura's breathing settled into the rhythm of sleep. I took hold of the two puppets, pulled the dog out of the monster's mouth, and told them to quiet down. I asked them if they missed him as much as I did. They stopped their fighting, looked at each other, and both shook their heads "yes." At least I was not alone. I stuck them into a ledge above me and stretched out in my berth for the night.

"Hey, Gene, where the fuck are we?" Laura shouted down to me from the helm. I was below, once again mopping out the bilge. Green slimy liquid was oozing up around the floorboards and migrating toward the bow. I twisted around and looked up to see she was smiling. I wasn't worried, nor was she, really. There wasn't much to worry about with the Rhode Island shore only six miles to leeward, lost somewhere in the August haze.

The wind was between fourteen to sixteen knots, hardly very strong, but out here, off of Rhode Island, the seas were rough. Long waves that rolled in from the open Atlantic rebounded against the rising bottom contour this close to land. The seas grew steep and lumpy. The motion was not the majestic rise and fall between broadly spaced wave peaks that Laura and I had experienced sailing to St. Vincent. Though we saw no land, the very rolling nature of the seas told us it was not far off.

Laura, with her legs wedged across the cockpit seats, worked the tiller and avoided the biggest waves. They heaved up in front of us, unexpectedly, like scary cut outs in a spook house. She knew her boat and she was good at it. I was still down below in the lurching cabin trying to plot our course on her little navigation board in my lap.

"Hey, Gene, do you think the head's still leaking green stuff?" She was up in the fresh air, while I was trying to plot or guess exactly where we were and how close we could sail to the rocks and fish traps surrounding Sakonnet Point, our first landfall before Newport.

"Hang on down there," she warned me from the cockpit. "Big wave!" I felt the bow point up sharply, pause for a second, then nose into a rogue wave. Above me on the deck I could hear solid water crashing over the bow. As we slid off the back of the next roller the boat wallowed a bit from side to side, and that's when more yucky green liquid came slopping up from the bilge. She was *Lady Clorox* no more.

By four that afternoon we sailed into Newport Harbor. We tacked our way toward the dock of the Newport Yacht Club in the northeast corner. I did not bother her with all the memories that this city, this harbor, even this very marina held for me. Rather I got on the radio and in a cool and professional voice made docking arrangements. Up on deck I put out lines and fenders and brought down the mainsail. As we came in close I jumped onto the end of C Dock and went about the routine of setting up breast lines, spring lines and fenders. I washed down the boat's decks and even filled up the fresh water tank.

When I was done the boat sparkled and smelled clean, and the decks dried quickly in the late afternoon sun. Walking back from the clubhouse at the top of the seawall, I then realized that we were tied to the same dock Kevin and I had used on our first trip to Newport, ten years earlier in the Tanzer 22. I began to have this spooky feeling that I was moving through parallel times, then and now.

At dusk Laura and I walked around the town and docks and boutiques looking for a place to eat. It was a weekday night, and though it had become a major tourist attraction, Newport was mercifully uncrowded that evening. Laura understood all that this place meant to me. For years she'd received our postcards showing the mansions along Bellevue Avenue or the America's Cup yachts during a race.

We wandered around the waterfront, passing the Aquidnick Lobster Company, with its huge tanks filled with live lobsters. Eventually we made our way over to the Black Pearl Restaurant. This was a popular nightspot effecting the atmosphere of a colonial tavern with sawdust on the planked floors, copper lanterns, and old nautical prints everywhere. Its smoky corners were a favorite hangout for big shots and dealmakers. On weekends the crowd was raucous and the wait interminable.

We ordered drinks and when the waitress left Laura leaned toward me. "Right now I know all you can feel is his loss and all the sadness of what you went through. But that isn't everything—that's not the end. In the future, believe me, in years to come, what you'll remember is all the fun you guys had with each other, all the stuff you did together, and it won't be so painful anymore."

Lulled by the sound of dishes from the kitchen, I listened, and appreciated her feelings for me. She was speaking from the heart. Neither of us were smokers, and our hands lay a little nervously on the wooden table. She moved her hand up to my forearm and held me there. Her fingers gripped me where the arm grew thick, the way Roman soldiers used to do. The gesture said, be here, now, with me.

The last time we had seen each other had been on a June afternoon, a month before Kevin died. We sat around her swimming pool with sections of the Sunday *New York Times* scattered on the patio all around us. Though we each held a section of the paper open, we did not read it. Instead, she talked to me about death, and what to expect.

"It's not like in the movies . . . not very often. People are always afraid they won't be able to face it, to watch someone die. But they can. It's very peaceful," she said. "It just happens and then they are gone. It's very gentle." I said nothing, but I think she knew I appreciated her honesty. Of course, she was also saying, You *can* do this, you don't have to be a specialist.

She was right. The end was like a whisper. Kevin had almost died sometime after a horrendous thunderstorm the night of July fifteenth. But I would not let him. He grew restless around 2:00 or 3:00 a.m. His breathing grew irregular, with quick and shallow gasps. He became panicky and his forehead felt clammy. He had pulled off the oxygen tube and began coughing. He had trouble swallowing. His throat was filling up with mucus that he could not get down. I sat with him, raised his chest and kept coaxing him to try harder to swallow. It was as if he had simply forgotten this basic reflex, and I only had to remind him where to look for it. Still, he was choking.

Then, with no more concern than when lifting scraps out of a sink drain, I reached into his mouth and cleared his airway. I pulled out all the gloppy mucus that was choking him. I did not even bother with gloves. Soon he breathed easily and calmly again, and we both went back to sleep. In my ignorance I had in fact just intervened in the initial stages of death, what is called Cheyne-Stokes, or the death rattle. But I could not let go of him in the middle of the night. I imagined something better.

The next morning both Sue and I were taking turns looking after him. At 8:00 a.m. I went to move our cars. When I came back into the house, Sue looked down the stairs and said to me, "You'd better come up, right now."

She was next to him. He had turned very pale, his skin was a translucent yellow, and again he was not breathing right. I sat beside him in the bed and held him. He calmed down as he felt my arms encircle his shoulders and his mother hold his hands.

Again his breathing grew labored. He sounded congested and gurgled a little from far back in his throat. I pulled him close to me and cooed softly, and rocked him just a little. Then he was quiet and very still. He had died in my arms. I held him for a long time. Sue left us alone. She went into the dining room and I knew she was weeping there.

I had in fact orchestrated his death to the last breath. I thought over and over, *Who was I to be so lucky?* Twenty minutes later the warmth had left his body, forever. His blue eyes were strangely clear, no longer bloodshot or frightened. I knew that I had just been changed in ways that would take me a long time to fully understand, but already I was filled with gratitude.

Laura and I finished our meal and then talked about tomorrow; what time we had to get under way and what sightseeing we might be able to squeeze in. We strolled around Banister's Wharf and gawked without envy at the opulent yachts crowded in two deep along the waterfront.

We walked along the seawall until we reached a small park, and sat on a bench across the harbor from the yacht club. "You haven't talked about it at all, but I know you must be thinking about him," Laura said to me at last.

"Of course, I remember all the fun we had, especially here in Newport. We made so many trips," I answered. "But I'm still haunted by the sight of him those last weeks, how he fell apart, just turned into a frightened child mentally, near the end."

"It can be worse than Alzheimer's, and this comes right at the prime of life. Bodies we can usually fix. But not the brain . . . not so easily."

I needed to tell someone about those last few weeks, just before he came home. "His memory was all messed up and he was starting to have double vision. Dr. Tapper was considering whether to give him Ampho-something, or maybe try surgery and remove most of his damaged lungs."

"Yes, now I remember," Laura interrupted me. "Amphotericin B. It's an awful drug, Ampho-terrible, we call it, because of the side effects. But you knew that they were probably wasting their time?"

"And his," I added bluntly. By then Sue and I realized it was too late for heroic measures; even Dr. Ryan, the pulmonary surgeon, told us to take him home. Operating would have been futile; his lungs were already ruined by fungus.

I often stayed late in his hospital room, long past visiting hours. No one bothered us. I might rub his legs or his bony shoulders a while. Sometimes I would even lie next to him in his bed just to feel him close again. Once I actually fell asleep there. I longed so much for him to be home with me again.

"Then one night I found him gently fingering a toy grasshopper that Sue had given him. Immediately I knew, just as I always knew what his confused gibberish meant. I knew what was going on. I knew his mind so well, sometimes I was his mind. He was moving backward, shedding the mental faculties that were progressively being destroyed by this fungal infection."

"Which fungus was it?" Laura asked me.

"Aspergillus." I answered her. "That's what destroyed his lungs. It took over a month to finally identify it, and by then he had virtually no lung capacity left."

"They're the worst," she said, looking down at the pavement. "Incredibly hard to kill," she went on, almost to herself, "especially at that stage."

"You two were closer than lots of married couples I know. You felt what was happening to him as your own. That's very scary."

"Yeah," I told her, "and I also knew that I had to let him go . . . for both of us. I had to separate my life from his and realize that it wasn't my tragedy. You told me that, or was it Hal, my therapist?" We looked at each other for a second, and I remembered our talk at the swimming pool. "Maybe you both said that, in different ways."

So eventually, I would play with the grasshopper, making him jump over the bed and eat up the other animals. It was another way to be with him, and if that was all that was left for us, I was still thankful. I was quiet for a while, feeling weary of talking about this.

"It's pretty amazing what you can do when you have to," Laura reminded me. "You learned a lot about meds and dosages and that stuff with infusion pumps. And you helped someone die very beautifully."

We did not speak as we strolled back to the yacht club. Next to us the harbor water was still and black. We sat together on the porch of the empty yacht club and looked across to the lights of Newport. The random clunking of halyards slapping against hundreds of masts filled the quiet night.

"He wasn't home very long after the hospital, was he?" Laura began.

"Less than a week. Five days. I was very clear about wanting him to die quickly, and easily." I told her. "The full reality that he was about to die hit me the night he asked for his dog," I continued.

We were together in his hospital room, once again long after visiting hours. He asked me in this thin and childlike voice, "Is Kasha there?" as if she was waiting out in the hall for him. All the resonance had gone out of his voice. He sounded small and afraid, like a little kid. The dog had died three years earlier.

I tried to recall for him the day the dog had collapsed in Prospect Park, and how I had to carry her home, all fifty pounds of her. "Do you remember now?" I asked him. She was panting and weak and we tried to give her some water. Then she died, lying between us on the bedroom carpet. "Do you remember that day?" I asked him again. For a while he did remember, but I knew from his face, how he stared up at the ceiling, that he was already someplace else.

"When she died, Kevin felt that was the start of his first getting sick."

"Some kind of symbiosis between man and dog?" Laura said and shifted on the bench. She sat cross-legged, facing me.

"No, much simpler," I told her. "For many weeks afterward he had trouble in his throat, difficulty swallowing. He assumed it was his emotions being held in, all the sadness he wouldn't let himself express, literally constricting his heart. Then he began to have difficulty just eating."

"Sounds like ulcers in his esophagus," Laura speculated. She was right; it turned out to be a *Candida* infection, classic AIDS symptoms. Neither of us had even been tested back then, I told her, feeling a bit naive.

"God, Gene, you don't know how angry that makes me. It was all so unnecessary; our lives are still haunted by that asshole Reagan."

"Maybe, but I've never lingered on that," I answered her. "I saw it as a kind of war, like an undeclared war, and some of us were not going to come home."

"Well, that's one way to live with it, I guess," she said diffidently. She absently tried to pull some of the kinks from her hair.

"But Kasha," I continued, "of course she wasn't outside his hospital room. Though he imagined she was there, he wanted her to be there. It didn't matter how she had died anymore. He was moving closer to her. And that was when I realized he was actually getting ready to die. He was preparing himself."

I stood up to stretch and leaned closer to her and asked, "Are you okay? Or have I become like the Ancient Mariner, telling my story to anyone willing to listen, and depressing everyone?"

"No, of course I want you to tell me about this. You have to; that's important. It's just that I've seen a lot of death, really terrible traumas, but that's different. I'm more protected than I ever realized by my role and all my training. I don't look into the face of death, really, I look at damaged tissue and arteries and muscles and I decide where to begin sewing things back up. There's almost always *something* I can do. The hardest thing is to just watch, helpless."

After a few minutes we got up and walked down the dock to the boat. The tide had gone out and the ramp hung at a steep angle down from the seawall. As I stepped aboard, the boat felt familiar to me—its sounds, its closeness, and even its smell. It was not like the security of a house made of brick and fixed to the street. No, it was more like a cradle, a rocking horse, a magic carpet, a walnut shell, or someone's arms. It was magical, since it both held you and took you someplace.

We said good night to each other, once again, inside the main cabin. We stood there in the semidarkness for a moment. "Oh Gene," she said to me with a sigh, and she hugged me. She rested her head against my shoulder and for an instant I wondered if she was going to cry. I held her too, and pressed my chin against her temple. Just that small contact of our skin felt good, real and comforting. It made me feel tall and strong, like a man, like a hero. We were both tired, but I knew that this had been the turning point of the trip, for me at least. "Thanks," was all I said, almost in a whisper, as we separated. I realized then how much she missed him and had been trying not to feel the loss. They were the same age.

Lying in my berth, I wanted to remember something about Kevin that was not tainted with memories of Lenox Hill Hospital or AIDS, or CMV or AZT, or DDI or any of the other hated acronyms we had come to live with. I closed my eyes and I went back to our apartment on Canal Street. I remembered a huge snowfall one winter. The city was paralyzed and it was wonderful. Kevin wanted to take the dogs out to play, so we drove down to Battery Park, below the Financial District. It was nighttime and the snow was almost two feet deep. The center lawn of the park had not been touched yet, not plowed or even walked on. There was an eerie light everywhere. Though the sky was overcast, the lights from the skyscrapers overlooking the park lit up the surface of the snow. Kevin wore his old duffel coat with its monklike hood and elkhorn toggles. We climbed over the fence and dropped the dogs onto the fresh snow.

Kevin started to tramp through the drifts, walking briskly and shuffling his big boots with some kind of mysterious purpose. After a few seconds he would stop, take a few giant steps sideways, and start again. He kept making turns and stops, and the dog kept following him, bounding over snow up to her shoulders. My dog, Auggie, was rolling on her back, happily growling to herself.

When he was done he called me over, and together we stepped back to study the results. He had drawn three colossal letters, ten feet long, like trenches gouged through the snow. "KAO" it said, for Kevin Abend-Olsen. "Abend" was Sue and Jules in New Jersey, and "Olsen" was for Kurt from Denmark. It was not very creative, or very original. It was just a way of saying what we all want to say: I was here.

I thought of this moment between us, this memory. I owned it now, completely, along with countless others. I felt somehow I had earned the right to his total existence within me. As if the act of consciously letting him go—that supreme act of faith—had now given me special rights. So convinced was I of the inviolable bond between us, the very merging of our destinies, that I had no need to keep any holy relics. I could be cavalier in disposing of his personal effects, his clothing and possessions. These things were as irrelevant as the hollow shell of his body, the "him" that I knew had become suffused throughout my being. I had lived my entire life convinced of the unbearable aloneness each of us must accept. Maybe I was wrong.

After he died, I had imagined our individual lives as a set of railroad tracks. Somewhere there had been a crossover, and that was our time together. Beyond that point the tracks continued once again, parallel but separate. It was a simple and comforting metaphor.

That night on the boat I saw a new image of the trajectories of our lives. I saw two planets traversing space on their own paths yet drawn inexorably together, until finally they collided in a blinding burst of stardust. This fusion produced a new and ever-expanding entity, a new celestial body that was catapulted outward on a new orbit. At its molten core there glowed an amalgam of the material of both previous planets.

With this image I did not have to search for happy memories or sentimental keepsakes to help me remember him. This Gene was the result, the product, of that fusion, that relationship. I fell asleep quickly afterward, reminding myself that I had been sailing with Laura for only two days, yet I felt as if I had crossed an ocean already.

The following evening *Penn Central,* with her crew of two, ghosted into Stonington Connecticut, about 9:30 p.m. All around us the lights of the docks and restaurants were shimmering in the still and inky water. Even before we picked up a mooring, we were met by

Laura's new boyfriend. He rowed over in a dinghy to meet us. His name was David, a new David. As he climbed aboard I knew that the dynamic of things would change now. My special time alone with Laura was over, my mission done.

# 19

## IN THE COMPANY OF APPLES

*The Ohio River, November 1992*

The plane to Cincinnati left on time, which was good since I was already nervous. This would be my third plane trip away from home since he had died; Nantucket with Laura, Florida with the ashes, and now Ohio.

It was a Friday flight, midday out of Kennedy. The wonderful old TWA terminal that had been the architectural masterpiece of the sixties was now a pathetic nightmare of form no longer suiting function. The once imaginative birdlike building did not have enough space to deal with the volume of people and luggage and snack bars crowded inside. The interior space had too many long corridors full of drama back then, but now they were just another obstacle to getting to the damn plane. In short, flying had become so routine in the past thirty years that no one really wanted or expected striking terminal architecture; they wanted to get through it without much delay or fuss.

At least this was not my first time doing it all alone. I got the car parked in the long-term lot, and Kevin was not there to remind me where to turn. He was not there to tell me anything. He was not there.

Still, I love flying. It remains one of the reasons to celebrate living in this world at this time. I loved that moment when the plane stopped for the last time as it turned onto the runway, the headlights came on and the brakes clamped hard against a final run-up of the jets. You could feel the whole airframe straining to rush ahead, and that was the time to pull the seatbelt tighter and set my stopwatch to zero.

Then the brakes came off and it felt good. You could feel all the bumps and seams in the pavement ten feet below, through the tires, shocks, landing gear, air frame, fuselage, cabin deck, and seat cushion. As the speed picked up enough lift was generated over the wings' surfaces and we took off. Next came the heavy thump-thump of the landing gear dropping down under its own weight, which meant one thing, that we were off the ground and flying.

We cross over Long Island, then over the Sound, over Connecticut toward upstate New York, the Pennsylvania countryside, and, beyond that, the Ohio River.

We are heading inland this time, away from the coast. Less than two hours later we are flying parallel with the Ohio River, an endlessly twisting muddy snake with no sense of purpose to its turns and back turns, a river that seems to spend as much time going in the wrong direction. Something big comes up on the horizon. It's a power plant with a huge cooling tower and fueling docks along the river. Soon it is gone and we are banking gently north and losing altitude. We begin the initial approach for Cincinnati Airport, which is actually located in Kentucky, and that is my destination.

We circle the city, crossing over the downtown. Below us is a circular stadium planted on the river's edge.

We are over a runway again, landing gear down, flaps and slats fully extended. Several huge factory buildings rush by. I feel I am closer to the center of American industry, where things are really made.

We touch, bounce, touch again harder, and finally there is a tremendous rushing noise as we reverse thrust. The speed brake panels pop up and I'm pressed back into the seat. We slow down, the engines get very quiet, and I can feel the brakes slowing us as we head for our gate. I can smell the hot brake pads. *Kentucky,* I keep thinking. *What is here? What does it look like? Will I like him?*

I feel light and bouncy as I come down the ramp that meets the terminal's corridor. It looks new here, cleaner than anything in New York. The carpet feels nice to walk on, the sound is soft, and the sunlight is mellowed by the tinted glass that looks out on the airfield.

He is there, waiting. I was not sure I would remember exactly what he looked like. We have not seen each other in almost two years. He is sitting against the back of a long waiting bench, and looks a bit uncomfortable like that, not fully seated, not fully standing. It's as if he's reluctant to appear too visible standing his full height, and yet too jumpy to stay seated.

He's wearing black jeans. They look okay, a little tight, I think. He's not fat but probably wears the same size clothes he did ten years ago when he was thinner. Looks a bit nervous, not certain when to stand erect, when to greet me officially. Should I shake hands? Embrace? Kiss?

Ten more feet. He looks healthy, better than I remember back in Washington. He's bald; that's right, I had forgotten. Too bad, he seems self-conscious. Can't blame him. Why have I been so lucky? Life is weird.

"Hello," he says in a cheery way, full of uncertainty about me. I drop both bags and stick out my right hand, the familiar man-to-man greeting. He's not weak, but not a macho bone crusher. I don't have very big hands, but they are strong enough. I've never punched anybody in the face in my entire life. I wonder if he has.

"It's so nice and new here," I say, looking around at the terminal's half-mile long arrival corridor, eager to put him at ease. He looks better standing up, but he still tends to stoop ever so slightly to talk to me. I'm smaller and more compact, I think to myself, and I like it that way.

"Oh, they've been expanding this terminal for years. It's suddenly become a big hub. You might like to see the great old mosaics in the main lobby. Let me help you."

"Oh, no, that's okay," I answer, and swing the knapsack around my shoulders. I reach down for the suitcase, and notice him looking at my forearm.

He looks a bit at a loss, with me lugging my stuff and him leading the way empty-handed. "It's okay, really. I feel more balanced this way. I get panicky if I don't feel the weight and think I've lost something."

"Well, if you're sure. But it's a long walk, so let me help you whenever you feel tired, or want to switch."

He walks a bit funny, a bit of a waddle, and still I cannot keep up with him. Must be those long legs. Frank shows me immense mosaics of great moments in the history of Cincinnati's industry. The terminal is wonderfully new and airy. We walk outside, and at last I am in Kentucky. The car is parked just across from the terminal. There is no broken glass anywhere. The car is an old VW Rabbit with a diesel engine. There are junk and food wrappers on the floor inside, and he quickly tries to gather them up and make the front seat look more presentable for his guest. I am touched. We drive out of the airport, and I am astonished that parking costs less than two dollars.

"Are you tired? Do you want to see downtown Cincinnati before we drive back? It's a long trip, and we should get something to eat pretty soon. I assume you must be hungry?" He was not this nervous when I visited him with Kevin, when he lived in Washington, DC. What am I looking for out here?

"Yeah, I'd like to see the city," I tell him. "This is my first time here. But I'm worried about leaving my stuff in the car."

"We can lock it in the backseat. It'll be safe."

"That kind of makes me nervous. I never like to be separated from my luggage when I travel. An old habit," I answer cautiously.

"You don't have to worry that much. This isn't like New York. Cars just don't get broken into out here. People are much nicer. Let me show you the old Union Station."

Sure, I think, if I lose my luggage then I lose everything. I can't lose anything anymore in my life. Everything must stay connected and close to me. Everything good is always stolen. Every bike I had was stolen; every car I had was broken into. It's just me, now, with no one else to look after me.

We left just the suitcase in the backseat and I kept only the knapsack. I could not even contemplate losing all the medicine, glasses, Kevin's pictures, and the finger puppets that I kept in there.

It was almost dusk when we finally left the big city for the highway heading east. I had no idea how far it was. I did not care. We were driving. He was talking. We were comparing our experiences in the world of journalism during the years since college. He seemed interested in my background, hungry for details that seemed so distant and trivial to me. My major. My grades. My thesis paper. My brothers. My house in Brooklyn. What my father did. My mother's education. All details. All bullshit. I was here. I was still alive. I had seen everything. Kevin had died in July. This was November.

He drove pretty fast, seemed good at shifting gears, but looked kind of cramped inside the little Volkswagen. Apples rolled around the backseat and floor, bumping into each other each time we accelerated. We drove for hours, always east. I had never seen roads so smooth and fast, so well marked and graded. The whole system seemed to be designed to get people from one end of the state to the other quickly and safely. I was not used to that. I was accustomed to an adversarial relationship between my car and the highway, a daily game of Russian roulette. This was a different place, Kentucky.

I liked him. He was easy to talk to. Happy to have company. He had come all this way just to pick me up at the airport. Shit, was it dark out there beyond the highway. The little Rabbit pulled us along noisily. He told me a bizarre story of his previous car, a Nissan, being destroyed when a friend rolled it over somewhere out west. At least he used to have a better car, I thought. And what was all that about his dog's ashes getting tossed around inside the wrecked car? I did not want to talk about ashes anymore.

We stopped at last in a small Victorian-looking town along the Ohio River. It was Augusta, and we ate dinner at an authentic country inn. It was good, probably the best food in this part of the state, he bragged. Great black bean soup. The cook was Cuban, no wonder. Another diaspora in my own lifetime. He seemed to glow a bit more now, with food in him and candles flickering on the wooden tables. I forgot about my luggage in the car. He was so eager to please me and

I was touched. We both ate flan for dessert. It was the first dessert I had eaten in four months. It was good, but I had lost interest in sweets, along with movies and other diversions.

It was colder afterward, but we walked down the steep bank to the edge of the river. One of the country's great rivers, I thought, but not like the Hudson. All the time I was aware of being far inland.

We peed into the river like kids, with steam rising in the night air. So many stars. A towboat inched past, pushing a string of flat barges, and soundlessly disappeared around a bend to the west. Creepy river, so many bends.

Another hour inside the drafty VW with no radio. We did not need the music. He never stopped asking questions about me, my life, my work, my friends. None of it important. Just information without substance. The real stuff falls between the questions, doesn't he realize that? The stuff that matters you find out when you stop asking questions and wait.

No, I've never heard of Maysville. Didn't know there were once more millionaires living there than anyplace else in America. This is Flemingsburg. That used to be the one Jewish-owned business. A dry-goods shop. Nice people. Store empty ten years already. The high school on the left with the white columns. Had to find a date for the prom. He acted in some of the student plays, but never felt comfortable, always afraid.

In the town not a soul is awake at this hour. We leave town for a smaller two-lane road that begins to climb steeply. The foothills of the Appalachians, he tells me. Limestone cliffs are heaved up everywhere along the road. Low mountains form parallel ridges, different from the geology back home. There are black bands between the rocks, shale oil, he informs me. The real cash crop here is tobacco, burly leaf only, perfect for cigarettes. Everyone grows it. An allotment system controls prices and keeps things fair.

This is the orchard. This is all our land, oh yes, that too, and all the way down that road too. About 700 acres. But only a small part is used for growing apples. Too hilly. Too rocky. Too wooded. It's terrible soil, too full of clay, and new rocks push up every year. Not enough good bottom land to go around. This is our road, he says, turning left up another short hill. Lights are on inside the house. No. No one else is here with us. The rest of the family lives in North Carolina. It's just us; we're all alone up here. It's okay to pee outside, he prods me with a gentle push. We all do it here. Feels more natural—you city people waste too much water.

I did not know we were going to be alone. Kind of changes things a bit, I think. Three different bedrooms upstairs, just like Goldilocks. No. No one locks doors out here in the country. Wouldn't make much difference anyway, he adds. If someone was fixin' to get you, they would. We all just know each other in a place like this. The family has had the orchard for three generations. We're like an institution, he adds, as we climb upstairs. Which room would you like? This is where I sleep.

I chose the small back bedroom. Its proportions felt right. I was tired, finally. But the house was so full of its own history and secrets I did not feel comfortable yet. Since we'd met, I had asked almost no questions about how his parents had each died. I would learn it all when I needed to. This little room seemed the least burdened with secrets. In the back corner of the house it felt almost forgotten. The bedsprings were squeaky. Hundreds of ladybugs lay everywhere, most of them dead. Too many to worry about.

It seemed silly to go to bed separately in this empty house, so haunted by his missing parents. How could I lie there and listen to him shift around alone in his own creaky bed? He looked okay, I thought again. Looked good in those black Levi's and work boots. I climbed out of my bed, wearing just my underwear.

"Want some company?" I stood next to his ridiculously high bed, feeling more like a kid in my briefs and T-shirt. He may have seen something else.

"Oh. Sure." He seemed very surprised. "That would be very nice. Want to get in with me?"

"No. Not in here. It's too high, makes me afraid I'll fall out in the night and crash on the floor. Why don't we go in the other room? I like it better in there."

"You sure? This is my favorite room. It has the most wonderful sunlight over the fields in the morning."

"Well, actually, it gives me the creeps to sleep in the same bed that you grew up in. You probably had your first wet dream here too." I picked up a copy of *First Hand* magazine on the night table. "Is this your porno? It's two years old."

"Well, I like to look at it still, sometimes. The guys never get any older even if we do." He took his own pillow and we walked back to the little secret bedroom. He turned off all the lights, kicked off his underwear, and slid into the other side of the bed. He rolled onto his right side to face me. Lying in the bed together, for the first time our heads were level. He looked at me, almost shyly, and just said, "Hello." I realized how happy he felt then, to have me there in that house. Such a big house to be alone in, I thought, out in the country. I wiggled over a little closer to him and felt his body warmth. Lying there, I realized how tense I had been all day, maybe for months or even years. I took a deep breath and raised my arms up behind my head. I grabbed the brass railings of the headboard, and flexed all my muscles.

"Look at you," he said, and touched me at last. Did I expect this would happen, right away? His hands felt good. No one had touched me in so long, not like that. He was looking at me, even in the semidarkness, and I could tell what he thought.

"You're so solid up here. You have great shoulders. You must work out a lot. I bet you could pick me up."

"Nothing special," I answered, trying to be modest but loving the attention. "Just a chinning bar. I don't want to get all pumped up."

"You don't need to. You're all muscle already. And your skin, it's so nice to touch you. Your skin feels just like velvet, it's so smooth." He ran his fingertips across my arms and chest. Then I took his hand and said in a whisper, "Touch my stomach, please, just lightly." Waves flowed over me, and my solar plexus felt like the center of the universe. I closed my eyes and felt almost an overload of pleasure, yet his hand kept exploring. He found my cock, which of course had become erect and hard.

"Can I touch this too?" he asked me, already knowing the answer.

"Oh, you feel so good," he said, with his face very close to me in the dark.

"So do you," I replied, and then asked him, "Hold me."

"Sure. Come here," he said, and I rolled over so we could embrace each other completely. I felt his body and his limbs wrap all over me, like an octopus. The distance between us, the formalities of getting acquainted with a stranger, all seemed to evaporate.

*How could this be happening, so quickly and so easily?* I thought. I expected years to go by before I went to bed with another man. He touched me like I was some kind of hunk, one of those muscle types. Like he'd never had his hands on a guy this solid before, or at least not this cooperative, and he seemed more amazed than I was.

I fell asleep easily after we had sex. I felt loved and watched over. Though I knew I was far from home, I was not homesick. Early in the morning I had a dream.

*Kevin appears in the room during the morning. He looks so wonderful. Trim, tall, tan, healthy, and incredibly happy. Frank does not see him. He is here to say hello to me, to be sure I am okay. I am baffled. He is supposed to be dead. Here he is again, standing right over me. He looks so wonderful. I can actually touch him. This is not a dream. He bends over the bed closer to me. He feels so good, so solid. I feel the fuzzy hair on his arms, his nice long biceps. I smell something so clean and boyish, both him and his clothes. He wears faded khakis and a striped polo shirt. I know that shirt. I can see freckles across the ridge of his collarbone. He gives me a little kiss on the lips. I can taste him, and now I know he really is here with me. I am living this and observing it together. This is just so wonderful again. The room is filled with sunlight. I have not felt this happy in years, just like a little kid.*

I awoke slowly, with one arm still around Frank. I remembered the dream, and sat up.

"What's the matter?" Frank asked me.

"I think he was here."

"Huh? Who? Oh. Did you have a dream about Kevin?"

"I'm not certain it was a dream. I felt him so completely. I could taste him." Frank rose up in the bed. He looked troubled and asked me, "Are you feeling guilty?"

"For what?"

"Well, you know, sleeping with someone else, with me, and so soon?"

"No, not at all. He was happy for me. That's what was so wonderful. It's as if he wanted to share it with me, to be with me just because I felt so good. You realize this is my first time?"

"I kind of assumed that. I wasn't sure if you were ready, but you let me."

"No, that was great. I love fucking. It just feels so bizarre. This is not the first time I felt he visited me. I know he was with me. I never thought about this kind of thing before."

Sleeping with Frank did feel good. But I could not tell him what was wrong, really. Yes, I did feel guilty. Frank's touch felt so wonderful on my skin; and how I came, with a huge orgasm that shocked me. Was I going to have to make a choice? Whom did I want more: Frank already deep inside me last night, or Kevin, making his presence briefly real to me? How could I move ahead so quickly like this? Just three weeks ago I had been in Florida, on the Donzi, with his ashes. I wanted him back so badly, even my blood craved him, searched for him in my veins. But here was Frank, so giving and also so needing what I could give him. Poor Kevin; he was so beautiful. His life had just barely started. I had loved him so much.

"Do you miss him now?" Frank asked and slipped his arm around my shoulder, a little hesitantly. He was not sure how to deal with all this intense stuff from me. This was still only our first day together.

"Yes. Of course. I'll always miss him," I answered, and then I pictured Kevin as he had looked a few minutes earlier. "It's just so wrong. You're not supposed to die at thirty-six. Hold me, please. Harder." I leaned against him in the bed. He ran his hands through my hair.

"I know. I know, puppy."

For those few moments, I let myself sink into Frank's arms, yielded, accepted, let the hurt course through me like a terrible orgasm. Finally, I pulled myself away, and struggled to sit up and wipe my face. "Sorry about all that. It just catches up with me at times."

"No. You have nothing to be sorry about. You're a beautiful man. I only hope I can love someone that much in my life. I envy you that you can cry for him."

"Thank you," I whispered, and drew in a deep breath at last.

"You okay now?" Frank asked.

"Yeah, I guess so." I wiped my eyes and sat up cross-legged in the bed. I pushed the patchwork quilts aside and began to stretch.

Frank smiled and asked, "Are you hungry yet? Want some breakfast?"

"A real Kentucky breakfast?" I said with enthusiasm.

"You bet." Frank was up and pulling on his jeans. "Ever have fried apples and country ham?"

"Sounds pretty he-man to me. Then do we go out and cut down some trees with a chainsaw?"

"Well, no. We just pick the apples; we don't cut the trees down."

"Oh. Don't you all keep dynamite around?"

"That's for coal mining, silly, and that's in Pike County in another part of the state. Land o' Goshen, you city boys just don't know shit or shinola about anything important."

"I never pay full price, like you goyim do."

"Why don't you take a shower? You've got dried come all over you."

"How'd that get there?" I said, looking down at my own chest.

"Well, the tooth fairy didn't put it there," Frank said, buttoning up his pants.

"Is there another fairy in the house?"

"Come down for breakfast and you might find out."

Frank left me alone. Soon I heard pans rattling below in the kitchen.

I glanced at the two finger puppets on the nightstand. The little dog and the yellow monster looked back at me, and seemed unsure what was going to happen next. Quite a night? I asked them.

I stayed a week, surprised that I did not miss the ocean or the boat or Brooklyn. The air was clean, the nights cold and full of stars. I helped Frank rearrange all the fussy old furniture in the living room.

We were trying to make the place more livable, less like a museum. Queers were naturally good at that sort of thing, he said to me the next evening.

In the barn the smell of thousands of fresh apples piled in oak bins was intoxicating. I got used to not locking the doors at night. The first couple of days, whenever one of the orchard staff was around Frank seemed somewhat self-conscious about having a "guest" stay with him in the house. By the third day he showed me how to drive the Ford tractor. It had ten gears, each one slower than the next. The brake was so stiff I had to stand on it to make the thing stop. Maybe it was all the vibration, but I got a hard-on every time I drove it, with my butt bouncing against the seat each time it rolled over rocks and furrows.

When I left I hugged everyone who worked there and Frank drove me back to the airport. He would stay with me in Brooklyn the next time he came to New York. On the nightstand of the small bedroom where we had slept I left the two finger puppets. I felt a little guilty at first, leaving them so far from home. But they could amuse each other and it was probably good for them to get used to some new places now.

# 20

## THE DINGHY

*Eastchester Bay, January 1993*

Nothing moved on Eastchester Bay. On the water the lights from shore reflected so they seemed doubled. The bay was still and obsidian and the air was just on the edge of winter. Far off in the distance were the lights of Manhattan; the two square fingers of the Trade Center and the Empire State with its glowing peak. In the clear January night everything was in sharp focus. Three miles away the lights of the Throgs Neck Bridge sparkled in the still air.

I stood at the edge of the seawall, staring out across this familiar bay, not seeing any one thing in particular, just recalling all we had done together. So many years, so many times up here, and always the water. All those summer weekends that ended long after dark with the water, as now, peaceful. Looking down at the wooden docks, imperceptibly rocking in the stillness, of everything that we did together what I most remembered was the dinghy, little *Ivan Kolodko.*

I could see Kevin as he sailed back and forth, using the anchored yachts as fixed obstacles to maneuver around. He had grown confident and would tack at the last instant. I no longer needed to be his source of knowledge of this anachronistic and slightly elitist sport.

When finished, he would sail back to the dock and swing the boat sharply up into the wind, and then land right alongside the float with a snotty little nudge. He was learning not only the skills, but also that sense of grace and an almost arrogant minimum of motion needed to handle any boat.

Only an occasional plop from a curious fish made the slightest disturbance as I stood at the seawall that cold January night. It was late, after 10:00 p.m. Everyone had gone home hours ago, leaving me completely alone.

My day had gone well. I had finished installing shelves in the yacht club's cramped attic storeroom. Things were never well organized around here, and there was a certain appropriateness that I, a compulsive listmaker and carpenter, was chosen to be the House Chairman.

Of course, I loved fixing and organizing. I often started working alone and soon found I had unexpected helpers, all eager for some way to contribute their time to the club. All they lacked were tools and directions. During the winter and spring, with all the boats out of the water, club members were happy for any excuse to spend a day up here. At least that way they could be near the water and glance longingly through the clubhouse windows at their boats all packed up under canvas or plastic tarps.

The tiny room on the top floor had been a hopeless clutter of lightbulbs, party dishes, and toilet paper all stacked in a mess on the floor. I put up shelves on two walls, simple tiers of cheap pine boards. *Order out of chaos,* I had thought as I packed up my tools an hour ago. With everything neatly stowed on the shelves, the room seemed bigger for the first time. But would it stay that way?

In the stillness that January night, my thoughts were interrupted by a hissing sound. It came from somewhere under the clubhouse, below the window of the men's room. I lifted a steel plate that gave access to a crawl space and I listened again. More hissing, water leaking in some miserable hard-to-reach spot. I got a flashlight, and now I could see a light spray of mist from a pinhole in a water line leading to some fixtures above. Another problem, and a potential disaster if there was a freeze tonight. I dropped the steel plate back and hoped that I would remember to call the plumber Monday morning. I wanted to stay with the mood I felt then, not crawl around in the dirt below the toilets holding a flashlight in my mouth.

But the spell had been broken by the pressing reality of being responsible for the upkeep of this seventy-year-old ramshackle clubhouse. Every single corner cried out for repairs. Peeling paint, rotting trim, stuck-open windows, broken rain gutters, bare electric wires, corroded and dripping water lines. No wonder they needed me here. And I loved it. It gave me a purpose, and without Kevin I would need that involvement and continuity. Leaks were sealed and windows were closed.

He had died last July. This was January, the beginning of a new year. Now I could say it had happened "last year." Somehow that seemed important, this inexorable movement of time.

I stared for a last time at the bay, at the familiar lights along the bridges winking vacantly in the night. I turned to go home and as I walked away from the water I wondered if I would ever again love someone so completely.

# 21

## ESTUARY

*Upper New York Bay, August 1995*

What is he doing down there so long? "Hey, Frank. Come up and look. We're almost at Hell Gate." I hoped he could hear me above the clatter of the engine.

"What? What's going to hell?" He shouted up at me, still sleepy and confused. He did not enjoy getting started at 5:30 a.m.

"It's Hell Gate," I repeated, louder this time. "We're almost there. Come on up and look!"

The massive arch bridge filled the horizon ahead of us. We would be under the two bridges in less than three minutes. For the moment we were the only craft on the East River. We would be alone as we rushed with the current past Hell Gate and began the run down river.

I looked through the boat's companionway to see what was keeping him. With four hours' sleep I was running on nervous energy and still trying to be in control of everything. My role was to be the perfect skipper: confident, cool, knowledgeable, and nimble as a cat about the decks.

In the cabin Frank was still moving around like a zombie. I thought he was exaggerating the difficulty of getting dressed in the confines of the boat. He was up forward, sitting on the v-berth and pulling on his sneakers. His pants were just halfway up his hips, and his shirt was halfway around his shoulders. If he were careful he could stand up in the middle of the main cabin. So he dressed this way, in stages. It all seemed so difficult for him to feel at home on a small sailboat.

"What's Frank doing?" Braden asked with impatience. Of course, he shared my need to *be there* all the time, to take everything in, to be ready and on deck. He too was a sailboat skipper, and he thought like me. Braden looked aft from his perch on top of the cabin roof. In one hand was a mug of coffee. The other hand he used to shield his eyes from the orange ball of the sun, rising dead astern.

"Miss Frank is taking her time," I told Braden with a straight face. "He's finishing his *toilette* before appearing on deck." Braden rolled his eyes, then smiled and spun around to face forward again. The giant railroad bridge was almost on top of us. In spite of its enormous bulk of steel trusses, the massive arch sprung across the river with the clarity of a kid's Slinky toy. Only the black paint made it look sinister and overly heavy, like something out of industrial London.

With the bridge so close, it looked as if our mast would not clear beneath it. But in fact the bridge had a vertical clearance of 134 feet above the water. My mast stood forty-six feet six inches high.

Below, Frank was hobbling around in the main cabin. At six-feet-two his head just brushed the carpet headliner. Yet he habitually kept his neck crooked while down below. He was almost ready; I did not need to pester him anymore. In fact, he was really being a good sport about this. It was not his cup of tea. He'd rather wake in his own bed on a summer morning, slip on his robe, and fetch the familiar blue plastic sack holding the *New York Times,* waiting on the front step of our house.

Not today. This was a sailing trip and there were tides to catch. The south-flowing ebb started at Hell Gate at 6:23 a.m. We left the mooring on City Island at 5:30 and entered the river beneath the Throgs Neck Bridge right at the change of the tide cycle, that mysterious moment called "slack water." Yes, I could have left a little later, not made everyone get up so early, but this way we had the full six hours of fair tide down the river, past the Battery, through Upper New York Bay, and right out the Narrows. It was like a free ride, the only cost was some lost sleep. Besides, there was something exciting, intoxicating, about getting up just before sun-up.

Frank did not agree: I could tell by the way he fumbled with his clothing in an uninspired manner. His pants were still dangling and his shirt was wide open. Fuck it! I wanted to shout down to him. Join us, see this great city awaken in the first beams of golden sun exploding off the high-rise windows.

Above us the massive arches of the Hell Gate Railroad Bridge covered the morning sky with a lattice of rails and wooden ties. There were four sets of tracks across this bridge, and I had been told once that the bridge had been purposely overbuilt back in 1917 so that it could handle the simultaneous crossing of four fully loaded coal trains. It is still the only four-track railroad bridge in the world. Those were the glory days of the Pennsylvania Railroad.

Again I peeked into the cabin. "Oh Frank, we're all waiting for you," I called with encouragement. But he was heading back to the v-berth again for something, probably his glasses. He turned around, straightened them across his nose, and then strode purposefully aft, where he immediately smashed his head on the supporting crossbeam set into the cabin ceiling alongside the mast. I heard a dull thud of skull against wood and winced in sympathy. He had stood his full height just a second too soon before he entered the taller part of the main cabin. At least the crosspiece was teak and not oak.

"Are you okay?" I yelled down. Of course he was not, but what else do you say? I turned to the nearest crew member, saying, "Dennis, here, just take the wheel and keep us in midstream." I did not even look back to see if he understood, but in one jump, like they do in those old U-boat movies, vaulted down the companionway steps to get to Frank. He was standing in the middle of the cabin, dazed, angry, and holding his head.

"Oh, what did you do to yourself?" I said, and tried to put my arms up to him. He stood a full head taller than I. I was never sure if my mothering concern like this would be seen as further proof that I was the root cause for these frequent bumps and accidents Frank had on board.

"Shit!" he blurted out angrily while holding one hand to his head. He held his glasses in his other hand; they had apparently bounced off from the shock. I could not see if there was any blood yet. "I was rushing; you kept calling me up and I forgot to duck."

Turning around to the galley sink, I made a quick compress with a dish towel and gently pressed it to his head. Could he tell that I cared, or was I just once again being the omnipresent captain, taking care of all problems?

"Did you have your tea yet?" I asked, trying to distract him. I moved his hand aside and looked at the bump on his forehead. It was already swelling up and there was a small cut, but no blood.

"No. Is there any made?" he asked, a little sulkily.

"There's only hot coffee. I can fix you some tea. I'll make you an ice compress. Go up and take the helm from Dennis. He's probably terrified by now."

Like an animal let out of his cage, Frank stood his full height once out in the open cockpit. Thankfully the main boom was safely above him.

This boat, which seemed to fit so comfortably around me, was an alien and unpredictable place to Frank. Where I could curl up and nap in the main cabin on any of the soft settees, he hung over the same cushion like a St. Bernard who had outgrown his puppy basket. I dropped a tea bag into a mug and poured in hot water.

When I looked up again Frank was standing on the stern, facing aft, obviously taking a piss over the rail. Dennis was still behind the wheel, looking nervous, as if something might happen at any moment.

"You coming up, Gene?" Dennis asked in a very encouraging way.

"Here, take this for Frank." I passed him the mug of tea and climbed into the cockpit, where I felt the growing warmth of an August day. The air still smelled moist from the morning, but I knew from the red sun behind us that the day would be hot. A dirty haze already blurred the horizon.

Frank was perking up. There was color in his face and he was almost smiling. The open space and the sight of the New York skyline obviously inspired him. It was a very special view that residents of those dense clusters of high-rises on the Upper East Side, sleeping behind their air-conditioned windows, would never enjoy.

So many millions, I thought wistfully, just a few hundred yards away from us. So many souls dreaming, waking, fucking, shitting, brewing coffee, and scheming to make some purpose of their lives. And here we were, explorers in our own our little vessel, pushing along toward the open sea. The great sleeping Moloch of New York City did not notice us as we steamed quietly through his very arteries at 6:45 that morning.

Frank took the wheel from Dennis, who was glad to be freed of responsibility for steering the boat through the infamous waters of Hell Gate. He went up to the bow where he could enjoy the view. This was his first trip down the river.

Frank managed to drink his tea, steer the boat, and keep the soggy cold compress on his forehead.

"Does it still hurt?" I asked him, pointing to my own forehead.

"Only when I think too hard," he said, and took another sip of his tea.

"Do you want me to put some kind of bandage on that?"

"Not yet, but you can bring me up a bowl of cereal if you're going below. I can't eat down there with the engine running." As I went down again, I remembered the time that I had neglected to warn Frank that I had not removed the lowest of the four hatch boards in the companionway. As I expected, he promptly bashed his shins on the top edge; once again attacked by my boat. That was unnecessary, I had scolded myself. Yet why did I do it? Why did I need to prove that he was a clod and did not belong on a boat? Was I that insecure about outsiders invading my special world here? In truth, he did like sailing. He even liked it when it was rough and most people would have been afraid.

In the cabin I noted that the Loran set above the nav table was flashing a speed of 9.2 knots, over the ground. We were certainly in the maximum current now. I marveled that something so small, barely the size of a paperback book, could process so much information. What a world we live in.

The streets of uptown Manhattan clipped past us as if we were on a subway train. Seventy-Fifth, Seventy-Fourth, Seventy-Third, and for a few seconds as we passed the wider opening of Seventy-Second Street, we could see straight across the Upper East Side with Central Park off in the hazy distance. Traffic was still light. It was almost 7:05

and joggers were already out in their sweats, doing warmup routines along the promenade of the FDR Drive.

From the bow, Braden gave a wave to a tall man walking six or seven yapping dogs on separate leashes. The guy wore a tank top and gym shorts, and even from this distance looked athletic and muscular. With the dexterity of a stagecoach driver, he shifted the entire bundle of leashes to one hand in order to give us a friendly wave in response. Good legs, I thought, setting down my binoculars, and felt my mood improving.

On the foredeck, Dennis and Braden stood at the bow in rapture as the entire length of the East River opened up before us. Soon we would pass beneath the Queensborough Bridge. The chart showed 131 feet of clearance.

With Roosevelt Island on our port and the stone seawall of Manhattan on the opposite bank, this reach felt more like a canal than a river. Further down in the East Thirties the river grew wide and impressive looking.

Of course, it was not really a river at all. No mountain lake or spring gave birth to the East River. It was merely part of an estuary, what the Dutch would have called a *kill:* a stretch of water connecting two larger bodies of water, in this case Long Island Sound and Upper New York Bay.

Braden stood at the very point of the bow, one foot propped up on the railing, and he held onto the forestay for balance. Dennis, a bit more cautious, sat next to Braden on top of the anchor hatch. They were close, lightly touching each other as the boat pitched and rolled in the rebounding wakes of the narrow channel. They seemed to have a pleasant familiarity near each other, a bit like puppies from the same litter. The usual conventions of privacy and propriety get sacrificed pretty quickly on any small yacht. For some guests it was a terrible strain. For others it could be a novel relief from our unspoken rules of distance, and a chance to get undressed, sleep, and eat in Scoutlike companionship. At times my cabin below had the look of a bunkhouse with young men in their underwear climbing over one another. Like this morning, with the four of us groping around in the dark, some still naked, some in their briefs, all scratching and yawning and probably wondering, *Why the hell are we doing this?*

"What happened to my granola?" Frank asked. "Is there any fruit down below? I'm getting a headache from not eating." I remembered that I was supposed to be making his breakfast. As I went below, I refilled Braden's coffee mug from the thermos. He had come aft and made himself comfortable again on top of the cabin.

"All the fruits are up here," Braden said to Frank with a smile. For a second, Frank seemed to forget about being hungry and focused his interest on Braden. Braden was that way with everyone, open, gregarious, and flirtatious. I thought Frank might even leave the helm and start horsing around with him. Instead, he narrowed his eyes, looked at the wiry and muscular younger man, and said, "I need a fresh banana to slide into my bowl."

"Jesus, Frank," I said, "it's not even eight a.m. and you're already prowling for dick?"

"I'm not prowling anywhere. I've already found it." He remained at the wheel looking at Braden, who was sitting cross-legged facing aft on the cabin top. Feigning modesty, he held one hand over his crotch. "I'm speechless," he replied.

"Don't get your hopes too high," I said quietly to Frank. "But you can try. I did for a while back also." I went below to get Frank his cereal.

There was once a time when his longings for these casual encounters—"fresh meat" in his words—left me flustered. I was not jealous in the obvious way, just confused. During those first months I marveled at how he would touch me, stroke the skin across my stomach as if he had discovered an amazing plaything that was available anytime. In bed, when I sat astride him sometimes, he would run his hands up and down my arms, lightly tracing the curves from shoulder cap to forearm.

He seemed to be so amazed at me, my availability, my readiness to make love anytime. I knew that I was the first person he had stayed with, lived with, for any length of time. I was not doing it for charity, to help him. He did not need help. He was confident both in and out of bed. I needed that attention, the feeling of still being viable, sexy, appealing, a hunk of meat, a guy.

I had assigned to Kevin the role of my source of delight. I was the troll in the tower, the old man with the money. Now I had all of Kevin's clothes, his sexy shirts from International Male, and even more important, his attitude. It was okay to wear pretty things, even around the house, just for the sake of looking clean and feeling attractive.

Yes, Frank made me feel wonderful, made me feel compact and dense, entitled to the space I occupied. I could play at being seductive, feel generous in giving myself and my body. I let him know that it was all right for his hands to conform to the curve of my butt. It was all right if he slapped me there, hard. Then I would have to assure him that it was also all right if he got a hard-on while doing this.

All the while, I kept thinking, he's roamed around for so long without living with a steady companion as I had with Kevin. I felt I had a lot to teach him, not about sex, but about feeling entitled to love, learning to expect it as a regular thing, like the sun and rain, every day. I suspected that he operated from a belief in scarcity, whether of money, good fortune, or love. Loving was like breathing and peeing and it flowed through us all like the tides, with its source unstoppable and ever renewed.

"Hey, Braden. Muscle boy!" I called to him. "Come and take the helm a while. I want to make some kind of breakfast for you guys."

"Now you're talking my language," Braden answered, and with the confident leap of someone who has spent years on small boats he made his way back to the cockpit to take Frank's place. "I'm starting to get faint, but I just don't want to go below. There's so much to see up here. But, Gene, I'm *staaarving,*" Braden told me as he clutched the scrawny place he had for a stomach. I went below to the galley and Frank followed me with his empty cereal bowl.

"Low body fat ratio," I said again knowingly to Frank, nodding my head toward Braden at the helm. Did I need to lecture Frank that being as spare and lean as Braden, albeit sheathed in nicely defined muscles, had some serious drawbacks during times of war and famine? During the past decade we had all come to regard with grave worry anyone who looked even a tad too thin. But did he understand the underlying message of my joke? I certainly was not taut and wiry like Braden, who was also twelve years younger. But I understood now that I had reserves of energy to help me get through difficult times, be it a missed meal or the death of a lover.

"You just wish you could look like that, all lean and hard," Frank taunted me. He had discarded the ice pack on his head and replaced it with a Band-Aid over the wound.

"Skin and bones," I said back. "Too brittle." But about Braden, he was right. "Yeah, maybe I used to, once," I answered, without any sarcasm, as I rummaged under the stove to find a frying pan. "But it was too neurotic, always wanting the unattainable. I'm not meant to be skinny and if I'm really lucky, I never will be."

"Want some help?" Dennis stuck his head through the main hatch and asked with a cheery smile.

"Be careful," Frank warned Dennis, looking up. "If you think he's like Napoleon running the boat, he's Hitler when it comes to running the galley."

I looked up, squinting, and asked Dennis, "Know anything about French toast?"

"Well, you need eggs and bread and then you—"

"Good. Then get your ass down here and help me make breakfast." Dennis carefully climbed off the cabin roof and made his way into the galley. "I'll set up everything for you on the table. You can do it like an assembly line."

"Why don't you let someone else cook? It's not very complicated." Frank asked me as Dennis looked around. He was reminding me of the many times I had complained of all the work of having company on board for a weekend. He was right. I had become the Martha Stewart of yachting, a marvel of cleanliness and efficiency. I washed the dishes as fast as I messed things up, I used small plates to hold all my cooking ingredients, and had everything thoughtfully precut, chopped, sliced, diced, and beaten before the final flourish of assembly. But in the process I had effectively excluded everyone from helping, no, participating, in the routine activities of the ship. They were crew, I reminded myself, not guests at an inn. They wanted to *do* things. Get them started and let go, I told myself. When things get rough, that was when they needed me.

"Okay cap'n, where do I start?" Dennis asked.

"Frank, you almost finished? Frank will give you a hand, Dennis. Everything's already out on the table, and he can light the stove for you." I poured myself a new cup of coffee and strode back through the companionway. They could handle this together, their own way.

"Dennis is making breakfast," I said to Braden, putting my mug next to his. I sat down and let out a relaxed sigh. "Isn't this lovely?" I said, like a potentate surveying his realm.

"Dennis can't cook for shit, Gene. He eats out of cans. You make such wonderful breakfasts."

"I'm learning to let go, to delegate. Beside, Frank's down there and he can show him everything." I leaned back and looked ahead to the broad vista of the river. The Manhattan and Brooklyn Bridges came into line as we slipped from the shadow of the Williamsburg Bridge.

To our left, the sad and decrepit piers of the Greenpoint waterfront and the woefully underused Brooklyn Navy Yard passed by. Further ahead lay the open harbor, the tip of Governor's Island, and silhouetted against the New Jersey shoreline, the Statue of Liberty.

I glanced into the cabin, thinking it seemed a little smoky down there. As Dennis stepped away from the stove I could see his flame was much too high. He had forgotten to turn the stove down once the burner had warmed up. I signaled to Frank with a pantomime gesture to turn down the control knob. For just a moment it felt nice to be able to communicate that way, wordless and clear.

Sitting comfortably behind the wheel, Braden smiled at me and said, "It was so beautiful this morning, when we first got up. Everything was so quiet." This was our first time alone since we had stood together on deck in the tentative predawn light. The sky was still dark, yet no longer nighttime. The air was cold and still, and a glow on the horizon presaged the rising of the sun. We stood on deck, quiet, reverent, and amazed. Though cold, we shared that brief moment of timeless awe at daybreak. Then we each peed from opposite sides of the boat.

"I'm never sure if I'm driving everyone crazy with my obsessive schedules. You know, like: 'We sail with the tide at dawn,'" I said, aping the gravelly voice of an old seadog.

"Oh no, that's the best part, being forced to do things exactly *because* the tide requires it, no matter how uncomfortable it is. That's what sailing should be like."

"Of course, you're a sailor," I said to Braden. "You know it's not the same as a weekend in the Berkshires. You know how I think."

"Look at it this way," he said, and held his palm up like a teacher making a point. "You're creating this event, this experience of a sailing trip, even for just a weekend, even here in New York Harbor. But it *feels* like being on a ship, on our own. You know—that we're self-sufficient, taking care of ourselves, cooking on board. I almost never do any real cooking, and you do it all the time. This feels like living aboard a ship, and the routine should feel different than at home. Right from the start we're aware of our need to deal with the elements, go with the current, get our power from the wind. God, Gene, you even wash dishes down below with saltwater. I think that's great. It's so . . ."

"Salty, eh?"

"Yes. It's very salty." Braden dropped one arm from the wheel to rest his hand on my bare leg. He looked off toward the horizon as he added, "You're so plugged into the traditions and even the superstitions of sailing. It really matters to you. I love that."

"Even when someone gets the pumps confused in the galley and they make coffee with seawater?" I asked Braden.

"That didn't really happen, did it?" he asked, frowning.

"That's what Kevin used to say my coffee tasted like."

"Your coffee is fine, but it's not Starbucks." Braden paused, then said in a different tone, "You almost never talk about him—Kevin. Not with me anyway. Do you miss him, or is that a stupid question?" Braden gave my leg a gentle squeeze. "Or maybe I shouldn't ask?"

"Ask anything. But no, I don't miss him in the way you might think. You see, it's as if I incorporated him into myself, as if we merged and I continue now as both of us."

"Frank told me about how you took his ashes to Florida, and you put them in the ocean."

"That's just the facts, not the emotional part, not the spiritual part. I *released* him. I never told anyone this, but I saw it as a kind of transubstantiation. Are you surprised that I think about such dogma?"

"You're not turning Catholic on us suddenly?" Braden asked with his brows arched.

"No. What I mean is, he *became* water, changed from one element to another. A couple of weeks after I returned from Florida I had this revelation: I had released him into the water, now he *was* water. I'm being metaphysical, of course. Wherever I would go, wherever there would be water, wherever I would sail or swim, he would be all around me."

Braden said nothing but closed his eyes a moment, and took a deep breath. Below us the Yanmar diesel steadily rattled on.

"I can tell how much you loved him. Your whole voice changes. That's him in the picture up in the v-berth?"

"Yes, on the forward bulkhead. It was taken in the Grenadines. Oh God, it's almost eight years ago now. We were sailing to Bequia. That's Saint Vincent in the background."

"I did look at it. Gene, I must tell you, he was gorgeous. I actually felt jealous when I first saw that picture. He really liked sailing, didn't he? Is this getting too personal? You look like you're about to cry."

Braden reached up and lightly passed his knuckles against my cheek. He steered the boat with one hand and brought his other arm around my shoulder. I closed my eyes and leaned against him a little. I took a long breath then straightened up again just as I saw Frank starting up the companionway.

Frank climbed up, trying to carry the folding cockpit table that hooked onto the binnacle. For a second it looked like he would have trouble stepping into the cockpit with his hands full so I reached out to help.

"Oh, no, that's all right," he said, then added, "Want me to take the wheel so you two can go below?" Braden slowly removed his long arm and playfully frizzled the back of my neck. Then he gave me a funny wink. I smiled, knowing how well we understood each other.

Behind Frank Dennis was balancing a tray of French toast along with plates and a bottle of maple syrup.

I set up the cockpit table and then asked Frank to relieve Braden while I went below to make another pot of coffee.

With the East River behind us, the entire upper bay opened up before us. On our right was the Battery and the copper green ferry buildings. We crossed between the slot where long ago great iron cannons from stone forts on both the Battery and the tip of Governor's Island could have fired upon us. Now Castle Clinton on the Manhattan side merely housed the ticket booth for the Statue of Liberty ferry and all of Governor's Island was soon to be abandoned by the U.S. Coast Guard.

There was a time when this great harbor intimidated me, with its big ships, deep water, buoys, currents, and huge logs floating up from old piers. I felt like a kid in my toy boat weaving between the legs of the grownups.

But this was no longer the grand harbor of my boyhood. Everything moved by truck now. What shipping remained avoided New York and used the modern container port out by Newark Airport. Now what mattered was being close to the New Jersey Turnpike, not Times Square.

I left the job of cleaning up the dishes to the others and went forward to sit alone at the bow. *Was he really out here with me?* I thought. *And what about Kurt, was he out here, too?* What about all the tugs and railroad barges that used to be a familiar sight on these waters years ago? Those jaunty New York Central tugs, with a tall stack and raked back pilot house? What became of the great Erie Lackawanna fleet of trains, barges, tugs, terminals, all with the big white E inside a red diamond? To port on the Red Hook waterfront loomed the immense concrete grain silos. There they have stood, empty and useless for half a century, too big to tear down, too big to use anymore.

This entire waterfront was ringed by derelict and collapsing piers, some of them no more than pitiful iron skeletons, lying like war victims with their bellies in the water. They stood as a testament to no greater tragedy than neglect.

Beyond Governor's Island optimistic ripples of wind skipped across the water. I decided to break out the spinnaker once everything was cleaned up below. That would certainly get everyone involved, but more important, it would keep me from mourning—or was it obsessing—so much loss I felt everywhere around me.

This was still a magnificent harbor: the view of downtown Manhattan, the emblematic torch of the Statue of Liberty, the Moorish towers of Ellis Island, the broad mouth of the Hudson River; it was impressive just for its scale and history.

Look at our crew, I reminded myself. Half of them are under forty, youngsters still building their careers, optimistic and hopeful. They don't need to know that Kevin's father, Kurt, once worked out here in the engine rooms of those phantom tugboats. It no longer mattered that Kurt had brought his bride, Kevin's future mother Marqueritte, into this harbor aboard the proud S.S. *Stockholm*.

"Just steer for the bridge," I told Braden, pointing to the Verrazano Narrows. "I need time to set up the spinnaker." From the cockpit locker I lugged out the big sail, stuffed into its bag, and went forward to hook it onto the bow. Kevin was history, I told myself, just like Kurt, and so was the Erie Lackawanna. I attached two ropes to both lower corners of the spinnaker and began the time-consuming operation of setting up all the lines. I led each sheet aft on opposite sides of the boat and back through the spare turning blocks and around the second set of winches in the cockpit.

Had I seen too much death already? Hardly. Others had lost so many more friends. I was still here, and very much alive. Now I lived with Frank, and for the moment, that was my future. I had never really given up hope and optimism. Quite the contrary, I smiled to myself, for I knew there were still wonders to behold.

Setting up the spinnaker pole came next, and I asked Braden to slack off the topping lift. I went forward again to hook up the ungainly thirteen-foot pole to a ring on the mast, just above my head. Next, I snapped on the downhaul tackle, lying slack on the foredeck. This was to keep the pole from flying up too high. Everything about this sail was a pain in the ass, and I knew they were watching me from the cockpit in total bafflement. The pole was necessary to hold the huge sail away from the boat once it was hoisted and flying. It would all make sense to them in a few minutes.

What about Howard, our friend who sold pharmaceuticals for Sandoz? Another major case of denial who only confronted his growing illness after a car accident. Howard's blood was splattered everywhere inside the crumpled interior of the Mazda ZX. Then, even after months of rehabilitation, he never looked the same again, never as robust. His nice suits no longer seemed to fit him quite as well, and something in his whole aspect was missing. When I called to talk one day, his sister said they had just come back from the cemetery. He had been Kevin's age, thirty-six.

I could never explain to the crew what all these lines, blocks, and shackles were meant to do. Even after twenty years I often got them screwed up and I now stalked around the decks mumbling the name of each line to myself as I traced it with my finger to be sure each would run fair. I felt like a magician arranging his tricks before the curtain rose. Last, I clipped the halyard to the head of the sail and came back aft.

You can teach them, I thought to myself as I appeared preoccupied with my ropes. You know so much about boats; they admire you, and want to learn. They did not come along just for the food; they came along because of me. Teach, but don't push them around. It will never be like it was sailing with Kevin; let it go and be with them now.

I asked Frank to take over the helm from Braden since he had been through a few spinnaker sets with me already. I told Braden and Dennis to haul in the sheet and guy on opposite sides of the boat. I paused with the end of the halyard in my hand. Had I left Braden at the helm, that might have made Frank feel less valued, less trusted. Maybe this way, a kind of connection was reinforced, and whether he wanted it I was not sure, but Frank was now at the helm and carried a central role throughout this operation. Dennis had no idea what was going on, but was eager to follow orders and not screw up. Frank was cooperative as long as he felt I was not being bossy or arbitrary. He would never love sailing the way I did, but I could determine how much he might hate it, and along with boating, probably me.

Everyone was ready and getting nervous so I called out, "Okay, 'chute's going up," and started pulling on the halyard. From up forward I heard the crinkly fabric being yanked out of its bag. When I was halfway done pulling the halyard I turned to Braden and Dennis and yelled, "Go! Pull, pull, pull. Get it up!" Infected by my maniacal enthusiasm, they pulled on their lines like real sailors. As they did, the two opposite corners of the big sail separated while I continued to bring it up to the masthead. The wind got behind all those yards and yards of thin fabric and with a loud whomp the sail bellied out in front of us. As I cranked up the final few feet of the halyard I could already feel the power in the sail. All Frank had to do was just steer a steady course and keep the wind behind his right shoulder.

"That's incredible," Dennis exclaimed. "We're the biggest show in the harbor." The huge sail spread out in front of the mast, a sudden effusion of yellow, orange, and black bands. With the sail up and full, all the lines made sense to them now.

"Hey, we're up to six knots already," Dennis called out to us as he read from the knotmeter. I could see the sense of wonder in his face. He probably never imagined he would be sailing like this in the very waters beyond his own office window back there in Manhattan.

We were moving along majestically, and Frank knew well enough to keep his attention focused on the wind direction arrow at the top of the mast. This was the right way to sail out of New York Bay.

Kevin and I used to do this just by ourselves, I remembered, even gybing the unruly thing as people from the club watched with their mouths open, amazed at our guts and coordination.

Our speed began to drop as we got closer to the Verrazano Bridge. We drifted underneath mostly with the current, and beyond the Narrows the wind turned shifty and began to peter out entirely. We bounced around for a while with the big spinnaker filling and collapsing, just making a lot of noise. We would have to motor the rest of the way. By the time we got the sail down and all the lines brought in, I was tired, and noticed that Frank had gone below.

I found him stretched out up forward, in the v-berth. "Was that exciting? Were you nervous at all at the helm?" I asked.

"You always forget that I sailed out in San Francisco Bay where it blows a lot more than this. So don't be so patronizing, okay?"

"Sure, okay. I was just trying to say you did a good job, that's all. It can be tricky at the helm. That's why I never do it." A bit of a lie. I found it more convenient to be free to move around the boat rather than stuck behind the wheel. Frank also knew that I often gave the wheel to newcomers to let them feel the thrill of "driving" the boat.

"So, how's your head? Do you know who our President is? How many fingers am I holding up?" I asked, teasing him.

"Are there any trains that leave from Sandy Hook?" Frank asked me, with his eyes closed.

"You mean back to the city? You don't want to stay for the trip back tomorrow?" In all my manipulations I had never factored in Frank's bailing out in the middle. I felt a cold blade of panic and remorse inching inside my gut.

"Why do you want to leave?" I asked him. "You're not jealous about me and Braden, I hope. He feels a lot of affection for you too. We're not doing anything—you know that."

"Don't be stupid, or flatter yourself. I know how Braden is, and you don't see all those looks he keeps sending me. That's beside the point. I'm just in your way, and at least be honest enough to admit that."

Trapped from all sides, my throat tightened up.

"I'm sure there are buses from Atlantic Highlands. We could motor over to the marina, but it's a few miles from the anchorage in Sandy Hook. I want you to stay, really. I planned this with the four of us in mind right from the beginning."

"You just don't want to be doing it alone, that's all. That's nothing to be ashamed to admit. You had a wonderful life before, and you're used to doing things with someone. I'm not trying to get back at you or hurt you, I just don't want to be used as a replacement, as crew to fill the boat with happy faces for you."

The depth of his defensiveness tore through me, and I was desperate for a way out of this situation I felt no longer in control of.

"You don't have to look so hurt and panic stricken," Frank went on. "We've had a lot of good times with each other, and probably we still can, but not necessarily in a one-to-one relationship. That shouldn't surprise you. You're a good-looking man, you're in amazingly good health, and you're not going to die. You should realize that by now. Plenty of guys notice you and you should be out there enjoying what you really want."

I stood there with my hands jammed into my pockets. I felt I was being scolded and I was not sure if it would be better to just listen or take a stance, fight back. Either way seemed doomed. "Yeah, of course I check out skinny boys," I told Frank. "But I have nothing to say to them. Even with Kevin, my head was always spinning around. But we stayed together anyway."

"Because you loved him," Frank answered, and pushed himself up to a seated position, his back against the bulkhead. Now I had interrupted his nap, I thought. I began to feel weary myself. The excitement of the dawn departure, the river passage, the spinnaker work, all felt like elaborate pantomime shows to avoid something between us that had no easy answer. Whatever else was difficult about him, he was not someone to bury problems beneath the minutiae of routine chores, as I did.

Kevin had run off several times, but that was different. I had a deep hold on him, and he knew how I would cherish him forever no matter what he did. More important, I knew how much he needed me to keep his life together. He lived in fear of finding out that his own personality was vacant. Frank had a very well-developed sense of himself; he would never allow himself to need me, my body, my technical knowledge, my pushy and abrasive New York manners. And below that brittle and obdurate surface were minefields of bitterness and hurt. Kevin's whole life was really about finding a home, a safe harbor. With Frank the territory was more difficult—the past had been more successfully entombed. I dared not open with him the unfinished business I sensed remained between him and his parents. To me it was obvious—that necessary step of forgiveness, that painful act of completion that he kept running away from, which was the source of all the anger and bitchiness. All this I had felt since that first visit to the farm, the night three years earlier, when we slept in the little bedroom in the back of the house.

"I'll help you get back," I told Frank, "if you really want it. But I think you'll enjoy being with the rest of the guys this afternoon. I'm not trying to dangle anything to hold you. I want you here with me, no matter what you may think. You're not the easiest person to get along with and feel close to at times, you know."

Frank closed his eyes, and I saw an involuntary smile of acknowledgment cross his face. Then he said, "We're two middle-aged men with very fixed ideas of how we want to conduct our lives. I know that, and so do you."

I felt a bud of conciliation germinate. "Listen," I said, sitting down on the edge of the berth. "Whatever pulled us together comes under a different heading than 'love.' I know I cannot recreate again what I used to have." No, I sighed inwardly, it certainly was not the over-arching love I had experienced during the thirteen years with Kevin, whose picture was on the bulkhead above us.

"Maybe it's okay this way," Frank said, "as long as we allow each other a lot of freedom. But with both of us looking around all the time, I think it's inevitable someone's going to be hurt."

*Someone?* I thought. *Which someone?* It would probably be Frank, I realized. And so he was already protecting himself from disappointment, a peremptory strike to put some distance between us before he felt too close and at too much risk.

I could not guess where our relationship was going. Instead I kept hearing this insipid cliche, repeating in my thoughts: *"If it quacks like a duck, then it must be a duck. If it walks like a duck. . . ."* I could not get rid of this stupid bit of doggerel.

How was I supposed to know what love looked like anymore? Was it the idiotic infatuation for some guy in faded Levi's whose very maleness I wanted to ingest, to slobber over? It is not the same when you are fifty, with most of your life over, than when you were twenty-six or thirty-two, with the horizon so far off. Suddenly, my cherished infatuations no longer seemed adequate guidelines for a boyfriend.

"You're entitled to have someone to be in love with again," Frank went on, this time gently drumming his fingers on top of my own hand. Was he trying to show that he felt generous and in control here, considerate of my fears of living alone? Yet my instincts told me otherwise; I felt his own defensiveness at work. We were just so goddamned competitive with each other. What were we so afraid of losing all the time? What was I afraid of losing?

"I'd like you to stay. I think you'll have fun." I said this to him, and twisted my own fingers around his until our hands were interwoven. Had I been the one who began this game of profit and loss, in which nothing was done spontaneously, but first weighed against how much this was compromising my control? If I had, then I was getting sick of it; it was too much fucking work for me. I wanted to live with someone, do things together, and if that meant doing new things that I was not in control of, well then, okay, I'll try.

I ran my other hand lightly up and down Frank's arm. He did not move. I released his arm and slid down in the berth alongside him until my head rested in his lap. I do not think he expected this, and he remained still. Then he reached up and gently touched my hair, kind of messing it a bit, then patting it down again. I curled up a little closer against him. We said nothing for a while. I heard footsteps on the deck above us, but then decided that if they really needed me they could call me.

"Quack!" I said, and raised my head and snorted.

"Huh?" Frank asked, probably wondering what new trick I was planning.

I pretended to look around. "It must have been a duck going by," I said innocently, and let my head fall back against him.

"You're very strange," he said, sounding both amused and baffled.

"That's what my mother used to say."

I closed my eyes and could feel the boat rolling along without me doing anything.

# GLOSSARY OF SAILING TERMS

**aback:** Setting a sail with the wind on the leeward side.

**abeam:** Any object bearing at right angles to boat's centerline.

**aboard:** On the boat.

**adrift:** Loose or unlashed objects aboard. Also, a boat afloat not under control.

**aft:** Toward the stern or back of boat.

**alee:** To the side opposite from which the wind is blowing.

**aloft:** Above the deck, or up the mast.

**amidship:** The middle of the boat.

**astern:** Behind the boat.

**back winding:** Holding sail out on the windward side.

**backstay:** Wire supporting mast at stern.

**ballast:** Weight used to give boat stability and trim.

**beam:** The maximum width of a boat.

**bearing:** Direction by compass.

**beat:** To sail to windward.

**bilge:** Inside bottom of hull below the waterline.

**binnacle:** Fixed mounting that holds the boat's steering wheel along with the compass.

**blocks:** Pulleys.

**boom:** Spar to which foot of sail is fastened.

**bow:** The fore part of a boat.

**bulkhead:** Partition inside boat, also a seawall on land.

**buoy:** A float used to mark an obstacle or channel in the water.

**C&C:** A yacht manufacturer, originally based in Ontario, Canada. Now producing a new line in Fairport, Ohio. Known for fast boats, with racy lines.

**can:** A common buoy, cylinder shaped, usually black or green, and used to mark the left side of a channel when entering a harbor.

**capsize:** To turn over.

**cast off:** To untie or free a line.

**centerboard:** Thin plate of wood or metal, like an adjustable keel, to reduce leeway when sailing to windward.

**cleat:** Wood or metal fitting with horns to hold lines.

**clew:** The aft bottom corner of any sail.

**close hauled:** Sailing as near to the wind as possible.

**coaming:** Vertical boards around cockpit to keep water on deck from running into the cockpit seats.

**cockpit:** Above deck part of boat where steering gear is located.

**come about:** Change course when bow crosses the wind. *See* HELM'S ALEE.

**CQR anchor:** A patented type of yacht anchor, similar in shape to a plow, made of galvanized steel.

**cradle:** Framework to hold boat upright on land.

**cuddy:** A decked shelter, smaller than a cabin.

**dead reckoning:** Rough calculation of distance and course made good, cf., "Deduced reconnaissance."

**dinghy:** A small boat, commonly 7-12 feet long, used for pleasure or to reach a larger boat. Also called a tender.

**down haul:** A line used to pull a sail down.

**draft:** Depth of underwater part of boat.

**ease off:** Let go or let out a line slowly.

**ebb tide:** When current is flowing back out to sea; receding.

**Eldridge:** *Eldridge Tide and Pilot Book,* published annually. A popular tide and current almanac for the East Coast of the U.S.; soft bound with a yellow cover.

**fall off:** To alter course away from the wind.

**fathom:** A measurement of six feet.

**fender:** Rubber bumper or similar soft object to prevent abrasion to the boat's sides.

**fid:** A short wood or metal spike used to work open knots.

**fo'c'sle:** Very old British contraction for forecastle, or the upraised bow section of a large fighting ship. Now the forwardmost living compartment of a ship, usually for crew quarters.

**foot:** Bottom of sail attached to boom.

**forestay:** Wire used to hold mast attached to bow; headstay.

**forward:** Toward the bow.

**foul:** Jammed, stuck; also, not clean.

**genoa jib:** A headsail, larger than a working jib, that overlaps the mast.

**gimbal:** Rings or pivots to keep a stove or compass level.

**gunwale:** Top edge of a boat at deck level. Pronounced gun'el. Originally, the top board above the deck upon which a naval gun could rest.

**gybe:** To change course with the wind astern; jibe.

**halyard:** Lines used for raising and lowering sails.

**handsomely:** Smoothly, moderately, opposite of rushed or abrupt. As in, "Bring the helm over handsomely."

**Harken Magic Box:** A self-contained block and tackle system patented by Harken Mfg. Company. The company is known for performance-oriented sailboat hardware.

**head:** The top corner of a sail; also, the toilet on a ship.

**head to wind:** Bow pointed into the wind, sails luffing.

**head up:** A command to bring a boat closer into the wind.

**heave to:** A storm tactic to hold a boat steady by balancing the sails and the rudder.

**heel:** Angle from the vertical at which boat sails; to lay over.

**helm's alee:** Command to come about or tack. *See* COME ABOUT.

**hike:** To climb out on the windward side to balance the boat.

**in irons:** When the boat does not respond to action of the rudder when head to wind.

**jib:** Small triangular sail carried forward of the mast.

**kedge:** (Noun) A small anchor.
(Verb) Using the anchor to haul the boat.

**keel:** Part of boat below the hull giving the boat lateral resistance and also containing the ballast weight.

**ketch:** Two-masted boat with the smaller mast aft but still in front of the rudder post. *Compare with* YAWL.

**knot:** Unit of speed, one nautical mile per hour (i.e., one minute of latitude, or 6,080 feet).

**lazarette:** Storage compartment way back in the stern.

**leech:** The after edge of a sail.

**leeward:** The downwind side (pronounced looward). Away from the wind.

**luff:** Forward edge of sail fastened to mast or stay.

**luff up:** A command to bring a boat head to wind.

**luffing:** Shaking of luff of the sail.

**mainsail:** The largest sail.

**mainsheet:** The line that controls the mainsail.

**make sail:** A command to set sail.

**mizzen:** The shorter mast on a yawl or ketch.

**mooring:** The chain or rope, buoy, and bottom anchor to which a boat is secured in a fixed spot in the water.

**nautical mile:** 6,080 feet. *See* KNOT.

**nun:** A common type of buoy, always red and conical shaped. Used to mark the right side of a channel when entering a harbor.

**off the wind:** Sailing a course away from the wind rather than to windward, which is called "on the wind."

**oilskins:** Traditional word for waterproof clothing; rain gear.

**painter:** The line used to tie the bow of a small boat.

**pinching:** Sailing too close to the wind.

**pointing:** Sailing close to the wind; ability varies by boat.

**port:** The left side of the boat.

**port tack:** Sailing with the wind coming from the port.

**quarter:** Position on boat between the beam and stern.

**range lights:** Vertical white lights indicating ship's direction.

**reaching:** When the boat sails with the wind abeam.

**reefing:** Reducing area of sail by partly lowering or furling.

**reeve:** To pass lines through a block or fairlead.

**rhumb line:** The straight line path on a chart.

**rig:** Mast and sails and attached wires and hardware for support.

**roller furler:** A system of winding a sail around a stay for storage or reefing. Usually the headsail.

**rudder:** Plate fastened vertically at stern of boat below the water used for steering.

**running:** Sailing with the wind astern.

**running lights:** Required standardized lights for each vessel for night use.

**scope:** Length of mooring or anchor line let out.

**shackle:** A U-shaped metal fitting with a pin or screw across the open end used for joining lines, chains, or wires.

**sheets:** Lines used to control sails; jib sheet, mainsheet, etc.

**shrouds:** Wires holding up mast at sides of boat and attached at the deck.

**sloop:** A single-masted boat with a mainsail and jib.

**spar:** Term for mast, booms, or other poles that handle sails.

**spinnaker:** A large, lightweight sail carried forward of the mast when running downwind.

**spreader:** Horizontal strut on the mast used for support with wire shrouds.

**sprit (sail):** Traditional rig, four-sided sail, with head held up on a thin spar called a sprit.

**starboard:** Right side of boat.

**stern:** The aft or back part of a boat.

**tack:** (Noun) The lower forward corner of a sail.
(Verb) To sail a zigzag course toward the wind.

**tender:** (Adj.) A boat that is prone to heel over easily; opposite of stiff.
(Noun) A small boat, used to reach a larger boat. A dinghy.

**tiller:** Stick or bar device that controls the rudder for steering.

**topping lift:** Line used to hold up boom or other spar.

**transom:** The sternmost part of the hull.

**traveler:** Fixed track with sliding car to adjust position of mainsail from side to side of boat.

**trim:** To set the sails at the correct angle to the wind; to pull in the sheets.

**turnbuckles:** A threaded metal coupling that may be shortened or extended. Used for tightening wires holding up the mast.

**vang:** A line or tackle to steady the boom when off the wind.

**v-berth:** Berth in a forward cabin following the shape of the boat as it narrows at the bow.

**way:** Movement through water, i.e., headway or sternway.

**weather helm:** The tendency of a boat to head up into the wind.

**well found:** A well-equipped vessel with all gear in good shape.

**winch:** A stationary device with a drum around which rope or chain is wound by means of a crank handle; windlass.

**windward:** Toward the wind.

**yawl:** A two-masted sailboat, where the aftermost mast, called the mizzen, is the shorter of the two, and is positioned aft of the boat's rudder post.

# ABOUT THE AUTHOR

**E. M. Kahn** graduated from Bard College in 1969 with a degree in political science. After trying his hand as a reporter at several different newspapers along the East Coast, he turned to carpentry. For many years, Mr. Kahn's custom woodworking shop—Evergreen Studio—has built fixtures for showrooms on 34th Street as well as trade shows and other high-traffic retail stores.

In the spring of 1975, his life was changed when he took sailing lessons almost as a lark. Since then, he has owned six boats and has sailed extensively in the northeast and the Caribbean. He sold his last boat in 2000. He is involved with the Knickerbocker Sailing Association (KSA)—New York's first gay sailing club—and is a former member of the Harlem Yacht Club on City Island. He still does custom woodworking and sails occasionally.

***Order a copy of this book with this form or online at:***
***http://www.haworthpress.com/store/product.asp?sku=5130***

**DEEP WATER**
**A Sailor's Passage**

________in softbound at $14.95 (ISBN: 1-56023-517-9)

Or order online and use special offer code HEC25 in the shopping cart.

COST OF BOOKS________

POSTAGE & HANDLING________
*(US: $4.00 for first book & $1.50 for each additional book)*
*(Outside US: $5.00 for first book & $2.00 for each additional book)*

SUBTOTAL________

IN CANADA: ADD 7% GST________

STATE TAX________
*(NJ, NY, OH, MN, CA, IL, IN, & SD residents, add appropriate local sales tax)*

**FINAL TOTAL**________
*(If paying in Canadian funds, convert using the current exchange rate, UNESCO coupons welcome)*

☐ **BILL ME LATER:** (Bill-me option is good on US/Canada/Mexico orders only; not good to jobbers, wholesalers, or subscription agencies.)

☐ Check here if billing address is different from shipping address and attach purchase order and billing address information.

Signature________________

☐ **PAYMENT ENCLOSED:** $________

☐ **PLEASE CHARGE TO MY CREDIT CARD.**

☐ Visa ☐ MasterCard ☐ AmEx ☐ Discover
☐ Diner's Club ☐ Eurocard ☐ JCB

Account #________________

Exp. Date________________

Signature________________

Prices in US dollars and subject to change without notice.

NAME________________
INSTITUTION________________
ADDRESS________________
CITY________________
STATE/ZIP________________
COUNTRY________________ COUNTY (NY residents only)________________
TEL________________ FAX________________
E-MAIL________________

May we use your e-mail address for confirmations and other types of information? ☐ Yes ☐ No
We appreciate receiving your e-mail address and fax number. Haworth would like to e-mail or fax special discount offers to you, as a preferred customer. **We will never share, rent, or exchange your e-mail address or fax number.** We regard such actions as an invasion of your privacy.

*Order From Your Local Bookstore or Directly From*

**The Haworth Press, Inc.**

10 Alice Street, Binghamton, New York 13904-1580 • USA
TELEPHONE: 1-800-HAWORTH (1-800-429-6784) / Outside US/Canada: (607) 722-5857
FAX: 1-800-895-0582 / Outside US/Canada: (607) 771-0012
E-mailto: orders@haworthpress.com

**For orders outside US and Canada,** you may wish to order through your local sales representative, distributor, or bookseller.
For information, see http://haworthpress.com/distributors

*(Discounts are available for individual orders in US and Canada only, not booksellers/distributors.)*

PLEASE PHOTOCOPY THIS FORM FOR YOUR PERSONAL USE.

http://www.HaworthPress.com BOF04